Sarah Roig was born in Palma de Mallorca, Spain, in September of 1999. She has studied at King Richard III College in Mallorca for most of her youth and is currently studying her second year of BA in Media and Communications at Goldsmiths University of London. She started writing her first novel, *No Price, No Time*, when she was 16 and has been remodelling it as she grew up to be 18. She also writes poetry and film scripts in her spare time. She is an ambitious upcoming writer who is hardworking and aspires to be able to live from her passion as such.

You know who you are, thank you.

Sarah Roig

No Price, No Time

AUSTIN MACAULEY PUBLISHERS™

LONDON • CAMBRIDGE • NEW YORK • SHARJAH

A CIP catalogue record for this title is available from the British Library.

ISBN 9781528942140 (Paperback)
ISBN 9781528971027 (ePub e-book)

www.austinmacauley.com

First Published (2019)
Austin Macauley Publishers Ltd
25 Canada Square
Canary Wharf
London
E14 5LQ

All my love letters to you.

First Take

I don't know where to begin; maybe it's better if I don't. To be completely honest with you, I'm not sure why I'm even writing this; I guess it's something you do without any particular reason to do it, which is probably what I like most about it. This could be one of the many stereotyped novels that are published every year and even only some of them get a good critique from some important magazine like *The New Yorker*; or are considered 'good books' by the public's judgment. The good thing about this book is that it's not really a book; I get to say this because David Antin already did in his own way, "It always caused me conflict to be considered a poet. If Robert Lowell is a poet, I don't want to be a poet. If Robert Frost was a poet, I don't want to be a poet. If Socrates was a poet, I'll consider it." If *Twilight* is a book, then I don't want this to be a book. If *The Catcher in the Rye* is a book, I'll consider it.

Maybe it's not even necessary for somebody to meet you and greet you as they strangle your flesh with theirs when you cordially shake hands because that's what you're supposed to do when you meet someone, but maybe it only takes nothing to interact with someone else. This introduction, or whatever it is, is starting to feel a helluva lot like some philosophical sermon Agnes Danell would tend to start talking about when she's trying to cover the emptiness that she is. Hoping in this way that her meaningless words will make any sense whatsoever, disguising the bareness in her mind with false intellectual frosting. I'd really hate for that to be the first impression you have of me; I'm not sure I even want to give you one. So I'm going to stop, I don't want to create false allusions. You probably don't really even know who Agnes Danell is and knowing about her isn't really something you'd like to know. Agnes Danell is the co-captain of one of those cheerleading squads you tend to see in MTV musicals like Macy Gray's *Beauty in the World* and she also drives one of those brand new Cadillacs everyone used to want. I'm really only mentioning her because she is my closest reference to a spoilt superficial shallow society.

You might be wondering what a strange and peculiar introduction to begin a book, and I agree. There are millions of versions of the introductions to this book; I knew the moment I wrote my first that it wasn't going to be my last, only because I barely wrote anything. I've written at least 10 books since I was 14. Every time I was about to finish one, I hated it and started another. This isn't really the most usual way to begin a book in order to convince you that you're going to love it until you reach page 10 and you realise you can't continue reading anymore; either you're not interested because this isn't the type of love story you had in mind or you are basically bored and can't have any more of this. Maybe your parents told you to buy this book, maybe your friends told you about it or maybe, simply, you were just curious because you just saw it hanging out of a shelf or thrown in the floor and decided to be one of those people who pick it up—maybe even, you bought it by mistake. I'm saying this now because I don't want any misunderstandings, this isn't a love story and it's definitely not a guidebook of any sort. I am not some type of Martin Luther King that can fix it (which is not really what I'm looking forward to be). It's as simple as this: you can't be Martin Luther King if there's already been a Martin Luther King. You can't be J D Salinger if there's already been a J D Salinger and you certainly can't be Jim Jarmusch if there still is a Jim Jarmusch. But you can be you through what they were and forgot to be.

I pretty much hated anything to do with marketing and business in my high school, so selling a product to a costumer isn't really my forte, but I bet if this book ever gets published, they'll know exactly what to do. I'll consent them to do anything but create an appealing book cover to mind game your conscience into overthinking whether you are or you aren't going to like the damn book, and all that propaganda about 'judging a book by its cover', well, in this case, how can you judge a book by its cover if it doesn't even have one? I want it plain, I want to sell it as it is: 200 white pages with long black skylines stuck in a margin.

I'm going to be straightforward and honest; unless you're prepared to hear the truth come out of a liar, then stop reading. The most probable thing you'll do is criticise how bad it is, which in a way is good, at least you might've found your criteria or maybe you will just opt for being some phony that, if ever were to come across me someday, would stop me in the middle of the street and give me some phony typical comment like, "I loved your book," when you didn't, but you thought it was the polite thing to do or the convenient thing to do. I don't like phony people. My intentions aren't to sweeten you with poetic words in order to compel you to meditate on whether you're going to like it or not, but it talks about you and I know how narcissistic we all are, being the centre of attention and all is what we seek for wherever we go, and you might begin to unconsciously deny it to yourself at this point, but it'll still be there. So we might as well admit it for once, and as in this book you are going to be the centre of attention, my bet is you'll love it. You'll even dare to think it's dedicated to you, even if it's not.

Maybe you haven't realised but in this whole introduction, I haven't talked about myself at any moment: you don't know my name, my age, what I like, the friends I have, what I believe in or where I'm from, and to be truthful, all those things are irrelevant to know who the abstraction behind the typewriter is. Everything really just begins with some name, to classify ourselves as a real somebody, although I feel the purpose of it just represents a nobody and I don't want to be a nobody. It's unnecessary to tag who I am under some lousy name; I am not a product on sale. You don't need this name to reassure that I am someone with boiling blood running through her veins, flesh and cold bones—even though I am something abstract, something yet to be discovered. If you're scared you have nothing to refer me with; then don't, a name shouldn't be the reason why you can, but my principles of what I see, what I feel and what I say of those combined.

Even after reading all this, you must have an idea of who I am or who I could be. You've missed a detail; you don't know me, nobody knows me. Not even you know each other, but the idea you've created of one another in this absurd way that just prevents you from getting to know yourself. So my best guess now is, after all the crap I just made you read, you must be starting to wonder who am I? If I'm not what you thought I was, well, you see it's like Hamlet's old saying, "To be or not to be." I'm not what I seem, and I don't seem what I am, I'm just simply an idea created by my ideas and isn't that terrifying.

"…there is an idea of a Patrick Bateman, some kind of abstraction, but there is no real me, only an entity, something illusory, and though I can hide my cold gaze and you can shake my hand and feel flesh gripping yours, and maybe you can even sense our lifestyles are probably comparable: I simply am not there."

—BRET EASTON ELLIS
American Psycho, 1991

Seq. 1 Int. Bedroom

I am laid on my bed looking at the ceiling; what's a better way to start a book than lying on a bed? My room is big and that sometimes stops me from thinking because I get distracted with any silly little thing inside its chaos. My bed is on one side beside the useless wardrobe masqueraded in David Bowie and Lou Reed posters, not to mention the one of Santana that's looking back at me. My bed is really comfortable as it absorbs the shape of my body once I lay on it for a while, but I don't much like the wardrobe, it just takes up too much space. My writing desk is by the window because I like looking at the views, although they aren't really that beautiful. The bathroom is part of my room, which I find lucky, only my parents and I have a bathroom in our rooms, my brother doesn't. It is probably because I'm older and my parents need their privacy. I quite much like this space, but it's a space that's easy to replace, that's what makes me like it most.

As I've mentioned in my lousy introduction, I'm not very enthusiastic about names or surnames for that matter, so you'll probably never know mine. My name doesn't have any strange urban story behind it that could interest you. It's a state of the US and it appears to be the name of a building in New York, where old Chapman decided to murder the ex-leader of The Beatles. I carry *The Catcher in the Rye* with me wherever I go and I still haven't master planned in murdering Bob Dylan. Fame killed John Lennon, not Chapman. Although I don't really want to get into this topic, but if fame wasn't given such an importance, maybe Chapman would've never killed old John, he'd be too busy buying *Franny & Zooey* in Barnes and Nobles, and be headed down Park Avenue for a coffee as he walks his dog and looks at the sky hoping today it won't rain even though it's Autumn, and he knows that at this time of the year in New York, it probably will.

If you haven't figured what shoddy name my parents decided to give me once the umbilical cord was cut, then you're going to enjoy this book way more. And if you have figured it out, well, what can I say, I am no longer the one in control as you know something about me but I know nothing about you. I recently turned seventeen, although when I say recently, I mean last year and apparently, it's the age in which everything's supposed to happen, and by everything people mean:

Drinking
Having sexual intercourse
Experimenting drugs
Going out
Drinking
Sex
More sex
Finding who you are
Stressing about the future
Stressing about the past
Stressing
Falling 'in love'
Falling 'out of love'
Meeting people
Losing friends
Hating your parents
Loving your parents
Depression
Realisation
More sex, I guess

I feel like this list could be going on for hours and I really don't want to bore you with all that nonsense you've probably already heard about a dozen times anyways in any *Teen Vogue* or *Cosmopolitan* magazine in a long car ride or in a sleepover with your closest friends. Some of it is true and some of it is just bull that the American stereotype crap movies have put into our heads. It's what bad cinema does to you: it encourages you to continue believing in the possibility of the stupid, instead of lightening a path like *Dead Poets Society*, which convinces you of the extinction of the ignorant. To be completely honest with you, dear reader, everyone prefers idiocy, including you and me. I feel like I should have some coffee; I'm starting to talk like someone who has no idea what she's talking about, although, maybe I do have a conscience about this paragraph. I am conscious that I need caffeine even though I find coffee absurd, and the taste has never gotten to like me, it's as if it repelled me drinking it; I think that's probably why I try to drink so much coffee lately, it's not because the caffeine has been underlined as a natural stimulant that awakens your brain and nervous system and so on, but because for however much I drink of it, it will never like me, my lips don't correspond to its flavour, neither does my tongue, or glands, which usually end up swollen because I always burn myself when drinking coffee.

In my room, as I think and scribble down all these thoughts as if they are going to make any sense, my gaze gets lost and finds itself on the brown corkboard pinned to the wall above my writing desk. The brown corkboard is bashed with photographs and stickers from known brands like *Vans*; I even notice *The Smiths* patch falling off from one side. I want to get up and pin it properly, but if it did fall, I'd do that later. I bought it in England when I went to visit my older brother. I have an older brother as I have a younger brother, they don't have any names either, although if we're really going to get to know each other, you'd be interested to know my little brother wants to be an actor. Maybe if he ever gets to do anything you'd ever watch, you might find out his name. My older one is one of those business English men. He is proper English now: nobody would've said he'd grown up in the valley. He is meaning to get married soon; I didn't hear this from him though. My dad read it in an English paper that got trashed in the can near our house, which my father later picked up to use in his studio so the floor wouldn't get spit with paint that is impossible to clean off.

My older brother and I didn't really get along at first, he'd always take me to these really boring parties because he hadn't gotten his license yet and I did. So my mum made me drive him around, which was quite ironic as I was two years younger than him at the time. It was really embarrassing for him. "Leave me here," he'd say and two minutes later without hyperbolic exaggeration, he'd come back and tell me to drive him over to Bruce's house because his friends were going there now. That was one of the first times I realised the society we live in, depends on trends; I think it takes out the fun in everything. It's like those parties that no one really feels like going to but ends up going to only because everyone else they know is going, and not because it'd be rude not to show up but because if you didn't, nobody'd remember to invite you for the next one—it's all about maintaining a social status. It's just the flock and how it works, they go where everyone else does, just how my brother did. I think it's all bullshit. All I said earlier on that list is just bullshit, what I'm saying is that what happens to you when you're seventeen is the same crap that happened to you when you were sixteen and that will probably happen to you when you're eighteen. Maybe you mature, whatever that's supposed to mean, or you become more childish, your age has nothing to do with it. I've just thought about it because one of Yoko Ono's quotes is staring at me from over the corkboard, I read it in my head, *'Some people are old at 18 and some are young at 90. Time is a concept that humans created'.*

I met this clown once at one of those birthday parties your parents always throw you when you're turning twelve and they invite all your classmates you stop being friends with once you become a sophomore. They'd also invite all my classmates' parents and their pets. I've noticed parents really like to have a lot of people at their child's birthday, maybe it's because they can't celebrate theirs anymore. They order dozens of junk food such as cupcakes and cookies, and inflate a bouncing castle in the back garden so the neighbours can see they can afford one, as well as all those balloons and bright colours covering the sky and garden grass, because it's more expensive. The clown my parents rented for my birthday party had pale white skin and a big red fluffy nose that covered all his corrupted expressions. He wouldn't stop smiling with his dirty teeth, and his eyes wouldn't stop glowing with his hidden dark circles and his face was inflated just like the balloons he sold. He wore colourful clothes that could've been bleached by the tears he didn't show. I always saw him at the same spot in one corner of our backyard, sat on this really uncomfortable chair without saying anything, he just blew balloons and tried to make children laugh by poking his squeaky red nose. I never dared to go and ask him if he could give me a balloon too. You must be wondering why I'm telling you this now, but that's where you got it all wrong because I'm not telling you anything, my mind must've dazzled after finding this photograph of my first birthday party.

It's 7.50 am; I woke up 20 minutes ago. I'm used to waking up this early to go to school so I don't really mind. My mother used to wake me up, but since she left, and my dad is always busy, he forgets to wake up my little brother and me. I've learnt to be a morning person even if I don't want to. I used to have *New Order* playing as my alarm but it became rather annoying so I replaced it for *Sid Vicious'* scream in *God Save the Queen*, which I think is even worse now that I am waking up to it. I can't remember the last time I saw my little brother, I'm actually not even sure if he might be sleeping in his room right now. He died some days ago; it's actually been a long time since I saw him. Don't ask me how he died because I don't know; I don't even know if he's actually dead or if he's simply disappeared. I just remember my dad buying him this massive present for his birthday last week, with one of those new PlayStation 4 inside it and that was the last day I saw him. My dad doesn't seem worried by the fact that his son does no longer exist; I think he's too wacked out to notice, but I notice. If my mum was here, she'd probably notice too and she'd expect me to hang a poster around our neighbourhood with the title 'LOST BOY' or something, but she's not here to tell me to do it, so I'll probably won't end up doing it.

I would talk to you about my mother, but I don't think it'll make her very happy if I started describing her private life on a public book. Although, I agree with Allen Ginsberg's theory that 'Poetry is the outlet for people to say in public what is known in private', but the only difference with this situation is this isn't poetry and it's not my mother's. It's mine, therefore, she has no reason for having her private life exposed publicly by her egocentric daughter. She gets very upset, very fast. If I did publish anything about her, *God knows* what she'd do; she'd probably have one of those fits in her room to not have the thrive of beating me up and then after she'd cooled off, she'd take those 10 deep breaths her yoga instructor recommends her to make, and then she'd go to the spa with Frankie, her publicist friend and they'd both moan about how mercenary and fickle teenagers are. That's one of the reasons why she decided one day to just leave us; she got upset. We had a discussion, and the next morning, we all woke up with a small envelope at the end of our beds. I found it weird that nobody woke up when she left them; evidently, on each of the letters, it said something different or at least I hope it does. My dad made us promise the morning we found them that we were never to show one another what the letter said, and so the mystery lies in my family for two years now, which is not a long time, but if you think about it, it is. I sometimes even suspect my dad helped her get away in some way—he did seem awfully calm about the whole situation at the start, but then again, so did I and I certainly know I didn't help her in any way.

The thing is, only I'm aware that a thirteen-year-old boy is non-existent, but nowadays, it's quite normal that so many kids are disappearing. Steve Jobs and Bill Gates are accomplices of kidnapping children all around the world, even if one of them is dead. I wonder why they'd want so many children, I mean; I think my brother is pretty useless. He sure has no idea of how to cooperate at home, I doubt he'd be able to handle the biggest businesses of modern technology; he only knows how to use the products. And how many more iPhones are there left to be made? I mean, is there really going to be some iPhone 50 plus or whatever they add to it that makes it look new and appealing to get the audiences' attention, and convince them into buying it. It's not the president or the government that are in control anymore, its publicity and the media. They give you what you want, even when you're not aware you consciously want it. We want what everyone else wants, which completely deviates the idea that we are all diverse individuals, if we are so easily bought by the same commodities.

I stand up from my bed to go open the windows so more light trespasses my room. I look out of the window; I have to because the view isn't normally beautiful, but today, it appears like a longing beauty. It's a view I might not see for a long time, at least not like this, from the window of this rigorous room in this house in this precise neighbourhood. I'm not the only one staring out the window this morning, the sun is staring at me from his and I can feel my face starting to get red. I move away from the window. The sun isn't that powerful to leave me sunburn from only facing it two or three minutes, but I have very sensitive skin. I look around the room for a while, as if I were waltzing in a Russian ball. I do this because I don't want to forget where everything is. I like knowing where things are once I've left them there; I like people knowing who I am once I've shown them, too. I head to the bathroom to wash my face so I can feel refreshed and awake. I put one of those special creams for sensitive skin and smear it all over my face like some tourist on a beach. I massage it carefully so it's absorbed properly; my mother showed me how to do this. I look at myself and think twice before putting any make-up on. I decide not to put anything on; I don't really like make-up that much on me anyways. I look at my face, from the end of one eyebrow to the other one and then I look towards my eyes, and it annoys me how they follow my movement so I can't really look at each of them separately. I look at my nose, I don't like it so I distort my look back to my eyebrows, and turn my face sideways. I like my nose now. I look at my lips and unconsciously smile. I stop smiling once I've realised this and confront the mirror, as I breathe all over my reflected image, leaving an unrecognisable fog. I step away from the mirror and head back to my room, and I lie on my bed again for the last time this day.

Seq. 2 Int. Bedroom/Kitchen

Today, I would usually do what I do every day before going to that educational institution for posh spoiled brats which has been so wrongly predominated as a 'school', as in a place where you are supposed to learn, or so that's what the dictionary says. I would put my uniform on, disgusted; I hate the patterns it's decorated with and the wool irritates my skin. It's not that I'm allergic, but it just makes my legs go all red and itchy, making me look like a dehydrated shrimp in an expensive seafood restaurant. Especially, above all, I hate the fact of being forced to wear this uniform. I hate being forced into doing things just for the hell of it; at least if I was given an equitable reason, I wouldn't mind it as much. I'd simply do it because I want to, because I'd find it amusing or interesting, either of both but I'd do it.

My routine bores me, it's monotonous and this uniform is partly guilty, at least I know I'd plead it as such on a court. It only changes on the weekends, and not even then, when I feel like getting high or getting drunk at some stupid party with people I've never seen before and hope I'll never see again. I've been to quite an abundance of parties these past few weekends and probably that's why I am so exhausted, even though I've awoken holding hands with the sun. It was Eddie's party last week, and the two weekends before, it was this girl's party, she threw two for the hell of it and because she happens to be filthy rich or so I read in the schools' newspaper over in the gossip column, this girl in my literature class writes. Now I feel like going to a party is like going to a circus where you can either choose to be part of the audience, backstage or on the stage, only here the performers don't get paid. I sometimes don't even know who's the host or if it really is somebody's birthday. I'm just there. Mainly, to get drunk. I want to disrupt my routine covered in hash with a new one that'll make me forget not go down a spiral into a dark hole, or end up like one of those crackheads that reside in South Central. I'm scared I'm just affectionate to hash, it creates my weekends too predictable, although alcohol doesn't do much of a difference either on the long term. I should probably stop depending so much on the side effects of drugs to achieve…what do I want to achieve? If it's fame, I can't have it and still be a writer, I'd just be another manipulating idiot, and there are already too many of those. I'm not saying I don't want fame; I guess I just want it separate from my dreams. I don't think fame and dreams are a symbiosis, I guess I just want my dreams to stay as dreams because I can visit them more often in my sleep, and have the assurance they're always going to be there, they're never going to end. I ask myself this question a lot, why do I depend on the side effects of drugs? And I always answer it in my head, but I'd never be capable of writing it down or telling a soul. Anyways, as I was explaining, I feel like I'm stuck in the same day like a groundhog until I start doing different choices like one of those movies they continuously make with the intention of provoking a somewhat change in people, a realisation, sort of like a climax moment. Getting drunk is really starting a partnership with the host of the party or any member of the party; I never thought business would be so easy as to share a bottle of expensive vodka followed by some tequila shots.

What I love about being drunk is I'm completely unconscious of any of my actions, what I hate about being drunk is I'm not conscious about everybody else's. I think it's the only time in our pathetic lives in which we don't care what people think, we just do it, like the phony Nike ad starring some skinny model. Hopefully, the bloody bastards who were with you when you were in an uncontrolled condition will forget what you did or said, but they probably won't, that's what I hate most about us, we only like it when it gets bad, when it gives us an opportunity of being the biggest *sonuva bitches* we can ever be. It's exhausting how we always feel the need to be awful to one another, creating it a form of entertainment; no wonder cinema is going out of business. If it's the Hollywood lifestyle you're looking for the only thing you need is to go to parties, and fancy dinners, or brunch.

I've emerged out of the feathery blankets that felt like a heavenly brush from Dante when he wrote about Beatrice. I put on this white strapless top I stole from some sleepover I got invited to. I put on my favourite pair of jeans and I tie my shoes as I grab my bag pack, and hesitate before grabbing my sunglasses and decide to leave them there as a reminder that I leave all my filters back home. I go downstairs and enter the dirty kitchen. It'd be clean if the cleaning lady hadn't gone back to Rumania or wherever it is she's from. To all this, *Love test* from *The Growlers* is playing. I wonder now, how can you even try to continue reading without playing that song? I clean the kitchen and I prepare breakfast replacing my mum's maternal habitudes; it was only my brother and I who actually ate together at the table now. I sometimes miss my mother, especially when we are at the breakfast table. It's so quiet. I say I miss her sometimes because I don't think she deserves any feeling towards her, not even anger, although what I miss is not her but what her role in this family was and how it affected each one of us. I didn't cry when she left. I kind of expected it to happen, she wasn't happy and when you're not happy, you try very hard to look happy until you kill yourself or leave, I'm glad she left. She continuously said I didn't love her. In a way, I feel like it was my fault she left, so I can't really hate her, but I hate what she's done to my dad and to my brother. They didn't deserve to be left alone. Anyways, now she's not here telling each one of us what to do, and what calcium or iron pills to take or what's the right food to eat in the morning so we have enough energy for the whole day without getting fat. She prevented the increase of weight at all cost in our family; she always brought her business home which was this new partnership with a friend of hers where they are responsible for Dolly Parton's and Courtney Love's facial renewal. Cobain's probably laughing at me from his grave because I bet he's even seen it in the news. My mother lived in a constant agony always preoccupied about our diets and whether acne had hit on us yet or not, she obviously wanted the best for us, I'm aware, but then again, she didn't give a damn. If not, she wouldn't have just left three useless wacked heads to deal with life's essential evil necessities by themselves, it's more as if she was preoccupied by the image of the perfect American family. I sometimes wondered if she'd confused our life for the realities she often watched when she had a break from work.

Today, I'm running away, even screaming it in this piece of paper makes it sound strange and not convincing. It's quite a selfish thing to do too and it begins to terrify me that I'm actually going to do this: leaving my dad here alone with my brother, doing the exact thing I hate my mother for, but it's not like they didn't expect it to happen. I'm not going to dramatize it, because it's not really such a big deal. I've been talking about running away ever since I read *The Catcher in the Rye* when I was thirteen, and I've read it about 13 times since then. It's the only book I carry with me wherever I go, as well as *13.99$* written by my favourite French writer, Frederic Beigbeder and *Less than Zero* by Bret Easton Ellis. I had planned this through for ten years, saving up all the salary and some good tips I got every week from my bummer job at Moon-shadows, some overpriced beachside bar in Malibu a couple minutes from my house. Its decorations are outrageous, although everything a tourist with money is looking for, and they've even got their own DJ to play the music, only he's forced to play music he doesn't like. I stole my dad 200$ late last night when he fell asleep, just in case; it's not like he's going to need them more than me. I forgot to tell you where I'm from or where I live, but I'm guessing you've already found out after all the references of places I'm making. We all live in the same place, only undercover with different names, cultures and people to locate them, but it's the same crap wherever you go only some are better camouflaged. But I mean, if you live in Los Angeles, especially near Hollywood, where everybody is an emblematic prostitute in all their departments, brown-nosing to a 'God' with a restricted salary who drinks too much, and lies about heaven and what not, you really rethink twice if it's the same everywhere. I live where earth keeps all the commands to control the world; I live in the backstage set of the world's reality. Los Angeles is the Oracle of entertainment, media and publicity. Los Angeles is the reason why we don't have time to think, we are too busy thinking we're busy with something that we don't know is irrelevant. But people love being distracted from the real screen that is their life. Everything in life is a business now, created to rip us off. It's a bit like what Frederic Beigbeder said in *13.99$*, 'It's not publicity that imitates life, it's life that imitates publicity'. We are living in the expanded new set of Truman's Show and here, there aren't any hidden back doors at the end of the sea, and if there were, I doubt we'd go in looking for them; we're too comfortable staring at its redundant saturation tones at the apparent 'unreachable' horizon hiding our freedom. How can we be so idle as to not wake up in the morning and admit that what we want is out there, and it's not some materialist construction—but a hidden spectre of our desires we can never seem to satisfy.

I'm in the middle of eating my breakfast when my brother out-of-the-bloom shows up. I'm saying out-of-the-bloom because lately, it's not like he's showed his face a lot around the house. So I'm guessing now I can quit worrying about whether he's still alive or not and if I should or shouldn't go around the neighbourhood hanging 'Lost Boy' posters. He sits on the chair in front of me at the table as I stand up to go make him something to eat.

"Are you going to make scrambled eggs?" he asks, with his nose stuck to his plate as he sits down.

"And toast," I add, proud of how good I'm preparing the breakfast today. "Are you sick?" I ask as I hear him cough and catch him looking for headache pills when I turn around to look at him. I'm actually not sure if he's looking for headache pills but my mum always said they were in the kitchen somewhere

"I'm just tired, haven't had much sleep lately," he complains as he continues his helpless research for medication in the wooden shelves packed with food even though it's on the other side of the room from where he's looking. "And hungry, and very not bothered to go to school," he adds as he grumbles and gives up his search as he sits down again, and I hand him the pan with the scrambled eggs so he serves himself.

"Did you go out last night?" I ask as I leave my plate on the side beside him and go over to get the medicine he's so desperately in need for. He didn't usually go out on school days or any days, but recently, he'd made some new friends he wouldn't even talk about that brought him home far too late than usual, and as my dad is never home at night and I usually don't check up on him before going to bed, he does whatever he wants. This whole conversation with my brother feels like a schemed kitchen commercial.

"No, I just stayed watching Teen Wolf for far longer than I expected, I might skip school today if it's cool with you," he says, before taking another bite of his toast.

"What do you mean you're not going to school?" I ask, alerted and in the typical phony tone parents tend to give their children when they're amused by something their kids have asked or said that doesn't go in accordance with their expectations. The problem with my little brother is that he's 14 and he thinks he's 18.

"I don't feel like going. Can't I just skip it?" he groans, rolling his eyes the same way I used to roll my eyes when I wanted to get something my way.

"I don't see why not. It's your problem if you get caught," I simply answer in my most irked tone and sincerely, I couldn't give a damn of whether he went to school or not. I would've if it was any other day but today, I am more worried about picking up the train in time than my lousy brother missing his trigonometry class for once.

"Yeah, I know but I just need you to back me up, you know. Just in case Head McDowell calls in asking for me and all," he says as he starts emptying his schoolbag and piling all his books on the table as he replaces them with energy drinks from the fridge and bags of chips from the closet, and in a glimpse, he's already headed to the door.

"Where are you going to?" I ask, in a scream with the hope he'd hear me before he steps foot out of the house and starts cruising down the street with his skate.

"We're just going to be at the skate park and maybe later grab some waves, I'll call you later," he shouts back, out of breath before he closes the door in my face, preventing anything else to come out from my mouth. I could hear his adrenaline running down the stairs like it were the happiest day in his life and it probably was going to be one of the greatest days in his life until he arrived home later that night or early the morning after, rushed into my room to tell me all about his day, and realise I was no longer there. You must be thinking what a lousy conversation to portray, and it's true, it is— but my brother, the same as my mother, can't really sit down and talk about something that doesn't concern him or his plans.

I was also going to skip school today anyways so I couldn't really start acting like it was the wrong thing to do when I was about to do the same exact thing, only much worse. I know I could be running away after school but I couldn't risk being seen by those I considered calling my friends. I was mad about my best friends, because they're the same as me, they're mad about life. I haven't really spoken about them yet, not because I don't think they're important enough, but because the timing is wrong. If I started talking about them now, nostalgia would ravage all my feelings and I wouldn't be able to leave. That's the only reason why I'm not still fast asleep in bed or writing the novel that depresses the hell out of me, also because I don't know what to write sometimes. I feel like what I write is just a whole load of crap. I don't even know if I'm a good writer, I just know I like doing it and I mean for something I like, I'm not going to stop just because I'm unsure of the fact of whether I'm good at it or not.

"Tout est provisoire: l'amour, l'art, la planète Terre, vous, moi. La mort est tellement intéluctable qu'elle prend tout le monde par surprise. Comment savoir si cette journée n'es pas le dernière? On croit qu'on a le temps. Et puis, tout d'un coup, ça y est, on se noie, fin du temps réglementaire. La mort est le seul rendez-vous que ne soit pas noté dans votre organiser."

—Frederic Beigbeder
99 Francs, 2007

Seq. 3 Int. Bedroom

I'm used to asking myself questions about merely everything and maybe that's a virtue or a defect. But as they say, curiosity killed the cat, and I'm actually not sure if that's a saying or not, I just remember having heard it in a conversation between Pamela Anderson's cheap interpret and this old hairy man with a Rolex watch on his right wrist and a gold Cartier bracelet on his left. He was watching her artificial breasts so intensely, he could've fallen down the doomed thin line that separated them from each other, as they tamed the bikini bra that kept them prisoners. I actually liked working down at that beachside bar, now I'm going to miss it. I learnt so much from all those costumers that went through it, even more than what I learn at school. After all you're reading, I suspect you must've analysed what type of person I must be, I'm sure you know all about Kant and Steiner's theories, so I'm not that surprised. For starters, none of the bull I've just written actually interests me, although I feel some things like these have to be said sometimes, so people know they're actually here and that they're not the result of someone's dull imagination.

I've been trying to adapt to solitude like a chameleon adapts to the colours around him, only it'd be much easier to do it stoned. I've been accommodating to being alone ever since I decided I was actually going to do it, that I was running away, leaving behind only some thoughtful letters to my dad, my brother, my Uncle Lloyd and even one for Andy, although I knew he wasn't going to read it, I still wanted to leave him something behind. The concept is that you can exceed of existence whilst still existing—my English teacher once told me this when I was failing all my exams, so I've created of it my own Keating's 'carpe diem'. The type of people that fear being alone are those that end up wasting their salary on therapists anyways, and I don't want to be like them. Excluding Woody Allen, I actually don't know why Woody Allen always goes to so many therapists; a therapist should go see him. In a way, going to a therapist is like going to a brothel, only you're paying to have a

26

different type of oral relation, although maybe if you leave in a good tip.

Anyways, it's just another way of avoiding solitude because you're with someone, we always do end up being with someone and I find that rather tragic to be true. After all you've read, you might think I'm an anti-social. I wish even I was capable of such privation. I'm not anti-social; in fact, I'm very social, even too social at times. I am hated and I might be loved but not right now, right now, I am forgotten.

I'll actually give you a brief synopsis of this book, I know on the back of its cover you might think you've read something just to make sure you're going to like it or not or some little hint of what it's about. But I don't think that happened when you got hold of this book, I don't want you being a sneaky bastard that goes through the back door when you can always knock. You're always so worried if you're going to like something or not that you don't risk your gut anymore, who would've thought we'd been savage animals in pre-history. Now that you know who I am, I just want to see if you really want to know me or if all these pages were just a whim to entertain yourself for a while. Perhaps, you were on a long car ride and this was the first thing you grabbed, or you're just sat in the floor at Barns and Novels picking out books, and reading their beginnings to see which one captivates you the most. Or it's just like one of those typical whims we all go through in our early naïve years in high school when we feel like we've fallen in love with the first pretty thing that comes up to us, only to realise the next day that it was all about bosting our ego's. I am really going out of context here, feeling like I'm talking in one of those chick flicks which always end up being a laugh at how ridiculous love and friendships are portrayed so vacant.

I've wanted to write this book, or to actually finish it, for two years. I know I've said this before, but I didn't say it right. It devours me inside, eating every piece of me till leaving me disintegrated. I've got so many ideas that I don't know which ones the right one, probably this one isn't the one, but I think it's time for one of them to be and it was actually Mike's idea that I'd just get on with one idea, and he probably said that because he's been through all of it before. You see, he's also a writer, only a writer in denial. He writes raps, I consider them poems but he always rectifies it with just being a simple rap. He mainly acts like they're no good; he could write a book if he got to it but his ego is just too big because the streets of city have gotten hold of the wheels in his sake. He writes like a writer and he's an artist but he doesn't know it yet. I think he is someone who is so many things, but then again, it's not like I really know him that much. We've only spoken a couple of times, but those times were enough. I don't know how to explain it, but then again, some things like these should never really be explained, but you ought to meet him, you really do. If he weren't so cocky and arrogant at times, I'd consider calling him a friend.

Once we were waiting for the bus together, I was listening to music and so was he. I only looked at him twice from up to down to be sure it was him, and I know so did he. The reason why we actually started talking was because my phone went out of battery and I had to stop listening to music. I just stood there in an incomplete silence. As his music was so loud, you could hear he was playing *Tupac* for the repetition of *Hail Marys'* that pounded in his earlobe. I looked at him for the third time since we had stood there, and he lowered the music's volume until he took them off and looked at me.

"Hi," he'd said shyly, looking over to where I was standing.

"Hey," I'd said.

"Was that too loud?" he'd asked. "If it was I'm sorry, I just—you know don't notice."

"It was fine, don't worry," I'd said. "So, how's everything?" I'd asked. "It's been so long since I haven't seen you at the Ghetto Park." The Ghetto Park is where they'd all go to skate even though it wasn't a proper skate park like the ones in Venice Beach and Santa Monica—they liked it because nobody they knew went there, I used to go sometimes with Andy.

"Yeah, I've been studying and all, no time to skate you know," he'd said, looking down. "Everything's cool though, how are you hanging?"

"Everything's good, I'm just a little balked," I'd spontaneously said.

"Why?" he'd asked, looking down at his phone as he wrote something. "The bus is nearly here."

"Remember last time we spoke, I told you about the book I was writing?" I'd said.

"Yeah, how's it going? I'd like to get to read it someday," he'd said, the typical comment someone always says when you tell them you're doing something.

"It's going good, if it weren't, because my ideas change of scenery," I'd said. "I mean what I'm writing—it's…it's just a whole load of crap," I'd moaned as I took a deep breath and kneeled my back on the wall behind me whilst I'd closed my eyes in discretion.

"Now I want to start re-writing it all over again with another idea, but I'm tired of this always happening, I just want to finish it for once!" I'd exhaled breathless and exhausted of having to actually explain my pragmatic crisis to someone who didn't want to hear it. He was still writing something on his phone, and time had passed before he said anything.

"It's psychological. You demand too much from yourself," he'd said as he took one look at me from behind his shoulder. "Just think everyone will like it, if you're not happy with what you've done, then do it again, just over and over again," he'd said as he'd given me a tender smile.

"You're probably right. So, what are you writing over there?" I'd asked, even though sequential seconds after asking, I realised I didn't really want to know.

"Grocery list before I forget and my mum beats the shit out of me," he'd said cheekily, smiling down to his phone. "What was your book about?" he'd asked uninterestingly, and I never really liked talking about that subject with him or with anyone for that matter. I hate it when I'm asked what it's about, not even writing it now I know what it's about.

"It's not really anything, it just gives me headaches and I…I can't eat or even think really, it's all about this book," I'd divulged as I unburned all that dumb pressure.

"Well, it must be a hell of a book if you can't talk about it. You should eat though, no wonder you looking so pale," he'd said. "And this is Los Angeles, you either get a tan soon or you'll start looking like one of them tourists."

"I look pale?" I asked.

"Now don't go on and change the subject, yes you do. Now look, what I don't understand, and I'll probably not be able to, is if you're so unstable, why don't you stabilise? Why don't you like it? Why are you giving it so much importance?" he'd asked. "You don't depend on that damn book of yours, it has to be something else, like for example, a plus of who you are, but not the 100% you," he'd said. I knew he was probably right, but like any other human being, we don't tend to like the truth so we try to recess it before it arriving. At least, that's what I do with my lies. Then I'd felt like it was impossible to defer the topic, he clearly had no time for my doubts, and anyways, he was probably the only person I actually listen to and accept the truth from, even though I may not agree with it.

"You know, I think you're right, but I'm not human enough to be able to admit it to you," I'd replied honestly.

"Well, the bus is here so maybe you won't have to," he'd said as he approached the front door of the bus and I followed.

I remember we sat down in different seats, which I found completely ridiculous, but then again, we are ridiculous most of the time. I remember turning around to look for him when I found him bowed down with his face stuck to his damn phone again, writing incessantly.

"I'm so stupid sometimes," I'd said aloud. I remember I hoped he'd answer or say something. I also just happen to blab anything out when I'm mad at myself, or I overthink about it something too much that I forget I'm talking aloud—that's why most of the times my friends say I'm random, but it's just that I'm still a child. The problem is I never say what I'm really thinking, I try though, and I really do. But it just doesn't come out as I thought to say it in my head and I end up looking like someone who has no idea what she's talking about; a degenerate illiterate with a severe brain concussion.

"I'm a bit stupid too sometimes," he'd admitted proudly from the other side. I was surprised he'd even heard me, so I went over and sat with him.

"Well, we all are, but that doesn't mean we have to forget who can perform and who simply are," I'd pointed out once sat beside him.

"You think?" he'd questioned, not noticing I was sat beside him now. I caught a glimpse of what he was writing, and as I said earlier, it was one of those poems from my point of view and a rap from his.

"No, I don't think so. But that doesn't prevent me from thinking about it now and then. I don't have the privilege of believing in anything lately," I'd confessed in a sigh of hidden despair.

"What's wrong? You seem in need of love, I mean you haven't stopped sighing," he'd affirmed answering his own question as if love was the cure for everything.

"On the contrary; I've got spare. I could distribute it, if it were food and feed all Africa, and still I would have spare," I'd lied so happily and excitedly, it could've been confused with truth.

"Then what is it?" he'd asked perplexed.

"It's simple; I don't believe in anything because the truth is just a moment of falsity. I could stop this whole 'I'm interesting act' and tell you it could also be because *God* by *John Lennon* is playing right now, and I really can't deny that after listening to it right now and have been writing all week long can cause chaotic nuclear bombs in my way of thinking, leaving my head like Hiroshima," I'd finished proclaiming.

"Cool," he'd said thoughtfully. "In the end, you are mature after all," he'd added with an idyllic smile of august.

"What's that supposed to mean?" I'd demanded rather clueless of what he meant.

"Well, maybe you were 'performing' but you acted really immature before," he'd said ironically.

I didn't know whether to get offended or not, with him you never knew if he meant things in a good way or in a bad way.

"One day, I'll publish this conversation," I'd asserted with a smile.

"Are you thinking on taking all the cash and merit?" he'd asked sarcastically.

"Maybe I'll think about sharing the earnings with you," I'd said.

"That would be very wise, I mean, you might not be crazy after all and all you know," he'd reaffirmed looking at me sideways with a saucy glimpse.

He made everything look like a joke with complete seriousness and laughed more about life than I did for the looks of it. He didn't have time to hate anybody; he was too busy hating himself. He wasn't part of society, but everyone still knew who he was. It's like he won his respect with his negligence towards the mass. We got the bus together thousands of times after that but I didn't really feel like talking and from the looks of it, he didn't either, he just looked down at his phone and wrote constantly. We did smile at each other sometimes but that's something everybody does with about anybody at school when you happen to come across them somewhere else than a school corridor. I wish I knew more about him as to tell you all about him—I'd like to exploit this book from a character like him, but I think it's best if I don't. He already will, if he ever confronts his aspirations and worth, and shows the world all his words. It saddens me.

I'd start taking you through all of my friendships, and all the gossip and Intel on my social elite you're so keen to know about. Mike and I weren't friends, we just agreed on having a conversation a couple of times, but we couldn't be friends, although that doesn't mean I won't miss him. BD was a friend, we spent a lot of time together until she decided to disagree with her having a purpose in life and spent her free time going to a therapist her parents couldn't afford because she'd obsessed over being ill. So we stopped hanging out, although funnily enough, I didn't mind it. I would tell you all about her and everything but I know she wouldn't like that, she was always really preserved about herself and her secrets. Although don't be too deceived, I will obviously end up telling you why. I can't keep secrets in this book and I vowed not to lie. BD and I met at one of those lousy summer camps your parents usually send you to when you're at that age where you're just too intolerable to be coped with all summer. I'm just kidding, if that were the reason of our friendship, it would've ended the day we stepped foot out of that camp. We met at one of those lame parties Diane forced me to go sometimes because this boy, Trevor, went, and she really liked him I guess. When I met BD, she was nothing like the BD she is now. First time I saw her, I confused her for some sorority girl, although she had dark hair and her features were of an oriental trademark which resonated in her beauty that contrasted with the blonde crew she was hanging around with. We started being friends though, which was odd because I didn't really like her at the start until we started talking about music. We are friends because; I guess we both like the same music and Roberto Begnini's performance in *A Night on Earth*, so really, that's what brought us together. Ironic how around where I live, cinema is the moneymaking business but no one really knows anything about it anymore. When I met BD, I felt like I was in the '60s, when the psychedelic movement began to rise accompanied by Jim Morrison and Bob Dylan, as well as Patti Smith and the Beatles.

This book is actually about a letter that'll never be received, the book itself is a love letter. Every book is a love letter hidden under an attractive title and a plot as the background, and only one person in 7 billion can identify it to be theirs, because it talks to them or about them directly. This book could also be about a young frustrated writer that never finishes her book in which the most identified person in this case could end up being me, and that would completely humiliate *Narcissus*, the god of beauty and King of conceit, what a threat would it be to dedicate a book to myself as to drowning in my own reflection, although I don't know if even that would beat the narcissism of a society protected from itself through a looking glass.

A few things about me would be, I'm self-interested, but I do anything I can, not to be, the same way I'm a compulsive liar but I try not to lie. I promise. Like I said, I try. Lying's one of my pre-eminent skills because I'm good at it, I don't lie about things that could hurt somebody, and if I wanted to hurt somebody, I would go straight ahead and tell them the truth and shed down those curtains hiding an empty wallet, a sick family member, an unrequited love, a lost friendship or straight ahead to their insignificance in this world. The truth sometimes is so unbearable, I feel the obligation to lie so it can be bearable, but so do we all. In reality, this book can be about whatever you want; let's say that you're the ones writing it. I mean we all experience things in a different way, that's why we have different perspectives, thoughts, ideas; it's what makes whom, or what, we are authentic.

What the book really is about is how a girl, in this case me, grabs her things and just leaves for New York. Now that's a poster in the hood with the title *Lost Girl* in black, bold capital letters. A part of me thinks my mum, maybe, actually would come out of hiding if she found out. When I was little, I thought of going into a coma just to see if she'd care, if that'd be goddamn enough for her to come back. It's very selfish to do what I'm going to do, I know that, but at least I'm not committing suicide; I'm just becoming an orgasm. Running away is like committing suicide, only you don't die, you're just reborn all over again in another place and alone. I don't want you to think I'm some type of depressive loony maniac, or any tags you can come up to describe me for what I've just said, because you're wrong. I'm just tired of it all being the same. I'm just doing what everyone wishes they could do, but don't in fear of what people will think about them. I used to care; now I couldn't care less. Let them think, for once, let our brainless society attempt to find their missing over-rated organ. I'm quite an impatient person, and I get bored easily. It's already a lot, I've survived 17 years in this crap hole and I mean it's not like I'm not going to come back. I just really need to go to New York. I really need to publish my book. I feel like this book is my only way out of here, the only way of starting again whether it's here or there, but somewhere.

Seq. 4 Ext. Streets

Soon, I'll be writing from an uncomfortable seat in the train from Los Angeles to Chicago. Chicago isn't at all the destination, but the price was lower if I made a transition and from there, I can get a bus to Manhattan's Central Grand Station. It's going to be two days on the railway, with about 31 stops, but I don't really mind. I don't really mind staying one day in Chicago just for the hell of it. I've never actually been, so I might learn something, you never know when you could be learning something. I'm sure you've already pictured what my arrival to Chicago or New York will look like, some really bad American movie in which the director decides to tag it as a romantic tragi-comedy. Even though after watching it, you'll realise you haven't cried or laughed, simply you've seen sequential images in which you profoundly wish that they'd turn into reality because everyone seems exceedingly happy. I'm just going to ruin the intrigue of any movie; if you've seen *Sixteen Candles*, they're all going to be the same, only the story might be vaguely personalised, but they all follow the same pathetic trail. Bad movies show us what we think we want, so they are basically a prolonged bad propaganda commercial whilst good movies take us somewhere we hadn't even considered could exist; they surprise us. Reality is only reality because we recognise it to be; once you let it be manipulated by the wrong people, the only reality left for you is someone else's.

Movie frame with the intention of making you want to buy love as a product:

Int. Train with NYC views
MF: Girl sat on a chair
CF: Girl looking out of the window with her headphones on listening to 'some pathetic sad song'
Dramatic music
CF: Tear strolling down on face

Shots after…

Ext. Times Square
CF: Girl going out of train
Travelling shot of Manhattan
Camera turns back to girl
CF: Girl steps down and nearly falls
MF: Boy holding her before she fell
They fall in love

I don't think it's necessary even to explain what else happens because it's pretty obvious. It's predictable just like we're supposed to have planned our lives. They're predictable, we all know what's going to happen, and it's in the protocol, that's why it's so necessary to get good grades, a good job, a good husband, be a good person…a bloody goddamn good everything, what does good even mean? Another filthy materialist product, that's what good means now.

You are born. You go to kindergarten. You go to school. You go to high school. You go to university. You get a job. You find a husband. You get pregnant. You have two kids. You get divorced. You hate your job. Your kids start to be annoying. You make breakfast. You take the kids to school. You go to work. You eat at work. You get the kids from school. You go home. You cook dinner. You go to sleep. Repeat. You die. Everyone misses you for a day. Then they forget you.

The script is typical. What you'd like to be happening to you, that love was as easy as slowly descending some bus staircase to your favourite city and that suddenly, coincidently, out of nowhere, the boy of your dreams created by your ideals or by some high school crap movie stereotypical jock, appeared right in that moment that you needed him and suddenly, only with the glimpse of your eyes meeting, you'd be guilty of creating the most romantic love story ever heard of. If love were so easy, it wouldn't be love. It would be another crap Hollywood movie trying to fit more goddamn crap in your empty head; now we all know where the garbage goes after it's been picked up in the middle of the night, it's not the landfill or the incinerator, it's our heads, that's probably where the saying, 'you've got steam coming out of your ears' comes from, it's your head being polluted. This way they show you, once more, that they're capable of destroying the only 'real' thing left in this world: Love. The media is capable of doing that; after all, thanks to us, they're the ones who are in control. They're the escape routes that we use to get back in a cage covered in paradisiacal wallpapers. We are just lab rats on a first-class level.

It's ironic really, how much and how often we complain about this society, damn society and its rules and laws, and what we should and shouldn't do, or what paths we should follow, all this unnecessary shit we've created to feel some type of fullness in our pathetic lives so after we can complain, when we're the ones to blame, because complaining is a sort of entertainment nowadays. I'm not generalising, I don't know everyone in the world, but I do know some people, and those people know some people. It's all a process, of listening and observing when you're at a club, party, lunch, and any cynical social event organised to downgrade the people around you, but most importantly to let them humiliate you.

I've been walking a while now between thought and thought. My foot stepping on, every cement square on the ground that builds this yellow path towards some type of Oz. With my left hand, I'm looking for a cigarette in the back pocket of my jeans, as that's where I usually keep them. I don't like keeping the lousy propagandistic boxes with their enterprise's logo, so each time anyone even has a slight read at what the title says, no matter how lousy or ugly it is, you're providing cash for companies initiating all types of cancer around. I might sound like a complete phony, because really, I'm just about to smoke one. The fact that I smoke them out of my jeans instead of the pack, just slightly, remotely changes the whole concept I've just described because I'm smoking nicotine, not the brand and those two things, dear reader, are two completely different things on their own. I smoke to narcotise my anxieties. I also tend to smoke alone, for instance, when I am taking a walk like I am now or when I'm laid in my bed looking out the small window from my bedroom where sometimes a star or two are caught in its frame, or looking up the blank roof over my head, looking down my nose to see the smoke swirling around. I don't want people to know so I lit my cigarettes when there's nobody around as I don't want people around when I do so, smokers or non-smokers, they shouldn't have to endure being around me and that smoke that embodies me when I do. It's not healthy for them and it's not healthy for me, I mean, it's too baffling having all those perky eyes inspect the movement of my mouth and whether I'm doing it right, for things like these you *oughtta* be alone to be able to enjoy them. I think people stop seeing you as you are, once covered with all that smoke around you, it's hard to decrypt if you're who you say you are, and if what you're doing you're doing because you feel in possession of your circumstances, of your addiction, which all revolves with the first question, why did you start smoking?

I really hope I haven't outdistanced the train station, because if not, I will probably get caught and have to wait another day or two for the next train to Chicago. Everyone knows everyone where I live, so it's just about time for someone to spot my accustomed face and my dad's already receiving a call from the other side of Santa Monica LAPD. The train station isn't actually that far away, if I had to compare it with the distance from my house to my high school, it's quite long, but then again, if I had to compare it with the distance between my house and this guy from my school, Lou, it's quite near. Lou lives four blocks away, but they're really four big blocks. He usually skates past my house every morning to catch the school bus on time. I've never actually talked to him, I just know he lives there because, one day, we were having lunch and this girl, *whatdyoucallher* Agnes, started blabbering about how she had recently moved to Beverly Hills because her mother's new husband was one of those music producers or something, and then Lou got really defensive saying, "Well, I live in Santa Monica near the pier but when I get out of here, my parents are going to make sure I study somewhere like France or Italy." I didn't mean to listen to their lame conversation, but it was inevitable not hearing Agnes's squeaky voice, she just kept on blabbering about how many rooms she had now, and how even her dogs, Rory and Spouch, had their own room. It was rather a blast; I mean, I found it funny that people actually spoke about those types of things while they're eating. I mean, isn't it distracting, to eat and talk about things like who's got the best house, or who's square metres of land are greater, when you're seventeen. Even if I tried not to listen to their voices, it was inevitable to talk with Jean, who was sitting in front of me.

Jean and I usually sat together every day since BD stopped coming to school, for she finally succeeded in being diagnosed with something and they sent her away. Then there was also Diane, who's residing in a boarding school in England. I don't quite believe in the term 'best friend' or even 'friend' for that matter, but I suppose if I were to use it, given the circumstances and all, they'd be my friends. Jean and I had gotten really close since then, even though the only class we had in common was English Literature and we used to sit very far apart because, for once, it was the only class I actually was glad to endure and took advantage of the ticks the clock provided me with.

Thinking about it, I'm actually not sure if Lou and Agnes are friends or not, or they just happen to sometimes end up in the same table because their friends are friends or just because they want to sit around people to increase their social status in the school rank of popularity, if there is even such thing—maybe perhaps even because they just want to sit together. We are all always friends of friends I guess, but I bet if she wasn't so damn snobby all the time and his parents won more cash at the end of the month, Agnes and little old Lou would be together. He appears to be desperate to be like Agnes, maybe that's why he gets so mad at her for 'showing off' how many drones she has or how many yachts this step-father of hers has named after her to win her love or approval for his conventional marriage with her mother. It's funny how her mum used to work down at the dirtiest pub in Venice Beach before; I remember she even served Jean, Diane and me once one of those toxic beers I always ask for but never end up drinking. Now that hostile grave bartender cleans her hands with FIJI ostensible water under a four-metre porcelain fountain in the centre of a symmetrical majestic kaleidoscopic garden with an endless grand pool that leads to the panorama of the sapphire amplified ocean that beheads Los Angeles of going any further. So yes, maybe if the circumstances were different and we weren't all so damn superficial all the time, these two characters could perhaps end up together. Maybe if Lou wouldn't be so arrogant and proud all the time, he'd admit he's in love with Agnes, and if Agnes wouldn't aspire to follow the steps of her cocaine-maniac mother, she'd admit she's in love with Lou as well. I don't really give a damn about them to be honest, but the money; the money interfering is what bothers me.

"Why reproduce if you believe the world is ending?

Because the world is always ending for each of us and if one begins to withdraw from the possibilities of experience, then no one would take any of the risks involved with love."

—Ben Lerner
10:04, 2014

Seq. 5 Ext. Streets

I am still walking, it's far a longer walk than I expected. To be truthful, I think I might be facing Lou's house even though I've never seen how it is. I used to imagine it, when they were having their dreary conversations in the picnic tables out front beside where we used to sit. I imagined his house to be this small 20th Century 'American dream' incarnate household you could've spotted advertised in one of those real estate magazines in the lounge table, probably put there by your mother. It's the first time I've actually stopped to look at it, although it's not a really good idea I think, after I start walking away from it. Lou could've skated out of the front door anytime and could've spotted me, although we aren't friends, I still think our faces know one another without us saying so, especially since we are the only two kids that go to Kings High living on the same street.

I work, well, obviously soon I won't anymore. Actually, I hope old Lloyd doesn't give up my spot in the surf shop so I have it when I come back, if I do. I actually met Jean at the surf shop, even though we'd been going to school together since the first grade, and well, Diane and BD started to work there with me, the surf shop is called 'In Flux', near Santa Monica's pier. We all worked there for a while; I think they actually hate me because of it, although BD stopped coming because of her illness allusions and Diane stopped coming the second she left to study in England. Diane loved coming though, she always got to model and all, with the new bikinis that come in store and she really is one to love the attention from all the costumers that would complement her constantly, even if it wasn't directly at her. She loves the attention; I bet, every day at school she'd count down the hours to go to work and exhibit the flawless structure that embodied her, as if she'd been sculptured by Edgar Degas, whilst her plumped lips and rosy cheekbones were gently brushed by the delicate colours on Meyer's palette, you could've even assumed she'd inspired most of her 'Liaison Pittoresque' collection. She's Botticelli's Madonna defying the churches commandments, for being an atheist and deflowered.

I helped my Uncle Lloyd and my cousin, Andy, prepare the shop; it was intentionally my idea that they put it to work in the first place. I showed them some creative personalised logos I had been working on in my French classes when I was bored. They didn't hesitate a second, chose one of the designs and just went up for it. I like people like that, like my cousin and my uncle, they were always my favourite type of people. They never waited for anything; they just went up for it, for anything really. I think I spent most of the time with my uncle carving the boards or preparing the stock, and well, I used to spend every day with my cousin too. His mother had been diagnosed with cancer and died a few weeks later they inaugurated the opening of the shop. I'd never fully understood what death meant, because it really doesn't mean anything, it's nothing. I mistook what death was supposed to be when I felt it, whilst I was trying to understand it.

The dawn that shook the horizon was acid, and the abundant foam executed the waves every night, making it impossible for the sea to rage again. Noise had become a foreign vibration for me, as my senses had been evacuated by that fading presence. The surf shop only had customers dressed in black and the boards were all broken either by my uncle or me. Either way, the whole place was wrecked, as if a gang of delinquents with tights in their heads had shoplifted the whole place. There was no funeral because funerals only exist as a social interaction of superficial cries and lousy sad faces, and my uncle really couldn't go through that, hell, I couldn't go through that. I got really aggressive by then. Funerals are the worst construct the system has created so that not even in death we can be free; we are condemned to be buried under its rules, represented by mud with the deceit given to us by the church and religion that they'll be in heaven, if there's even a thing as such. Hell is not burning with flames and being condemned to slavery, hell is simply a couple of worms eating you up as you decay. We believe we'll be visiting someone, commemorating their minor existence, but visit whom? There's no one there anymore, there hasn't been anybody there for a while now. It might be that I'm just too cynical about death, and I don't know what I'm talking about and that I'm just exempting all this rage on this paper. I just hate funerals, I really do. I mean, what are they for? There are more people around you when you're dead than when you've barely been born. We celebrate death more than life to later feel regretful about it. My uncle never wanted his son to be remembered because a grave had his name beautifully carved on it with roman calligraphy, but because of the things he did and didn't do.

I had only started surfing four years ago with him and I think it took me about a year to learn how to surf properly, so it's not like surfing was everything I lived for. I was fine not ever doing it again, I didn't want to anyways. It sure was my cousin's though, he always told me when we were cleaning the boards behind the store that if he ever died, it had to be at sea. I actually remember most of that conversation because we used to have it too often for my taste.

We were coming back from the sea on this new military Land Rover he'd been saving for, which I didn't like very much. It was actually his father's, who he'd bought it off from, so it had the logo I'd designed for the shop and all, but you couldn't really see it. We entered through the back of the shop to not disturb the costumers and so Uncle Lloyd wouldn't have one of his fits. Andy grabbed his surfboard from the back of the truck and placed it in one corner, and then he helped me with mine. We got two beers from the mini-fridge and sat down as we drunk up. We didn't say anything, we were too breathless due to the dehydration to speak, I remember that day we'd been six hours in the sea trying to tame waves that had developed an instinct to kill. We grabbed the two surfboards, and placed them over the table to clean the salt and wax them again. He'd tell me how I'd gotten a big wave today, and we'd later practice my standing on the board with balance, as he'd throw tennis balls at me. He'd try to kick me off the board, as if he were the wave. It was good, he said, a good technique my uncle used to do with him so he strengthened his legs and abs. I always ended up in puddles of sweat after those lessons that only lasted five minutes because my uncle would get all mad about us not preparing the boards that had just arrived from his merchandiser. We put the radio on and started singing to whatever came on, usually it was *The Beach Boys* which always played on this '60s music canal, which my cousin was very fond of, he knew all the lyrics of most of the songs they played. We'd go on talking about my friends and how I was doing. He was always really keen about how my life was going on with school and all. He'd recently dropped out, although he was an A student, he told me he didn't want to go to university because he was going to live up in the sea, in a beautiful sailing boat with all his surf boards and just travel the world starting from the beginning of summer, but he never saw summer. That's when he always ended up telling me about death, although he didn't really like the subject after his mother's death, and tried to avoid it most of the time—but when it came to him in the sea, he always said, "You know I'll always be out there, in the sea and all, I'll die when I'm about 80 surfing." He got really emotional when it came around this subject.

My cousin drowned surfing about a year ago, it was unexpected and he didn't have a funeral like his mother, unfortunately, he was 19 instead of 80. I didn't cry, not because I wasn't blue, but because I was too destroyed to do so. I wanted to so badly, but I was unable to. I screamed, I screamed a lot, it was the type of scream Michael Corleone did when Mary got gunshot in the steps of *La casa della Opera di Sicilia*. I miss my cousin. I miss the waves too, everything that came together any day my cousin and I went to the bay. I tend to write more when I'm destroyed and I feel not sad or depressed but as if I'd perished. The way I felt when I was waiting for Andy's head to just pop out from the sea or grab one of the hanging legs that weren't on the board and take me down with him like he used to do when we fooled around like seven-year-olds, only that this time he didn't. This is too melancholic to even write about, not only melancholic but unnecessary, I don't want to profit from his death, to augment the size of these moronic paragraphs. I know you probably think I should've waited to throw this guilty weight on you, and that it would've probably created more suspense or leave you unexpected, and uncomfortable for a while which would probably just make you want to read more, even have the chance to psychoanalyse me properly, blame it all on the event of my cousin's death. That's why I'm telling, you know, I don't want you to do any of that, I just needed to write down somewhere.

Once, for the English coursework at school, we had to write a short story about anything we wanted, you know the typical assignment you get when you're in the 10th grade. My cousin's ashes had just happened and the only thing really that I felt I could talk about was death, either to mock about or torture myself. I often visualise the things I write as some movie scene, and that's pretty much what I did in this case. I couldn't quite pick a title that wouldn't demoralise my teacher too much, as for then the only things that mattered to me were getting good grades, which is quite odd due to the circumstances I was where I should've felt like failing everything and slip into depression. I just maybe wanted to write about death just so maybe I'd finally overcome what it means, simply stop avoiding it like everyone else does, like it was something surreal. People think by avoiding something it just

43

leaves, but they're wrong, its importance increases even more due to their intentional ignorance.

I never really named my story, I thought of various titles but none of them made the cut so I just left it blank, as you've probably realised already I'm not good with titles anyways. The story, what it was about, was this journalist from the *New York Times* or *The New Yorker* (I can't remember now), that lost his wife in a car accident late one night coming back from having seen *Rebel Without a Cause* in the Angelika. They'd be in the car discussing the movie and out of nowhere, a racoon jumped in the car's front window. The man got agitated and started to zigzag on the road he thought was vacant, to try to get rid of the racoon that was scaring his wife. The racoon wouldn't go away so he stopped the car at one corner of the street and went out of the car to scare the racoon away, but the man hadn't realised at what corner he'd left the car so, out of nowhere, a truck hit his car and murdered his wife.

The man was devastated after such disastrous event that he enclosed himself in his apartment for three years, he lost his job at *The New York Times,* and had to sell all the furniture in the house, even his books and vinyls and DVDs to be able to keep up paying the rent. He slept in one corner of the house, again, the wrong corner, for he could've seen the moon from the opposite one but, instead, he saw the neighbour's trashed home. He always wondered what his wife had thought of on the milliseconds before she died and from there, the story just really unravelled alone. The man decided to interview five different types of people:

- A little boy
- A teenager
- A graduate
- A mother
- An elder man

All of these people had been survivors of a coma or a resurrection at an OVR through electro-shots. He'd ask each and every one the same question, what did you think, or see or even feel before you closed your eyes? Before, I guess, you were put in an unconscious state. From their answers, he'd put his life together, he spoke with the director of *The New York Times* who decided to let him come back and publish his story. A couple of weeks later, after being published, he went to buy a Colt revolver 44 in this armoury store uptown cornering on E 63rd street with Madison Avenue, right a couple blocks from his lonely apartment on 72nd street and Lexington Av. He incidentally shot his head whilst playing with it and died on the corner with views to the window, from where you could see the moon. I don't remember what grade I got for that, I think I have that story stashed somewhere in the cellar with all the other trash from previous school years. I'm just talking about this because I don't want you to get too bored with each and every description of my voyage to a bloody train station. To be truthful, it's not like anything interesting has happen yet, I'm only getting closer.

Seq. 6 Ext. Train Station

When you get what you want, a part of you, for a moment before you get it, just stops wanting it. It's mainly fear, but we can't let fear be the obstacle of getting what we want, the same way we can't let the fear of failure be the only threat that stops our generation from achieving, anything really. Whether it's the person you love, that birthday present you've wanted since you were ten, that kiss you had been waiting for, that summer camp, having sex for the first time with someone special (or not), grabbing a train to some city once you've ticked it off your 'to-do list' it's stashed into a cellar. I think New York was the reincarnation of my cousin. Instead of dying into the nothingness, he'd become a place, my place. New York was the only place where I could be myself; something about it just got the best out of me. The same way my cousin did. It's ironic that the ideal place to be alone is in one of the capitals of the world that is packed with more people day-by-day; hour-by-hour for that matter.

We went to New York for the first time a couple years ago at Christmas when my mum was still here. My dad had gotten this e-mail from some well-known art gallerist down in Chelsea that wanted to represent him and display him for New Year's Eve, so New York's social elite snobs could buy it. They did end up buying it, all of it actually. I became completely fascinated by that lifestyle, it frustrated me then why I didn't live in New York already. Some really 'important' people, as some would call it, got invited, that really made my dad happy. I think my dad is a really talented passionate artist and he's gotten a lot better ever since my mum left. Pain really is the main ingredient to create a masterpiece. Aside from the evident, love and hate, but I think pain is made out of those two. It's as if they were the primary colours and pain was the combination, so hate was blue and love was red, pain would turn up purple. That's how I would describe colours to someone who's blind; I bet they'd understand me. I fell in love that Christmas, my brother would be so excited of going ice skating at Central Park,

46

every day he'd made me go with him, bribing me with caramel apple sticks before and after we went. He actually didn't even need to bribe me, because I loved ice skating with him, even though when I was angry I told him I didn't. Then we'd hurry the *hellaoutuvthere* and ran through all of Central Park as we threw snow at each other; that was the first time each of us had actually seen or felt snow, so we even took our gloves off. It never snows in Los Angeles. I am actually hoping it'll be snowing when I arrive in two-day night.

I just arrived at the train station, it took less to get here than I expected. I think I'm going to have to wait for a while, which actually bothers me a little, but I'll be fine. To be honest, right now, I feel a bit terrified of actually walking through those crystal doors, which are constantly opening and closing at the pattern of my constant hesitation. I start to imagine the reaction of my psychiatrist when my father calls her today to tell her I'm not going to be able to go to our meeting today because I had run away. I had specifically written in my dad's letter that after he'd read it, he had to go give that serpent a phone call. I think you can guess I am kind of freaked out to cross those doors. Only that I'm too proud to even admit things like that to myself sometimes, that's why I'm writing it down instead. I am actually being pushed inside by a mass of tourists who seem to be late for their train, for they really seem to be in a rush. I really hope they aren't going to Chicago. They actually look more like a stampede of flamingos with blonde wigs, colourful socks and flip-flops with some fake Nike and Adidas logotype on the front, but for sure, somewhere where it stands out so it's seen. I could actually imagine that posse going to Las Vegas and staying at one of those massive expensive five-star hotels that inveigle you like a lotus flower so you never want to leave. I imagine those fat bastards sat around their green numerated poker tables with two less hot female versions of Cindy Crawford and Naomi Campbell; everyone can be anyone this century. Our image isn't enough that we need to begin being a collection of others.

Inside the train station, I realise how long it'd been since I'd been in here. I forgot how much I loved train stations, there were so many people coming and going unceasingly, although after writing those words, I notice how cliché they sound. But I still wish it were like that every day, that life was just a train station of different people crossing each other all the time. One day, I think I'm going to spend my whole day sat on a train and not come down till the next day, and what I'd do would be listen to music and stare at the person in front of me, but not in a way that would make them feel uncomfortable or observed, I'd be gentile with my vision. I'd just interpret staring into space whilst I'd skilfully scrutinise their each and every move, but it wouldn't be someone in particular just everybody in general, at least the one's that caught my attention full enough.

I buy a ticket and head over to pass whichever control I have to go through. I sit down to wait on a bench in front of the train I'm supposed to get. A woman and a man are sat beside me whilst I wait for the train to arrive. He's reading the local newspaper and she's reading one of those magazines my mum used to have spread all over her beauty clinic, where all the girls are exuberant and all the men seem to be somehow an attractive bunch of slaves or at least that's the way they're portrayed. I mean, why would she read the damn magazine if it weren't for the abundance of attractive masculinity at her disposition to daydream about instead of spending her day looking at what is supposed to be the love of her life (according to her lousy phony vows at least). He's probably more interested about the Yankees or the Mets winning the next match anyways, so it's not like he's any better. There comes a moment in life when you just stop caring, everyone stops caring whether there aren't more craters in your face or if the new lipstick you're wearing is a darker red than the other, maybe it tastes less to death. Things you want someone to notice they never will. That's when you realise you're deteriorating slowly into some memory. That's when sex stops being sex, and starts feeling like the prescription drug your doctor gives you every month to keep your body functioning, but you no longer feel any pleasure by your own. You're just there, not giving a damn thing about anything anymore, waiting for it to happen—the orgasm that'll take you to the grave in all literal terms.

Looking at that woman makes me sick, but looking at that man even more, I'm deducing they're a couple because their luggage has the same Louis Vuitton pattern and practically the same size, and they tend to kneel over each other and smile to one another once in a while, as if insinuating a kiss that's not going to occur. I'm actually just trying to distract myself. I'm not nervous or anything, I'm just impatient. I get impatient sometimes, but I really need this train to arrive anytime soon. I'm just going to think about everything else so I take my mind off whatever pressure it's in. When I'm in the train, I'll be sat in front or beside someone I don't know and they won't know me. I'll try to get to know them without talking to them though. It's what I do; I have this obsession with scanning people, not scanning them but I guess as a writer, as what I think I am, I like making up stories on those that don't give me a chance to listen to theirs. They're the characters that create the story, not me. They are unpaid actors in my imagination: best part about this job is they don't know they're working, so it's much simpler for the director and avoids any complaints about not being paid. If I had to pay them, New York would be the unfocused vision of a myopic without his glasses, not being able to distinguish if a light bulb is, in fact, a light bulb or a goldenrod Pollock.

Do you think you have to experience something in order to know how it feels? Like love, do you have to be in love to know how it feels? It's more like you feel love when it's no longer there. It's how we work; we destroy what's beautiful to raise our self-esteem. Yes. I am describing love as a mechanism, as if love were a washing machine or a toaster or one of those stupid iPhones. I wish I wasn't lying, but I am. Unfortunately, love isn't a machine, that's what terrifies us the most: we can control what we create but not what creates us. Your heart can, in fact, be mechanised into a metal and so can your lungs into oxidised pipes, at least that's the sensation you get when you don't feel it anymore, that love. That's when you start to allude you're feeling manic-depressive and that's when you become a toaster. I remember my therapist was depressed, it's the whole reason behind why she got into the whole therapist business, which I found interesting and rather odd. You must be feeling beaten up after this melodramatic paragraph about love and depression, and probably the cause of most suicides and drug overdose in the art world. I am no Groucho Mars, I'll tell you that and I wasn't lying when I said this wasn't a romantic comedy like *Annie Hall* or *A Midsummer Night's Dream*. Woody Allen and Shakespeare mock society in a way I'd never be capable to do, I am no genius as I've said earlier, I'm just a somebody out of the bloom going somewhere or nowhere to dodge the truth of who I am which is so contradicting at times that I regret even writing all these revoking pages and pages.

"There are so many things Blair doesn't get about me, so many things she ultimately overlooked and things that she would never know, and there would always be a distance between us because there were too many shadows everywhere. Had she ever made promises to a faithless reflection in the mirror? Had she ever cried because she hated someone so much? Had she ever craved betrayal to the point where she pushed the crudest fantasies into reality, coming up with sequences that she and nobody else could read, moving the game as you play it? Could she locate the moment she went dead inside? Does she remember the year it took to become that way? The fades, the dissolves, the rewritten scenes, all the things you wipe away—I now want to explain all these things to her but I know I never will, the most important one being: I never liked anyone and I'm afraid of people."

—Bret Easton Ellis
Imperial Bedrooms, 2010

Seq. 7 Int. Train I

(I just wanted to tell you, mostly warn you and evidently, apologise in advance because I'll forget to do so later, but in this sequence of my rather unelaborated script, everything will be told with the purpose of not making any absolute sense whatsoever with the paragraph before or after. It'll be a constant switch between what I'm thinking and what I may actually be doing. I know it's confusing; hell, I'm confusing, all of these sequences are confusing, so I hope this serves as a precaution. This is my off voice in the novel, read me in parenthesis.)

To my disappointment, I have been given one of those cabins that isolate you from the rest of the passengers, as well as the rest. We are all inside our little claustrophobic cabins, probably because it's going to be a long ride. I agree it's more personal and solitary, but I really didn't want that. I get inside the cabin; it's small and has a small seat that occupies half the room although it looks really comfortable to lie down on. I put my bag under the sofa bed or whatever it was supposed to represent. I sit down. It feels like one of my grandmother's sofas, which was always stuffed with pillows. She had one of every colour and size, I always thought that was a very grandmotherly thing to have. The only difference is, here you have to stand up and walk to another wagon in order to eat something whereas at my grandma's house, you just sit there and she'll continuously bring a banquet of sweet delights, even if I haven't asked. My grandmother is dead; she's been dead for a while, although, funnily enough, I sometimes taste her delicious traditional artesian Italian biscuits, which I'll never taste again. I didn't like remembering that now, it just really wasn't the right time. I guess I'll be on my own in this claustrophobic space they've stuffed me in until Chicago

I wonder if they've all read each of their letters by now. I'd really like to know what they've thought of or might've said once spotted them. I start thinking about my dad bowed down in his room or his art studio reading it all over again. Thinking about that is

51

starting to make me feel a little blue. At least, now he'll know how I felt when he just ran off to work. He had a very busy schedule most of the time; going from one place to another, for instance, one day he'd be having dinner in New York, then breakfast in Miami and lunch in Argentina. That was his life, all over the place, everywhere, just how I wanted mine to be. He could disappear and appear whenever he felt like it; he was the only person I had ever met that knows how to be invisible and visible at the same place. He is the only one that ever really tried to understand me, now that no one does; only I try to understand myself and when I do try, I don't.

I can't remember the last time he was one week straight with my brother and I. I sometimes wonder if that's the reason why my mum just suddenly disappeared, she got bored of being so alone all the time, to be the one waiting. I hope she finds out I'm gone; I hope she feels like punishing me. I think it's the first time I'd like my mother to punish me, I promise I wouldn't answer back, I would give her the pleasure of telling me off just to see her again. She'd be screaming and shouting, maybe even getting emotional and crying, and in the meanwhile, I'd just stare at her like she was a scene from a David Lynch movie elapsing her movement in slow motion so it didn't complement her voice. The sound would start to get lower and rougher, and it would seem like she's getting further and further away, the closest she got. I imagined myself sat on a chair in our kitchen and she'd be standing in front of me with hell in her eyes, so she'd loose it. We'd entered *Twin Peaks'* famous red room as the lights fooled around with each other. Even lights feel sexual desire for one another; they'd be procreating raining red all over the walls as they got darker, such to the point of being considered mahogany, so we could finally drown our anger and remorse in a pool of a delectable Vin Rouge.

I've noticed these two hours in the train that a man two cabins left away from mine has been staring at the same piece of paper since he sat there. I often thought I should've hitchhiked my way to New York instead of wasting most of my money left on train tickets, in cabins I wasn't comfortable in. I thought I was going to sit as well as everybody else in a shared wagon, where we'd all be sat down one in front of the other or even beside one another at times. I guess since the voyage being so long, the construction of the train had to be fit for it. I was curious about all the places I was going to go through, I even regretted not being able to meet them in person and just have to stare blankly out of a window. We were going to go through Nevada first, although I highly doubt we'll be crossing Las

Vegas, and apparently, mid the way, we'd stop in Kansas City for a couple of hours so more people were ingested in the train as others where excreted. The man I was talking to you about is beginning to worry me, for the only thing he is capable of at this point is lying his head down with his eyes closed and his mouth opened. I begin to wonder if he's breathing and whether I should do something about it. He has a black coat all over him, covering any existence he has into an absent eclipse of a scorched full moon. He looks like all those creased papers that surround him and he holds his pencil between his frozen fingers as his rebellious ink runs all over the page. I soon realise it's monotonous, when the ink goes off the page, he gets another paper and replaces it for another, and the same sequence repeated on and on. I keep watching him; I really have nothing else to do anyways. Although now I'm starting to feel uncomfortable for he's stared back at me. He must've felt some type of force around him that led him to meet his ash-fallen eyes with mine. He has a sad look, the kind of look you have when you're either in love or alone and the cause of both those reasons is either you're alone because you're in love or you're in love because you don't want to be alone.

We were staring into each other's minuscule lit-up city carefully from two cabins away through the looking glass that parted us. We just sat there as if we've seen somebody we're supposed to recognise but don't, and the hesitation is there of whether standing up and greeting them or act like you never saw each other. I felt quite uncomfortable for a moment, but I just kept on looking at him until I gave up and turned down to my scribbled paper where I was writing all of this. My lenses were getting frosty so his image started to freeze to the point where his body started looking like a brushstroke of black paint on a white paper. I had fallen asleep, and you must be wondering, how can this be written if I'm asleep? Well, technically, I'm not but I could if I wanted to. Sleeping is the entrance to my studio, the same way an office door is to yours. I remember every detail of my dreams because, in a way, they're not really dreams. When I woke up, I sensed he'd lost any interest whatsoever in me, although I do find myself covered in a blanket that doesn't belong to me. Nothing really ever does belong to us; especially the people we love the most. I feel like what I say is just senseless. I also feel I talk too much about what I'm thinking instead of narrating to you whatever the hell it is I'm doing in some chronological Holden Cauffield order and I'm conscious that probably half of the thoughts I've written, you don't care much about reading so I think I'm going to stop. I'm breaking the promise I said at the start: no lying and only talking about you but the thing is, it'd be easier to talk about something if I didn't hate it so much. We like feeling identified with other people so we stop feeling so lonely, like there's someone else in the same state as us. But really, I don't like to be identified with anyone, not even with my favourite writer; I think it'd ruin me.

Seq. 8 Int. Train II

Let's stop talking about me. I also hate being the centre of attention; it gets to a point where it gets really boring, and I don't want this to feel like an autobiography, because it's not. Also it makes me too vulnerable and I get weary, same thing that happens to you when you start saying things of which you haven't even thought about. That always happens to me: saying bloody things without processing them through or on the contrary: procrastinating about things too much, I end up saying nothing of what I had planned. The truth is: I have no idea of how to write a book, I've read plenty of books but that doesn't mean I know how to make you feel what they make me feel when I read them. My best guess is you probably think I'm just some lousy fed-up teenager like the millions there are out there with adjusting to society issues and that I could've just written all my sorrows in some shitty blog—I don't quite believe in those. I know you're not really interested in hearing this but I don't give a damn, no one is interested in listening to anything these days anyways, we are too busy talking about things we don't know about. It's okay though, I don't really care what is of this book.

I'm tired of being sat on this train looking out of the same frosted window caused by the air conditioning in my cabinet, and worst thing is, I could freeze to death but they're not going to change it because they really couldn't give a damn about my second-class concerns. I'm in one of those cheap cabinets where you don't really get seen a lot or people don't really give a crap about you enough to see you, which is really what I was aiming for: not being noticed. I'm not interested in a cop passing by and spotting me, asking me for my ID and passport, and then realise I have some singular features that match a photo they've been sent all the way from LAPD of a girl that's 'missing'. Then they'd call my dad and I don't want that. I don't like people calling up my dad, he's busy working and all, and he would probably get madder by the fact that he's being disturbed at work than by the real reason of the call. I'd give them my uncle's phone or Frankie's phone; I haven't talked about

Frankie, she used to be Diane's mother once but since Diane is nowhere to be seen, and I don't mean it in a way in which you'd think she's dead, she's in an all-girls boarding school in one of those stodgy old towns in South England or something. If you haven't read *Picnic at Hanging Rock*, I can understand you're not feeling very relatable with what I'm talking about…and maybe you're in an all-girls boarding school and you are completely fascinated by it. It's not that I have something against boarding schools or concretely all-girls boarding schools, I just don't like them and I know you must be waiting for a real argument or an equitable reason as for why I am so repelled by those institutions, but then again, I'm repelled by any institution that wants to subjugate a mind into becoming a loaded bank account or a university degree.

I'm not really keen on talking about Diane, I hate talking about it anyways so I don't see why I'd even start, it's not like that's going to make her come back anyways, and it would be too late, because if she did, I wouldn't be there anymore to greet her. I wonder if she even knows I've ran away, actually I feel like I should feel terrible about it but I don't, although she's probably taking one of her advanced mathematic lessons to really have any time to think about it, which in a way reliefs me. She takes her exams very seriously, her future for that matter. She's really worried about the whole thing, hoping she can make it and all. I felt sorry for her at the start, it felt weird having lunch with someone who was so pressured by herself, covered in books on how a beetle breathes. She sometimes didn't have time to eat, and she'd skip having lunch with Jean, BD and I. She got really skinny since then, I was worried Uncle Lloyd would fire her. I didn't want her to get fired; she was fun to work with sometimes and Andy really liked her. I think he was one of the only people who thought there was more to her than what her perfection hid. I thought that too, she was a very pretty girl.

I know LA is known for Hollywood and the American dream but it's just what they're trying to sell to you: like the advertisement of the new Cillit Bang; the new cleaning sprays that doesn't really clean a damn, but you believe they do because you see the ad where they plague the idea of Grease Lightning only with a much catchier song to complement with its nonsense catchy slogan at the end. It's not that I hate advertising, everyone needs to make money the way they can, I just don't believe in it. The same way I don't believe in the stupid educational system we are forced to have in order to end up like the ones who imposed it, just to clone us. School exhausted me, I didn't only run away from everyone, I ran away from being forced to depend my future on a psychopathic probation of whether I'm good enough for this society or not. That's the main pressure now, especially when you're 17. You have to be good enough and if you're not, you're not even considered, they just get rid of you somehow, and your ideas that could be a threat to what keeps them financially functioning or just simply functioning for all that I care. They're all goddam sicarios without staining white sheets with blood but minds with corruption and pressure. The government and the media are the new Godfather. Puzo's masterpiece has been summarised into a couple of fat bastards around a table eating some donuts and burgers, like Tony Soprano, inside some horrendous important building's penthouse as they're having discussions of what to do next in order to continue being in control. That's the only thing they care about. I wish I could get myself to start writing about politics or extend my theories on our educational system, but that's really something you can read everywhere from many different people and I also feel I don't have much to say about a matter I'm no longer part of. I also don't want to dedicate this goddamn book to any of those bastards that remind me of the headmaster of my school, I don't want them to ever end up reading this, and laughing as they leave the book imprinted in sweaty or oil marks and crumbs.

I feel the wagon become stretcher and stretcher every sequential minute I've been spending here. It might be something psychological, a visual illusion, but I just feel it getting smaller, like I'm being jailed in my own self. I'm actually not getting anxious because I know it's not real, when I think too much I tend to get dizzy if I haven't had my pills, the pills my mum always prepared me at the breakfast table. Don't get overexcited, I'm not sick and this isn't a psychological thriller like *What Ever Happened to Baby Jane*. I'm just anaemic something most young women my age are; I mean BD is also anaemic. BD didn't like being told what to do or what to take so she really never took her pills. I remember we spoke about this once at a party. I didn't like talking about it at a party, specially that one. She was talking to me and I'd be examining the room, looking for this boy I'd talk a couple of times in the locker rooms. He's not really that important, it's not like I had a crush on him, but he was awfully handsome and I liked talking to him. Poor BD would just blab continuously about the whole vegan thing and the goddamn pills. I don't know if she was drunk or high but she just wouldn't stop talking about the goddamn pills all night. The minute I'd gotten an eye on Aaron, I left her sat in the sofa talking to whoever was on her right. I would've offered her to run away with me, she seemed to need it even more than me, but she was too depressed to do this whole trip, she also thought I was kidding whenever I mentioned it in one of our weed interventions at her pool that sometimes felt as if it was attached to the sea or the sky, you couldn't quite distinguish one from another because they had the similar shades of blue, especially in the dark when it was all pitch dark. It's weird how we never really realise when our friends need us; I felt really bad when she stopped coming to school.

No one ever believes me when I tell the truth, but when I lie, they do. Andy was the only one who knew when I was lying, but just because I never lied to him. I didn't have reasons to; he was going to catch me anyways, so why bother. He would've run away with me, but probably not to New York. He hated the city, thought it was too polluted just like LA only with no good waves. So if he had run away with me, we would've ended up in Sydney or Tahiti or some exotic lost place like that. I think I feel more inspired in a French lesson than in this tight wagon. In class, I always used to doodle everything that came up you know, scribbling as fast as I could before it ran away from me like a burglar. I was unable to do what they wanted me to do, but that made me do what I wanted to do: write. They would sometimes catch my ideas in a net and leave me empty. They forced me not to think, the purpose of school is to block your independent thoughts, and transform them into a whole that everyone shares and agrees on. They don't want you to think on your own, that's when you see things how they are, and if you do see things clearer, you could fuck up the famous 'system' everybody keeps talking about either against it or in favour, not having a clue of what it is as most of the things people blab about at dinners.

"Seen from across the street, he was like someone to whom the world had long since given notice to quit but who was compelled to stay in it, no longer belonging to it, but unable to leave it."

—Thomas Bernhard
Wittgensteins Nephew, 1982

Seq. 9 Int. Train V

I can't distinguish reality from fiction. I dreamed I was in my room and I woke up in the same wagon I've been sat on for the last past hours, but yet, I am confused of whether this is a dream or if my dreams are reality. I feel under the effect of a very powerful drug that still hasn't been given an illegal name yet. I think it might be the cold breeze, which constantly hush's in the back of my neck. Although it could also be the fact that I haven't eaten since I left my neighbourhood at eight am. I would tell you what time it was now if I owned a watch. I don't like watches; I don't like my time being counted. I feel really pressured living between the ticks of each of the clock's handle, running from it in case it caught up with me. I would spend my whole life running away from that handle until the day I started running slower and slower, and eventually, the handle trapped me. I don't want my life to be like that, I don't want time to be the turtle. Maybe you didn't get the moral of the fable then, because you were just a kid, I didn't get it either, I was just a kid too. I wish I were still just a child maybe I still am sometimes. We were too naïve then to understand its whole concept, where we are the rabbit and life is the turtle, if you stop and rest, thinking it'll never catch you because you're so presumably fast and the turtle is supposed to be so slow, you'll always win. That's really where all those 'live your life' hashtags come from. They don't want you to waste any minute of your time, but who gave time such importance? Actually, I did just right now by talking about it, and even though I answered my own supposedly rhetoric question, you can do so too. We are crossing Arizona right now, through route 40 which just trespasses the Coconino National Forest. I know all this because, fortunately, in my cabin, it's packed with pamphlets about the route and all, with all the best sightseeing pictures around the zone. It'd also be stupid not to be able to pinpoint the forest shaking in the window, as its branches plead for help leaving scratch marks all over. The panorama is exuberant and feverish, for such beauty can leave you hung-up. It's a view that's lurking with sweetness as well as snarls, as the emerald of its leaves cracks pathways to crystalline rivers that from here afar can't be spotted. Now I am thankful for going in train instead of hitchhiking my way up to the North.

The elder man from earlier hasn't stopped staring at me since I woke up; his chin decorated with artificial snow or cocaine. I'm not going to lie, that is definitely the type of man that looks after his beard the same way my grandmother looked after her roses. She loved her roses; the house was full of them, of each and every colour creating a kaleidoscopic illusion of uncertainty between the ethics provided by the proof of a rainbow or a paint explosion chimera. I don't know why she's got so many roses. I know it was my grandfather's favourite flower, and it'd be romantic and all to think that was the reason, which it probably was, but that would be depressing. Looking at all those roses and remembering every day that yes, they're beautiful, but he's not there to admire them anymore. When someone you love dies, you don't have to do things in order to remember them because they'll never know and by doing it, you'll just endure their absence too intensely, and no one should really go through that. Maybe it's immoral to say what I'm thinking but once they're dead, you've really got to let them go, otherwise you'll be left more defenceless than ever. It's sadist to want to feel pain, but sometimes feeling pain is the only way to wake up, even though you want to go to sleep. That's what I did when Andy died, I'd just sleep for days and days. My schoolbag seemed to weigh more, my dad's cooking tasted worse, weed got rougher, the sea seemed louder and wider like it'd be expanding its latitude to drain and drown the whole city if not drowning my cousin was enough, and especially of all my damn book became senseless, yet the only thing that kept me intrigued. Everything just seemed duller. Death tends to be that filter that just darkens the exposure and degrades the colour out of anything; it creates a dark grain in the photograph. Death is always described from the perspective of the living as Ludwig Wittgenstein described it, "Death is not an experience in life," so what are we really talking about when we talk about death? Nothing, I guess it's to keep our conscience calm as if it has some type of control over how to react to something we really can't explain or haven't endured yet. We talk about how others' deaths affect us, but not how our own death makes us feel, as if it were a mirror. You do realise I constantly repeat matters I really don't want to talk about, I guess I just want to clarify if I can speak so openly about it, it's because I don't think about it anymore, it's as if I were no longer connected to such occasion.

It's not much one can do to entertain themselves nowadays in the types of circumstances I am in, I feel like I've been blabbing for half an hour and yet I haven't even opened my mouth but broken my hand. I am writing all these thoughts on my black leather Italian booklet my dad gave me for my 10th birthday in order to write pretty much about anything. I've grown a dependency over that book as I've grown because, well, it is basically the interior design of me. When I write is the only moment when everything else just seems to get further in the distance, until I am just left alone in a hollow susceptible, achromatic space. I'm a black silhouette responsible for the rhythm of a shaking pencil tracing its shadow as it moves. But I'm not a prisoner of this abstract penitentiary, what's out there; on the other side is the prison. I'm a fugitive rebelling against an elite system. I'm just here in this three-dimensional outer space from reality where the echo of my pencil is like the peripteral octastyle doric supporting the Parthenon of Athens. Brian Eno and Pink Floyd are the tunes that keep my acropolis safe from the peasantry agora, which in this case is everybody.

All this fictional outer creation became corrupted by the cacophonic knock on the door of this minuscule cabinet. The old weakened look from the man was staring right at me from the other side of the door's windshield. I opened the door carefully, ignoring that thing your parents tell you to never do when you're seven or eight or nine or ten: that under no circumstance should you open the door to a stranger. I didn't see the man as a stranger, which was the only difference. I actually felt like I'd seen him before, like he was one of those déjà vu they talk about in the movies. I really hoped he didn't know my dad or my uncle, or even worse, my mother. I sometimes had imagined my mother's new lover; it was a thought that persecuted me. Maybe this old man is he, maybe my mother's given up and turned up to be like Agnes' mother. The man must be wondering why it's taking me such a long time to open the goddamn door completely. I don't want to describe to you every step I'm going to do in order to open this goddamn door to let this bohemian *sortalookingfella* walk inside and the step following after that. And I know you really don't want to hear that, and I'd really hate to tell it. I just hate having to talk about things that bore the hell out of me, concretely if I know they also bore the hell out of the other person. I know I've probably said I hate many things since you started reading this book, and you must've forgotten about half of them, but this one you won't forget because, funnily, it's something you do very often or something someone you know does very often and it is often known as slander, at least, in our generation.

The funny looking man enters and sits down in front of me with a crooked smile; I think the hidden secret behind that smile was to prove he still had all his teeth in their place so that I wouldn't think he was some old paedophile just because his face had stopped being his face ten years ago. We sat there in silence for about 69 seconds; I started to count them since he got in because I wanted to avoid having to think about what to say to him. I feel quite uncomfortable if I'm being honest with you, as his intimidating granite eyes reflect melancholy towards me. I am beginning to spawn a conspiracy that he's mute.

"It's kind of chilly in here," he says as he shrugs, and strokes his arms and legs to warm up. "Aren't you cold?" he asks.

"Sometimes," I say.

"You should really get that air conditioner fixed," he says.

"I'm not really cold," I say.

"What are you thinking about?" he asks.

"Do I know you?" I ask perplexed by the whole situation, I sure think that is a strange way of starting a conversation but at least I was having one for a change.

"I don't think we've ever met. My name is Anthony," he introduces himself, holding his hand out for me to shake.

"Nice to meet you, I'm Ronnie," I lie in a cynical smile as I shake his desiccated hand.

"Just Veronica?" he asks, sitting back on the seat and takes his zippo out of his left pocket. "Can I?" he asks, before actually lighting the thing up. He quite reminds me to my father, he always has a pipe in his hand or mouth whenever he's about to have a conversation with anyone.

"No, just Ronnie. And yes, you may," I simply say, just to be polite and all.

"Seems to me you don't want to be found, Miss Ronnie, been hiding your face since we left the train station," he assumes. He assumed right, although I was starting to get a little weird out by him. "Is Ronnie even your real name?"

"Unfortunately, sir, it is and why would you say I don't want to be found?" I ask intrigued, I didn't like feeling so ingenious.

"How old are you, kid?" he asks blowing the smoke in small circles out of the window. You see, you're not supposed to smoke, there's even a warning banner right outside my cabinet door indicating so.

"I'm seventeen, how old are you?" I ask, looking back into his eyes like he'd been doing all the time before.

He just laughs, maybe he's really old and he's taken it as an offense like elder people always do, they get so picky about things like these.

"I'm soon-to-be 50. You're pretty young to be on a 48h train all by yourself, kiddo," he marks out. I hate it when people call me kid or kiddo. Johnny and Hugo's friends called me that all the time; it feels like something you'd call your pet. Johnny and Hugo where one of my cousin's closest buddies, we occasionally went surfing with them, only thing is, they'd bring all their grown-up friends from the Valley.

"You're pretty old to be talking to a 17-year-old you don't know," I point out.

"I just thought we could keep each other company for a while, it gets lonely sometimes. And I know you've been looking over at me trying to figure out what it was I was doing," he says, taking another breath of his damn pipe and blowing it out the window, which didn't really change the fact that he was blowing it right in my face.

"Well, I thought you might've been sick or something and looked over to make sure I didn't have to call anyone to come help you. What was it you're doing anyways?" I ask as I wave the foul vapour out of my face.

"I'm meeting my daughters that have recently moved to Chicago with their foster family," he says, smiling to the carpet ground thoughtfully. He was probably thinking about his daughters jumping on him the moment they saw him or something.

"Foster family?" I ask.

"I had alcohol issues so they were taken from me after their mother died," he says as his facial glee expression disappears into a bitter one and I should've felt horrible.

"I don't know whether to believe you or not," I say doubtfully and it's true, why would he tell me all this personal bull—if he didn't know me and to be frank, I didn't really care either so there was no sense to this conversation.

"Why not?" he asks astound.

"You're opening up too much to a person you've just met," I indicate in suspicion.

"That's a better reason to open up, you know nothing of me, might as well talk about what grips me than keep up to a standardised polite conversation that'll bore both of us," he declares confidently. "And you can't judge me, at least not like the people who aren't considered strangers," he adds. I must say he does have a point. And what do people mean when they say they want an 'interesting conversation', what does an interesting conversation involve? Art, politics, literature and the exchange of a diversity of opinions on the matters that are being discussed—it could also involve astrology and the significance of emotions, and our favourite subject we don't talk about but we do with our looks and our gestures, with a sip of wine or a tender bite from a bleeding steak, the way you look at your watch or ask the waiter for the desserts menu, it's even said with the signature on the check after a wonderful dinner accompanied by an 'interesting conversation', and then it all ends up summarised in sex, the most interesting conversation of all.

"Why did your wife die then?" I dared to ask.

"What a personal question," he says.

"We are strangers after all, you said so yourself," I remind him awkwardly.

"She died, I don't know of what, I wasn't with her when it happened but they told me she wasn't happy," he confesses with what looks like a melancholic smile.

"In what way? Did she commit suicide or something like that?" I ask. I was always so damn inquisitive about death, it bothered the *hellouttame*. If she died because she wasn't happy, then why are so many people still alive? How can I have survived so much time? The concept of a mislead happiness is too easy to blame—happiness doesn't exist without unhappiness. The earlier you're told this, the earlier you'll accept pain because really and I'm quoting my English teacher, happiness is only found easily by the ignorant.

"Kid, I don't know why she wasn't happy," he said, taking another smoke at his old pipe.

"Well, did she kill herself?" I asked.

"She stuck her head in the oven," he said as he turned to look at me from his damn pipe. I didn't really feel like saying anything else after that, I was incited to make a related comment to Sylvia Plath but that would've been too gorgy. Death isn't always a topic that you can gossip about at an event dinner and certainly not with some constrained stranger in a train. I was getting startled at how personal he was getting; I wouldn't trust me with all this information; I could publish it someday.

"You got any folks?" he asks, changing the subject.

"Yes, I'm going to Chicago to visit my aunt," I lie.

"Do they know you're going to see your aunt?" he asks.

"Of course, they know, how the hell do you think I got in this train and who paid my ticket," I say irked.

"I don't know, kid, you seem to have a lot of wit if I'm being honest with you," he says. "What does your aunt do?" he asks. Adults always ask that, I don't know what it is about other people and their snooty jobs.

"She's a florist, she's my mother's sister, you see. I'm going to see her because my mother recently got pregnant again with this new husband of hers, and she'd like my aunt to come home for Christmas and all that, for the baby, of course," I lie convinced.

"Hell of a plan you've got there, kid, is it your first time in Chicago?" he asks, as he prepped his pipe with more tobacco to smoke. He was starting to create the typical small conversation I've always tried to avoid.

"Yes it is," I say.

"Any places you'd like to see?" he asks.

"Well, not at the moment really, I'm only staying for a day anyways," I say truthfully for once. "Tell me about your daughters?"

"What about them?" he asks, surprised, which quite bothered me to be honest.

"I don't know, you're the one asking all these irrelevant questions, might as well switch roles for a while," I said.

"Well, one is, I think, about your age and her name is Jaime, I'm not quite sure, I know their mother gave one of them a boy name, and the elder one's Helen I'm for sure and she's about 18 I'd guess, it's been a long time you see," he says nervously. I didn't answer from there and looked out the window covered in smoke.

"Got any idea of what you'd like to be when you grow up, kid?" he asks.

"I'd like to be a nobody but to get there, I ought to be a writer first," I say.

"Thought you might say that; you look like one but do you write as one too?" he asks, rhetorically of course.

"You'll find out if I ever get published," I say.

"Got yourself any muses?" he asks. "Some love story to write about?"

"What do you mean?" I ask amused.

"What inspires you, kid?" he asks as he takes another damn blow at his pipe, this time accidently throwing all the ash on my leather Italian bag without realising.

"Oh, right—I'm sorry but I'm not going to be able to answer to that," I say.

"Come on, kid, you oughtta be able to talk about what you love if you want to write about it. You oughtta be able to talk about anything," he says.

"Not really, I mean if I wanted to talk to you about it, I wouldn't write it, don't you reckon?" I ask. "And besides, what the hell does it matter what inspires me as long as I'm inspired."

"I understand, kid," he says, evidently not understanding but just being polite.

"Did you love her?" I ask, referring to his dead wife or ex-wife or God knows what.

"Have you ever loved somebody?" he asks, changing the subject. I hadn't, so I couldn't really answer and decided to change the topic before we started psychoanalysing one another to satisfy this silence everyone tries to avoid when being with someone. I feel like our dialogues are interviews we don't plan; it makes them look *helluvalot* like a conversation.

"If you like asking questions, you should learn how to answer them too," he says, for I was taking a longer time than expected in answering.

"I like to listen to what people answer," I say, although I was lying, for I mainly asked questions because it was a way of drawing more attention to myself.

"Why?" he asks perplexed. He didn't look like a 50-year-old, my mum was 50 and she never asked 'why', she already took for granted that she knew everything, which I'm sure, is something common in mothers.

"I guess I feel more secure with the person I'm with if I know everything about them but then again, you can't really know everything about anyone," I say.

"Do you ever answer the questions made back to you?" he asks.

"Depends on the question," I answer.

"Can I ask you a question? Do you fall in love often?" he questions the same idea with different words.

"Which of the both questions do you want me to answer?" I ask back. I actually didn't mind answering both; it wasn't that big of a deal. I just wanted to taunt him.

"Now, don't be clever with me and all, kid, I've been where you are so answer the question without a question," he says.

"I don't know what love is, how do you expect me to answer about something I've got no clue about?" I confess. I wasn't ashamed of it though. Love wasn't something I was interested in. Love is the best-sold product in the market this century; it's advertised as the best thing that can happen to you, or as a concept of an eternal hypothetical happiness. I mean, who would want to be happy their whole life? I know when you first read it you think it's a great idea, but it's not. It'd be great to find someone you can be unhappy with too. Even if those two are completely paradoxical through my inexperienced eyes, it seems right.

"What do you mean?" he asks alerted. He was starting to annoy the hell out of me with the damn conversation topic. I rather not talk, if we're talking about love. If we wore out the word so much, we will end up draining its mediocre meaning to which everyone's so goddamn dependent of.

"Never felt it before," I simply say, hoping he would notice I'm not very aesthetic about continuing talking to him, at least about this bloody matter.

"Do you want to?" he asks, not giving up.

"Should I want to?" I ask.

"You're doing that thing again of answering without answering," he says. I don't understand why he cared so much, what could intrigue him so much about my love interests unless he was trying to seduce me, which I doubt after telling me he is 50, and has two daughters.

"I don't know," I reply in agony. I tend to start getting really tense when I'm forced to continue doing something I don't want to.

"That's a vague response, when I was an English teacher in the University of Columbia, answers like that weren't accepted. I'd just politely demand the student to exit my class until he came up with a better response," he says. Finally, he said something that caught my attention. I was starting to think that he was an advert associate trying to get an idea for a new phony advertisement and I didn't really want to collaborate in one of those.

"Ivy league? My dad wanted me to apply to one of those and frankly, I'm quite glad I haven't," I say honestly.

"I'm just saying as someone with experience that a good technique to be a writer is to have a unique response than no one has come up with, yet," he advises.

"Not really, everyone's kind of come up with everything lately so the best thing I can do is reform somebody else's idea into what it would've looked like if it had been mine," I say as I try to find a comfier position to sit in, as he had really just invaded half of the seat in front of me and all his smoke was floating towards me instead out of the window, as if to cloak me. I'm beginning to realise this damn book is really a mere script with a couple of mad descriptions. This isn't going to be an autobiography if that's what you had in mind; hence I've already guaranteed you that earlier. I doubt anybody would like to read my autobiography; it'd be just too blank.

"You seem pretty sure about what you want, kid," he says.

"Please don't call me kid," I finally say. I'm glad I look more confident about who I am, that what I really am.

"Alright, kid," he says.

By not owning a watch, I realise I am living outside of time. Therefore, for me, it'll never be daytime or nighttime; it'll just be time at its different stages of colour shades. It will simply be the today, whether it's a modern era or we're back in the '60s will be irrelevant. I mean, for anything to last forever, you really ought to live outside of time. I will live in a day with no end, but who says it won't be the other way round? I'll live in a night with no end, or they both have no end and they overshadow one another creating of my surrounding an inexhaustible space of Turner brushstrokes in the night whilst it rains hail. Now the room is colder and the simple fragile white pieces of ice that collapse into a million tiny pieces when they delicately drop on my booklet like any tear trying to inspire this blank page that I have been staring for half an hour without knowing what to draw or write. I reckon we are crossing New Mexico by now, or so that's what Anthony said a few minutes ago—I'd always heard a lot about New Mexico, specially about El Paso which was probably where we were going to go through, but Anthony said we'd go by Albuquerque instead. The truth is the train was moving faster than what I'm narrating to you about.

Anthony and I aren't really talking; at least we haven't since our previous conversation, although, funnily, we're still together in my cabin. I was quite uncomfortable not being able to ask him to leave; I was still confused for why he'd end up sat in front of me in the first place. I'm glad he did though, for a while, I would've done the same sooner or later with someone who'd caught my attention even though not many people do. We just looked out the window, hoping to arrive to our destination with the hope of… What am I even writing? This isn't the product I want to sell to you. I felt like a third voice was narrating my thoughts dramatically like in those really drivel movies where it's supposed to be funny, but I just find ridiculous. Anyways, the truth is, after the last thing Anthony said, we spoke no more, although I quite felt like our conversation or whatever that was, had finished. He started to fall asleep as the silence we'd created began to have domain over my cabinet creating it so peaceful, no one would dare disturb that silence. Not even the stewardess passing by with that little trollies of hers piled with gruesome junk food dared to open the door to offer if we wanted anything. She also didn't disturb us because we both immediately faked sleep as we heard the soft wheels of the trolley approach us like she was a psychopath in a sinister movie. So the poor lady didn't really have a chance to sell us any of her expired products, maybe she was even an expired product. After that endless excruciating job, she's been obliged to do, her life's probable expired by now. I imagined her as a yoghurt.

"Did she go?" Anthony asks as he discreetly lifted his head out from the blankets like a kid making sure the monster was back in the wardrobe. He was quite childish for his age, which probably was the only thing I liked about him.

"She was deceived by our great acting skills. Instead of going directly to *The New Yorker,* I should deliberately change my plans and go towards Broadway!" I exclaim ironically.

"If you need a manager or the director of 'Hamilton' needs an extra hand, you know where to find me," he mocks.

"Uh, do your kids know you're coming to see them?" I ask.

"Not technically, but their foster parents do," he proclaims.

"Are they going to let you just take them away like that?" I ask doubtful.

"I doubt it, but I'll let them decide," he says nervously. I could feel how he was dying to change the subject. He was getting rather tense and looked preoccupied.

"They'll choose you I'm sure. You seem like a good dad," I lie, although I wish I hadn't.

"Would you like something to drink? I'm quite thirsty myself. Probably going to head to the mini bar at the end of this wagon," he offers.

"I'm good, thanks," I say.

Anthony stood up from his seat discretely but I still noticed his sweat patch left on the seat in front of me. I didn't say anything because it'd be rude and he did try to cover it, I didn't even find it funny, to be honest. I'd been thinking about this one time when Ronnie Havelock and Blair *whatshername.* Blair Carr, these two girls that I'd shared a room with at this lousy summer camp my parents made me go to when I was ten. We'd always play the rope even though we never really spoke, except this one time where they asked me if I'd like something to drink, being polite and all.

Anthony reminded me to them, especially Ronnie. I actually lied about my name being hers because she always made it look easy to be referred to as Ronnie and I must admit it's an easy name. She was so darn polite all the time like the way Anthony's just been. Being polite is good if done out of instinct than because you feel like you 'have to'. I lent Ronnie my bob pin once and never got it back.

Seq. 10 Int. Views of America

Outside, it didn't look like the typical rooftops that I used to mistake with yacht decks of some rich bastard's boat at the port in LA. Anthony and I have been sharing each other's company since he came back with his glass of sizzling champagne, which I found rather amusing. I thought he'd gone for a bottle of water or something. He was old, but he wasn't the repellent kind of old, the type I usually try to avoid when I'm walking at one end of the street and they're walking on the same one, and I just purposely change my path on to the other side. Don't jump to conclusions if you've read *Lolita* by Vladimir Nabokov, in fact, it's my mother's favourite book. It's not that I have something going on with old men, I just have a fear that, one day, I'll cross my mother's new husband in the same street. That is by far one of my worst nightmares, the other one probably I imagine would be after having my piercing conversation with Anthony about falling in love. Although, writing it and reading it now makes me feel corny and miserable. It also makes me feel susceptible and at unease with myself. Although, if I tell you some lousy truth, if I did fall in love, maybe I would be able to finish this goddamn book you can't wait to finish reading. Lately, I don't know what to write, I feel like I'm saying all these things, writing all of those words that not even one of them seems right once I've read it over. I know how I said we barely crossed New Mexico, but once you're in a train, you forget you're in motion—for we've barely entered the vacancy of Colorado, going through small towns I've never heard of before.

Anthony is twined in his seat queered by idleness. His head is held by the mirror on his right, in this way, preventing his head from being decapitated, although not even the mirror is liable enough to prevent his head from falling even lower as he begins to fall asleep. I, on the other hand, suffer insomnia. All night, I've been staring at that old mourning English professor with his two unknown daughters named Adrian and Helen. That's really all the information I have about him. He really has less about me, he's not as curious as his gauzy sphere-like glasses expose him to be. He's a precocious fraud, now I know another thing about him. I suddenly have this urge to wake him up and answer his goddamn question, but I knew the instant I approached him, I actually didn't want to wake him up. I end up whispering to myself in a sotto voice what he would've liked to hear if he weren't so passed out. So what love really is, what love is, I mean writing is falling in love continuously with love itself.

Sometimes I put my headphones on, not because I want to listen to music, but because I don't like people disturbing me. Headphones are the only invention that has successfully achieved to approach the principle of any respect whatsoever towards one another. Music is the only thing that nobody likes to interfere with. It's a religion, like Jesus Christ; only it exists. Oh, Father, please forgive me for I have sinned, for I have used your Preacher's name in vain! I feel it is unnecessary to talk about God if you don't mind, I don't really want to. In the pre-school, I used to go to a school which was Catholic and all, my parents aren't religious, and my dad was quite against my brother and me attending this school on the first place but it was the only school that would have us at that time. So every day, we'd have to go to church and confess, and then this priest on the other side of the confessional would make us do eight Hail Marys and eight Oh our Fathers as a way of God forgiving, whichever could've been our sins at that age. Our parents switched us schools when my uncle told them about the school my cousin went to.

Jean, BD and I often walked past the valley sometimes when we had to go get supplies for my uncle. We usually didn't really do anything together because they were older than me and didn't really like to hang out that much. I understood, I wasn't bothered by it really because I had other things to do anyway. We got along though, but people stop getting along sometimes. I guess it's something that happens so I didn't mind it as much. Although, at school, we usually hung out often. Anyhow, so this time when we were walking back from the Valley, we crossed this shop where they sold TVs and decided to go in, just to check them out and all. It was the first time we actually didn't have a curfew set by my uncle so we took advantage of it. We looked around the shop, it was nice. It was full of televisions playing different channels all the time, and you might've thought the shop was modern and all but it was full of dirt. The shop was very narrow and deep. I really wanted to see what was over at the dark point of the shop where the products were difficult to recognise at the certain distance I was. We didn't see anything we liked, but then again, we didn't come in because we wanted to buy anything. The counter lady was nice too; she'd smile at us all the time, just in case we'd steal something. As if it were easy to steal one of those five pound televisions. I'm telling you this because something odd happened. After we left the shop, smiling at the woman by the counter as she waved at us, probably shaming us for not buying anything. We went out and noticed all the TVs exposed in the display case were playing this lousy advertisement. If it weren't because it was nearly finished when we took a glance at it, I would've known what it was selling. What it was, you see, was a man smiling at us announcing the only way to find yourself is with this product. I've wanted to know what the product was since then, not because I want to buy it but I want to know what it is. It was the first laugh we shared mutually and actually looked at each other. I wanted to throw a rock at each of the televisions, but I couldn't. I just thought about the old lady sitting there doing her job and how it'd annoy her if we did something like that. So I decided not to. I never quite got to understand what was it he was trying to sell, and why was he so convinced of such lie. What bothered me the most was that his stupid superficial smile wasn't at all that superficial.

Kansas. Kansas. Kansas. This lousy description is what happens when you don't know how to describe a place that only makes you wish you could leave it as soon as possible. I couldn't put it in better words than Tennessee Williams, simply "America has only three cities: New York, San Francisco and New Orleans. Everywhere else is Cleveland." Kansas is just a quick stop retaining me from arriving to the only destination I want to invade. Not with guns, not with nuclear explosions but with art, literature, music. Burn the city down to create a new one. In Los Angeles, I felt like a girl made out of methanol paper in a flamboyant city that didn't stop scorching, leaving me ominous, this time the flames will be on my favour. The train driver announces, "We have arrived to Kansas. The train leaves again at 2h for those who continue the journey! Hope you come back soon!" His voice quivering with hypocrisy as his hazy words spread around the trains' headphones like chewing gum between a group of friends in a public high school or a private one. It really doesn't change what adjunct it has in beheading it, it's still a school, and it's still the purgatory because hell comes after when you go to college, if you do go. It seemed like Anthony's dreams had driven him into a deep coma, how much I envy him. Being in a coma is the best suicide one could survive; you're dreaming without knowing you're dreaming. You basically start a new life out of the creative neurons in your brain, out but inside a new paradisiac cage. It would be such a marvellous way to die, not dying in your mind. A way of telling everyone to, well, there's not a polite way to put it, and even if there were, I wouldn't use it. It wouldn't create the same effect, but, yeah, what I'm trying to say is, 'fuck off'.

At this point, you might be bored, maybe some might've not even gotten to this page and condemned me for making them waste their money on something they don't like. Probably this wasn't what you expected, but let's be realistic for once, let's reason with entity. I'm only seventeen. Now, the results of this book till now can either be one of two things: I'm a failure of a writer or you are a failure of a reader. I could guarantee you that it gets any better, but I'm not going to lie: it doesn't.

You must be wondering what's happened to Anthony by now, well, he's still breathing with his eyes closed, laid down in a rather uncomfortable position. Nothing other than the obvious has happened since I left you with my shameful description of Kansas. I'm just sat in the same place I was an hour ago, staring at the same man, the only thing that changes in this set is the thoughts in my head. The expositions of art of any mortal are nothing compared to what delves in the studio of my sub consciousness. I mean Freud would know.

My characters, they call me. They're looking for directions for they have forgotten their lines from the script and the director of Costume Department is stressed because production hasn't given him enough time to make up and dress all the actors for their given role. Worst thing is, *atrezo* isn't able of creating the described atmosphere I had visualised as to be my setting. It reminds me of that movie of Luis Buñuel where they just can't figure a way of getting out of the room, *The Exterminating Angel*. I disappear into the world where someone can be a cinema director without it being a trivial profession. I'm unsure of whether my dreams are controlling my reality or if my reality is controlling my dreams, either way I am falling asleep. If any idea arises and I don't write, it's because I am finally aroused by something other than bolstering views; if the idea is good enough, I will remember it once awoken and if not shame for it, but it'll be forgotten into the undiscovered part of my brain, not even a neurologist could examine.

"I don't think I can give you an answer. Oh, I could give you Freudian reasons with fancy talk, and that would be right as far as it went. But what you want are the reasons for the reasons, and I'm not able to give you those. Not for the others, anyway. For myself? Guilt. Shame. Fear. Self-belittlement. I discovered at an early age that I was—shall we be kind and say, different? It's a better, more general world than the other one. I indulged in certain practices that our society regards as shameful. And I got sick. It wasn't the practices, I don't think, it was the feeling that the great, deadly, pointing forefinger of society was pointing at me—and the great voice of millions chanting, 'Shame. Shame. Shame'. It's society's way of dealing with someone different."

—KEN KESEY
One Flew Over the Cuckoo's Nest, 1962

Seq. 11 Int. Train

I don't know who I am, not even after writing this ludicrous book I will, even though my intention is to be able to find out. I've also realised through the transition of writing this book that really a writer just narrates his or her life by creating a different dimension in which he would like to live his life, a different species of realities someone could choose from that satisfies us merely to the expectations of our dreams. It's like writing a book; this book is the 11:11 wish or the sensational astray that flashes in the dried dark space at an accelerated rhythm; the gentle blow of the birthday candles on your seventh or hundredth birthday. When I read a book, I think about the writer under the name of Holden Cauffield, Patrick Bateman, Sal Paradise, Amory Blaine…maybe what I'm reading is simply a lie of who they are, their mascaraed camouflage: the reflection of them to a mirror that won't answer, a reflection you can't sanction. Even though it's exactly the same person as you, the same face and colours mixed all together to create you. For some irrational reason, it doesn't follow your movement or answer your questions with the same answer. The mirror has converted into a frozen image of the most insecure moment of your life and sometimes that image is the image of a face that blazes.

That's how I woke up. When you dream, you never have the chance to see yourself die, because that's when you wake up. In my case, when I dream, I directly don't even see myself and if am about to, I wake up. For when I had opened my eyes, Anthony had disappeared. I'm not sure if the abandoned side of my imagination created him, or if he was actually real. Maybe he had to descend in Kansas and didn't say goodbye so he wouldn't have to wake me up. Either of both reasons, I am alone again. I'm not sure if this time I feel happy or sad about it, I think I directly don't even feel anything about it. I actually hope he just had to go to the men services which are on another wagon and that he'll come back. I can't explain something that doesn't have an explanation, like the fact that I've been staring to this page for an itemised amount of time and

Anthony hasn't returned yet. Maybe, if I take a nap again, when I wake up, he'll be back. The problem of this plan is that I'm not tired, and I can't really fall asleep unless I'm really tired. I haven't been diagnosed with insomnia but I just know I have it, I can't sleep and the truth is that I hate not sleeping, it's the only place where I'm awake.

I haven't written much since I got on the train, the constant twittering of the vehicle doesn't give me a pace to think in, everything is muddled up in here; it's almost like a scenario of my old bedroom. I say old, because it's no longer mine, and I'll probably never see it again. Patrick Bateman was a schizophrenic without a plan, at least I have one, and it appears to decorate one of the walls of the white box in which I sleep and eat, pinned to the board above my writing desk. In this way, I avoid being part of the society of narcissism where the TV is used as only resource of entertainment. My favourite channel was to look at that wall, it's my favourite movie set, I bet that not even Bergman, Kubrick or even Lynch with his great masterpiece such as *Twin Peaks*, had come up with this idea: a wall that resurrects ideas. Yes, I am like everybody else, because this idea of being different is just an excuse to be an asshole and no one telling you anything about it, but inside there, I was the metamorphosis of my ideas. And the best part was, I never went out. Even though you may have thought you saw me and that the lips you wished to kiss looked something like mine, and the eyes you desired to wake up in the morning with looking at you were my eyes and that perhaps my face was mine—'I was simply not there'. That's my favourite quote from *American Psycho*, Bret Easton Ellis really does know how to represent the madness of the narcissist oppressed prude society and its only imperfection was it wasn't based in Los Angeles. I bet it would've impacted more in New York, although I can't imagine how the high-class society of Wall Street and the Upper East Side must turn out to be. I'm not in the mood to start creating deceptions, there's nothing worse than Beverly Hills where everything is just compiled in materialistic expenses incorporated by a brand name and its ornaments.

You must be feeling like an extra low paid actor in *Groundhog Day* where Bill Murray is constantly trapped in time, reliving the same scene of his past day, over and over again. Only you feel I keep repeating myself, it's not on purpose, I promise. But you really couldn't expect to get hold of this book and assume it'll have an incessant amazing story, when it only has me. When I get really anxious, I trap myself in time and how ironic to talk about time when

I never actually look at it. Anthony has trapped me in time with the constant pestering in my brain of whether he was real or a furtive mirage. He most evidently was, as we had, had a conversation and I still have his coat beside me but I don't see why he'd disembark in Kansas when he was meant to go to Chicago to pick up his daughters, my best guess to resolve all this mystery is that he freaked out about them not wanting him back. I wish I knew more about his daughters so I could find them for him, even though that wouldn't help much. I don't even see a reason why I would do anything for him; I don't even know him and I quite disliked him after a while. What I most hate about him is he seemed something he wasn't, that leads me to the conclusion he was a liar. I bet Helen and Adrian don't even exist in the first place, it's a good technique to distract your languorous victim, making me think he was innocent and hurt, and children are always the perfect key to masquerade someone with innocence. I'm not a maniac, I am just mad; I suppose we all react differently to all types of madness.

I have actually decided to write him a letter; I'm not really inspired to write my novel now anyways. His sudden disappearance has gathered all my attention. I didn't know where he lived or anything, so I doubt he was ever going to receive it but I wrote it anyway.

Anthony,

I am writing you this letter because I have a question, which is triggering me since you disappeared. You see I'm not sure you were so incessantly truthful with me. I know your intentions weren't the same, as Humbert Humbert's but that doesn't change the fact that you meant any good. A little note would've been helpful to know you've left. I might never finish my book now because of the triggering thought of whether you were real or not and that's absolutely your fault. I'm actually surprised an English professor is such a liar as yourself, or maybe you've read too much Tennessee Williams and declare subconsciously that you 'misrepresent things to them. I don't tell the truth; I tell what ought to be the truth. And it that's sinful, then let me be damned for it!' I can even guarantee you Helen and Adrian don't even exist. I've met you for half an hour and I hope I never meet you again. This is actually quite a hating letter, I'm not used to writing these types of letters sincerely but now you've taken away my ideas by replacing them with the intrigue of your sudden disappearance, you bloody narcissist. It looks like you're trying to recreate a Cohen's movie, The Man Who Wasn't

There. *Only you are making the title literate for you were never here, if you were, it was just an illusion but I doubt even my imagination would be capable of creating such a bastard as yourself. So, I suggest you either write me back explaining yourself or you directly just come back. I don't think about you in the way 'Oh, I wish he were here'… I'm glad you're far away so I can burn down alone or freeze to death, either ways, your presence isn't acquired in the reunions of the Dreamers Club. Thanks to your repugnant transformation, you are no longer a member. It's not that I depreciate you, it's just you questioned my thoughts on love and now I hate you, I can't feel a mediate between love and hate, I doubt one even exists. It's either black or white, yes or no, love or hate. And in your case, it's an immense amount of hate. I must admit I've never tasted this delicacy before and I'm still questioning myself whether I like it or not…but let's summarise it in that I've tried it and I'll continue trying it. If Satan were real, I would tell you to burn in hell with him, but as he doesn't exist, you've got something worse coming for you; burning with me.*

Your dear not-travelling partner

I actually hope he never receives it. I don't want him to think he'd been of significance in my paused life. He actually didn't, but the fact of being alone made me scandalise everything that happened to me to a point of severe excess. Since we left Kansas, I haven't written anything more than that letter. I've just stared at the depressed countryside dreaming of becoming a city. Has it ever happened to you that you're experimenting not boredom, that would be too easy, but you're dying of disgust towards everything but still you just want to do everything? That's what's happening to me since I woke up. Write a song, finish this book, play the saxophone

I used to play the saxophone back home but even my mum took that away from me when she left. Most of our discussions were because I didn't play it enough for what it cost and to her musical ears was not good enough. She wasn't really a musician but she composed and played the piano since she was twelve. The house would always be suffused with music, and now silence was its perpetual replace. My dad hated that once she left. He loved the music in our house so now he'd always play Jazz or Bob Dylan in the garden. But anyways, that's not really what I want to talk about and I know it's not what you want to hear…

Learn to sing, make a movie, draw, draw plenty, draw what you imagine and what you don't, but just simply assassinate your hand so it's the dancing partner of a pencil. Run away, write, write so much so I can just leave, get out of there, accomplish my dreams, so I can actually, finally disappear. To abandon the whole world but still, secretly, wishing that nobody abandoned me. In definitive, I hate solidarity that's why I brag about it. If you say it's fascinating, maybe you'll end up believing it or at least, people won't think you want it. The only thing I feel right now is the pain in my head provoked by all these things occurring inside it at the same time. God, how much it hurts! I feel like the cells in my head are trying to excavate a hole in it to have a clearer view of all those things I so think about, to visualise what's been veiling on the other side of obscurity. It's killing me, they can't continue cleaving me. I'm losing my sense, losing eagerness; I'm losing sleep at the same time. I'm only capable of watching movies now. I've become everything I've always hated; depending on a machine and I'm still not even dying. At least from the movies I learn something: that I should stand up. I listen to music imagining I already know how to make mine; truth is, I'm an amateur in all senses, for I am feeble and do most of my actions abstractedly—just like all of you. I wish I was impulsive like my dreams. That is why when we are asleep, when we dream, we sometimes misinterpret dreams as the hidden realm of reality. Our dreams are our only liberation from the world, they're the ones who show us the truth of our feelings, our fears and our thoughts—we know the people we love when we see them as recreational stardust in our dreams. Even nightmares are better than the reality we have succumbed to living in. As Freud said, dreams are a 'detachment of the soul from the fetters of matter'. Maybe if we all dreamed awake, consequences would be abrupt, maybe we'd all stop being dreamers of our desires and desirable of our dreams.

Seq. 12 Int. Train II

There are so many things I want, like to be a kid again and do all of those many things. I look at the children running around in the cabin hallway and I see myself for a very vast moment, but I do. I never think about things like this, or by far say them out loud but for the first time, I've directly thought in a dramatic way as I looked at them, 'I wish they never grew'. Why would anyone want to? I hope the same thing that happened to me, doesn't happen to them; that they fall in love with someone's soul instead because they like the same game as you, become addicted to telephones, gossip, weed, alcohol, fight with their life-time friends for worst things than who's tag—learn to live without it being something you have to be taught. I want them to stay there, right here, in this moment and that they never egress form it. Without dysphoria, euphoria doesn't exist. Happiness is like love, it only happens once and you don't really get to choose when.

Be careful, wonderland doesn't exist; the more you take LSD, the more the rabbit's hole will diminish. I'm warning you that Neverland is a myth, I know, because when I jumped from the window glaring at the moon, I only saw how it got further away from me instead of letting me go. Although I didn't fall on the ground, I was ten when I killed my granddad by accidently falling on him. Maybe if it weren't for his uncalculated appearance, I would've arrived but I'm getting too dramatic, I know I'm crazy but there's just some things that shouldn't be published and that's one of them. You see, there are books written for writers to read and books written for an audience to read, I'm still not sure for which of those publics this book is recommended to, probably to neither, I'd only recommend it to myself really.

They say if you fall hard, it means you've reached the Zion. Father Christmas, the three kings, the tooth fairy don't exist. But the lost kids do, they're everywhere, I'm one of them. Holden Cauffield, Peter Pan and Woody Allen exist. Woody Allen brings gifts every year—a new movie. Holden Cauffield, instead of replacing your bloody tooth for money, keeps you away forever having to worry about the significance of it, and Peter Pan stops you from becoming what you don't want to become. That's where I am, looking out a window in immense apathy but thinking, thinking so much that my head hurts and the countryside of Missouri at my right bleaches. I dominate the world; it could disappear as soon as I dazed it completely by closing my eyes or I could give it more importance by keeping them wide open. The thing is, I don't belong to the world, on the contrary. Usually, I don't talk a lot about my childhood, feeling nostalgia from the past prevents me from feeling it from the present. I am going to be clear though, you may have misunderstood some things; it tends to happen when you think you've understood everything I am writing when you haven't, that's how the goddamn critics get their jobs. Now is where reality drives in and all my deliration is humiliated by truths like the window I jumped from, for instance, was one metre or so from the ground, it's one of those windows you jump from at night when you want to go out but you're grounded.

That just sounded like a rather depressing speech someone would give to a crowd of teenagers to prevent them from trying any drugs, even though, you know they obviously are. Thank God they are, we need more revelry in this generation, an anarchy that corrupts the established laws with culture and art. We are all so anxious of whether we're going to get admitted into the college we want to go to and what job would be a good idea just to survive in the 21st Century crisis with enough money. I say it'd be stupid not to experience the experiences of life. It's the pressure that kills teenagers, not drugs. And that just sounded like a revolution logo in a banner being walked around the streets the same way feminists defend their rights as women, teenagers should defend their rights as well, children. They are the dream makers, and if you just destroy them, you'll wake up to a clouded sky and a starless night. When I say you, I'm deliberately talking about all the prosaic parents, the teachers, the government, the media etc... Those who control this bloody system: anyone older than twelve because we only really live twelve years, the twelve years of innocence and actually not having a notion, a conscience of whether what we are doing or not is bad or good, just not driven by the systematisation which is later applied to us in our heads; the rest of our life is sat at a bus stop waiting for the one indicating death as the final destination. There are so many damn quotes and logos about freedom and being free, and all that hipster teenage bullshit phase, you've had your freedom until you were twelve, if you don't have it anymore is because you sold it in trade for a seat at a certain table at lunch, a good grade in Maths, a new brand car from your parents, all these appearances you summit yourself to which have been moulded by people who don't even know you.

When you're on a train, time doesn't even pass. I'm stuck in this perpetual turn in time where time doesn't even turn. I feel like I've been trapped in this cabin and that soon, I'll be transferred back to Santa Monica and I'll probably end up in a central education reformatory just to make sure I won't do anything as stupid as this again, they'll just hide me in my visionary cell, thing is, I don't have time to continue strolling around this empty space. I've got contractions all over my body preventing me from running away from running away. It's like this whole idea has become a non-fictional nightmare and I'm the main character. Since Anthony has left, I've just grown more frightened. Even though several hours have passed since the train left the state of California, I feel like I'm still stuck in it, not being able to extricate the diversity between reality and fiction. I'm confused of whether I'm still just asleep in my bedroom or have I seriously flied over the cuckoo's nest like Jack Nicholson to actually be in this train heading to Chicago for the night and then back again early in the morning up to New York. Funny thing is, I haven't even thought what I'm going to do once I get to Chicago; I don't know anybody there. Please, I beg you don't picture this great adventure I'm going to live, because I'm not, I already told you at the beginning that this wasn't a movie and I wasn't lying. This book has become more of a personal diary companion than a novel wanting to be published.

I'm no longer the writer of this book; the book is the one writing me. Maybe if I eat something all these allusions will become more vivid and I will see everything clearer in order to understand what's going on, if anything is going on. I feel like my cabinet has been excluded from the rest, I'm the maniac chosen to be in exile. My fears have been paralysed by the sweet voice of Gladys as she walks down the aisle with her food trolley as her only comrade, clamouring gingerly, "Tea time!" That voice took me out of my misery for a while. I'm not sure if her name is Anne, I had never really had the chance to speak to her or even have a glance at her nametag probably positioned on the left side of her gleaming breasts or even know if she has gleaming breasts and if she was beautiful at all. I have no idea of anything about her; I just know her voice zooms me out of a dream that was being thought over too much, making it look like a gunshot body in the back room of a successful club.

I dream of having a conversation with her, but even that type of dream is out of my league. I hadn't seen her yet, but the way she walked could describe her pureness accompanied by her angelical voice. I just heard slight parts of her conversation with other clients on the train. She would always say "Thank you" or "Welcome" or all these really polite things you're supposed to say to a stranger from a supposed higher class than you, if there're still things like those in the 21st Century, I thought we left it all in Dickens's *Great Expectations*. But they're not from a higher class than her; she's probably more intelligent than any other passenger in this train including myself. I imagine her tense as she's serving the tea, hoping she doesn't spill it on their Armani jackets and then get fired for it, people actually lose their jobs because of snobs like those. When she goes past my cabinet, I'll ask her to sit down with me, and shift working turns with the other stewardess. I didn't like the other one; she stomped around smelling like anger contaminating the air as it spread like pollution. If it weren't for the advantage of being locked in this two-metre squared box without holes, I would've stopped breathing a long time ago.

In the meantime, I was tempted to write Diane a letter to entertain my perpetual boredom. You must've noticed I like writing letters to those I love by now. I remember the first week she left, it was the only thing I did, even though I never got any responses. People never write you back, that's why you keep on writing to them. They just look at the letter and they either appreciate the romantic gesture or understand it's a manipulation. We spend all our lives evading from sensing any type of diverge emotions whilst we search for them persistently, unconsciously every second of our lives in flooded allies of darkness or in the floating corners of your bed when you're alone and you wonder if you should masturbate or go out with your friends. We really are masochists in a sadist world; I think it's the only real true confession that affects us the most. We depend on others so much we deny their whole existence alone. She never answered me, when things like these happen, the two choices are: accept the negligence or create excuses of why they haven't answered. I'm a masochist, my ideas exist because of the pain I unconsciously inflict on myself. I don't mean pain as in cutting my wrists and hurting myself ruthlessly. As it's unconscious, I don't really know where I get it from, I just know where it's hidden and I don't hesitate in finding it. Suffering is the dose that your doctor never diagnoses you with, but should. Painkillers don't kill any pain but increase it, and antidepressants provoke the contrary effect of its useless name. Stop searching for felicity on packed tablets. All those pills just prove how much you need to be depressed in order to even have a bare idea of being what, for you or this society, considers as 'happy'. You're all living a lie, I'm not the liar here, I say the truth too much only that if you're living in a lie, any truth I say to is considered a lie, it's not reverse psychology what you're suffering, it's simply fucked up psychology. Those pills only exist to earn a great quantity of money, the government knows how to dominate you and from it, they take advantage of your ignorance and corrupt you. Pills are like drugs, only they're legal. They know how to get you sick so then you buy what they've created to cure you. It's a moneymaking business. This generation should stop selling their soul to the devil also known as a psychiatrist.

The fact that Diane never answered increased my obsession with her departure. I couldn't write to her now anyways, it would risk her finding me or telling anyone where I was, I know she'd tell. I didn't want that, the thought of writing a letter is an unconscious feeling I have of wanting to be found, even though I believe I don't. Everybody's always leaving me, I guess by now, the tough thing to say would be that I don't care. But when you're alone, like I am right now, you can't be tough, you can't be anything but be what you really are and who you are when you're with yourself can't be spoken about, simply because you'd stop being that person, even if you thought you were talking about yourself cleanly, you weren't. And even that's frightening for me, so I'm just a nothing in a train, an everlasting train that seems to sink into the nothingness of the proceeding horizon as I blankly stare to the colours complied in the objects waiting to be liberated on the walls of this wagon.

I knew there were only a few seconds left till Anne knocked on the crystal windowpane of my cabinet. I wasn't hungry or thirsty, I was just interested in what her face looked like and if it looked like her voice had drawn it to be. I would even waste 5$ on any garbage food she had in there just to have a face to face conversation with her, and maybe after one minute of simple talk, she'd like to join me in my solidarity and gleam it with her beauty. I really admire beautiful women, they're the art that hasn't been exposed yet because of the ignorant cities they're hidden in, and also I'm not really what you'd consider to be vain. If you're someone like me, you never have time to be vain; I hardly ever look at a mirror. So I'm not sure what I actually look like, that's why I haven't described myself before, only someone who's really looking at me could be able to do that. Most of the time, I don't know what I'm writing, just because I write everything really fast so it doesn't achromatise, it just invades pages and pages until everything I've ever wanted to say out loud has been transplanted on paper; a writer's heart is not in his body but in the pages he writes. This book is the corpse I've been transported to after dying. The weather's happier than me and it's raining. I feel like New York is getting further away, the closer I get to it. I actually like not having a conversation with anybody. I'm actually not a writer; I don't know what I am; I am a refugee in the idea of being what I think I'd like to be, but that doesn't mean I am. Every word I type is a strike in my cell wall, not because I'm counting down the days to get out, but the days left to stay in, I've written 29982 words by now. Imagine a world where walking with clothes was obscene. I wonder if people would walk around naked or stay locked at home with their insecurities as the hidden key they can't find to get out. This chapter is giving me a headache since I started writing it, only because at this point, I'm not sure if to start another book again or just finish this damn one. I'm not writing to give you pleasure by reading me, I'm writing to survive at least a few months more or whatever is left for this goddamn book to finally reach its given end until I stop simply being here. I've mentioned this several times but that's not going to prevent me from doing it again, wouldn't life last longer if death were considered life too?

Gladys is here. She is what I thought she would be as I look over at her once she's knocked on the windowpane delicately so that her porcelain hands don't shatter to pieces. She knocked three times as I was still zoomed out to hear the first two knocks, but when her hand motioned for the last knock, I heard it in the highest intensified resolution you could've imagined. I'm not even sure that type of sound is even reachable for a human being. I should probably go find a doctor when I arrive to Chicago, maybe I'm deaf and I don't even know it. I saw the scene of her movement in an extreme close-up frame to complement the high resolution of the sound that would vibrate through the cabinet like an electronic charge. The image was clear, like my eye had been mutated to a HD cinematographic shot camera. I was no longer in a train, I was shooting a movie. The moment actually occurred much faster than what I've just described it; she just knocked one-third time.

"Yes, hello, come in," I say, eating my words like a packman as they blurted from my mouth. I don't really know what you're supposed to say, I hadn't planned that part of our conversation, only because I wasn't sure we were actually going to have one.

"Would you like anything?" she kindly asks with glitter in her eyes, trying to hide how long it took her to stick each and every one of those recycled diamonds to cover the sadness of her daily blue drizzle.

"What do you have to offer?" I ask, in my best interpretation of a polite voice I had heard in *Dangerous Liaisons*, although still not trying to sound too polite, I didn't want her to start thinking I was a dickhead like the rest of the stuck-ups she had recently attended but I still wanted to show some respect.

"Well, depends on what you like, ma'am," she says, but I wouldn't let her finish that sentence, I hate people talking to me like I'm somehow superior.

"I should be the one calling you ma'am, I'm only seventeen," I rectify her. She sure wasn't expecting that for the reaction she offered.

"Oh, okay, sorry, ma'—sorry," she says, blurting words without sense. I felt terrible now, I didn't mean to intimidate her; I didn't know she'd get so touchy about it.

"Are you okay?" I ask, concerned but not really that concerned. You're never really too concerned about anyone, but you think you're supposed to feel like that on certain matters. This is the most interesting thing that has happened to me since Anthony left.

"Yes, ma'—sorry," she repeated herself. She did it again; I really didn't know what to say now, apart that she had disappointed me. I hadn't imagined her to be that mechanic, she really didn't know any other way to direct to someone else if it wasn't with ma'am or sir. She had accepted her inferiority confusing it as a way of survival.

"I'd like a Kit Kat please," I just say so she wouldn't break down again, blurting, 'Yes, ma'—sorry' for the third time.

"We don't have any left, m—" she says, tempted once again to call me that ludicrous name. Now I was the one in an awkward position because I really didn't like anything else. She only had sweets and gooey melted chocolate bars which where most definitely expired.

"Well, then a water please," I ask politely with a phony smile now. I can't stand her, but it felt rude now telling her to leave without buying anything or tipping her or something.

"Cold or warm?" she asks as she searches for a water bottle. How long was this conversation going to continue playing? It felt like the broken beeping honk from Little Miss Sunshine's yellow Volkswagen.

"Cold, please," I say, wishing this was the last thing I'd have to say to her apart from the typical thank you and goodbye.

"No cold, sorry, would you like a tea?" she asked nervously but maintaining her polite '60s pinup waitress cover. I feel like I am in a survey of how much from one to ten I liked the food of the restaurant.

"Okay, what savours do you have?" I ask impatiently. Now I understand why it took her so long to get here if she'd been the same with all her other costumers.

"Mint," she says. She started to remind me of Candy, the inexperienced Jew prostitute in *Café Society*. I hate mint.

"Okay, I'll have that then please," I order cordially, hoping this would be the last time I would have to act so phony towards somebody.

"It'll be just a minute," she assures me, knowing it'd take her an hour at least. I knew she was lying anyways; she didn't even have a kettle with her. Which meant she'd have to go somewhere else to do the tea and she'd probably bring it cold in half an hour or so but at least I would get rid of her for a while. Not having to endure her repelling voice any longer was going to be a blessing.

I didn't say anything else to her, I just tipped her and she left silently with her squeaking empty trolley. It's true that appearances kill you; hers just murdered me but not skilfully enough because unfortunately, I'm still alive staring out the same dusted window at a different landscape from the one before. Did that mean I was going forwards or backwards? I seemed unable of finding any form of appealing entertainment that wasn't looking out the window to a landscape that never changed, it was monotonous.

"I keep picturing all these little kids playing some game in this big field of rye and all. Thousands of little kids, and nobody's around—nobody big, I mean—except me. And I'm standing on the edge of some crazy cliff. What I have to do, I have to catch everybody if they start to go over the cliff—I mean if they're running and they don't look where they're going, I have to come out from somewhere and catch them. That's all I do all day. I'd just be the catcher in the rye and all. I know it's crazy, but that's the only thing I'd really like to be."

—JD SALINGER
The Catcher in the Rye, 1951

Seq. 13 Int. Train III

I'm thinking I should quit writing, but even thoughts like that aren't allowed to be thought about anymore, given the circumstances. You see, when you start being lonely not in a diagnosed depressing way. You're just lonely, like a devil in heaven playing ball with all those filthy painted angels, a lost wolf in a moonlike city, or even a kid at a really crappy prep school or an adult at some annoying Christmas office party. You're just lonely, not meaning you feel lonely. That's what I've been trying to decipher since Gladys went to find my sleazy mint tea. I've lied myself into believing she'll be back any time soon, but since I don't know what time it is and how much time has gone past since she left with her aggravating broken self, I've just sat here, the same place I've been sat for the last hours in the exact same amount of solitude. I really think I should start walking around or something, I don't know much about science as I failed all of its three diverse courses that complete it: chemistry, physics and biology. But I know about poetry, and I know that if I continue sitting in this same spot for the rest of the ride, I'm going to become somewhat paralysed; not physically but mentally, any functioning creative neuron in my mind is just going to explode like those fireworks my cousin and I used to throw around Santa Monica Pier when it was New Year's eve. We sure scared the hell out of all those American dream families with their snobby robotic children that looked like they've just come out of an expensive golfing brand factory like Ralph Lauren or Tommy Hilfiger, just admiring the pier as if Paris or Rome didn't exist.

The third thing I hate most after my name and phony people is an ignorant, even more if they're a fat ignorant. They don't have to be even physically fat to annoy the hell out of me, I know they're fat just by looking at those stupid brands decorating their vast emptiness often confused, or even assimilated with a human being. Not even hate is a good enough word to reflect what I feel towards someone like that, the same way love isn't a good enough word to describe what you feel when you fall in love, because I can assure you it's not love if you have the capacity to talk about it. It's chickenpox or tuberculosis or some type of illness that itches through all your body and makes it hard to breath somehow, it's like your heart has been taken over control by an element you don't know about and it's no longer beats that keep you alive but that sensation we so confuse with asthma. Anyways, Andy's the one who put this idea in my head when I was ten, he used to go to one of the most expensive boarding schools outside the city, where all the kids from those stupid people you often see on TV laughing at jokes they don't consider funny or having idiotic conversations with people they've just met or can't stand. I'm so fed up with everyone being so busy, so goddamn busy in maintaining their cynical appearances just to satisfy the hell out of someone who's doing the exact same thing for them and the best thing is, neither of them give a single outstanding crap about each other, they're just too accustomed to be shallow as to dare be anything else. You can't be different anymore; being different is an appearance, it's probably the worst appearance of all only because it's the one everybody wants to have, and it's sold out, I checked on Amazon.

Their kids would just all go to the same school because, well, they've got the money but what they've also got is arrogance. They're raised into thinking their money is who they are because they've got full of it, enough money can make you think you don't need to know anything else but how to create more of it. Those people sicken me, my high school was also full of them only it was worse, because they were probably twice as more conceited with their appearance as the other kids from Andy's school without even coming from a fine family as you would say these days. Andy hated all those bloody snoopy bastards; I don't even know why he went there in the first place, probably because he'd gotten a scholarship. He was really good at all his subjects and all; he was good at everything actually, probably the brightest person I've ever met. I'd continue talking about my cousin, but you're probably not even interested and even if you were, I just don't feel like satisfying you, entertaining you with urban stories of my dead cousin just to depress the hell out of me. I'm not going to deny, it would fill a couple more pages of this endless book, as much as I'd love that to happen, I don't want it to.

I haven't seen anything catch my attention, the fact that nothing has caught my attention is because I've decided I don't want to look anymore where I'm supposed to look. If I could tear my eyes out and give them to some blind man in the streets of Chicago, I would,

I really would. I feel like my eyes and the fact of having them open is the reason why I can't see anything anymore the way I'd like to. A fog has stormed my iris, that's why if you ever saw me, you'd know who I was. Having a fog in your eyes doesn't mean they'll be grey, it just means they'll be colourless and yet for some, that might not know this, grey isn't dark, but it's not light either. The same way that I don't know isn't no but it's not yes either. I'm against indecisions but yet I'm the first one who isn't capable of taking one. I just prefer not basing how I feel on what I thought that one moment into a definite answer that'll prevail for the rest of my insignificant existence, as Fitzgerald said in *This Side of Paradise*, 'I love you—now'. Well, the good news is, we all agree that there's a problem, we stress plenty about that supposed problem, and it's the only thing we talk about, 'The Goddamn Problem'. But what we don't talk about or even haven't thought is how to fix the problem or even what that problem really is. I know many might've thought how but nobody says anything these days; you never know what could happen to you if you spoke too much. Its true liberty does exist, but it's got boundaries just so they've got us chained to their standards of what freedom is whilst we're naïve enough to think it's ours.

I miss talking to my friends like probably BD or Jean about things like these or just talking to them about anything really, at this point I don't even care if they start blabbing about any crap that goes through their minds, although, when I think about it properly without my solitude being the one to speak, I know I don't. How can I miss talking to something I've never had? I might've had friends, but you never really know if they really are your friends; what is a friend anyways these days if a shared silence is why they ruin it only because they can't stand it? I miss Mike, I did get better with him than any other bloody bastard I considered my friend. I know BD's not going to commit suicide; her vanity would be the first one to grab her hand before she jumped, dying isn't her way out, it's dreaming. I know BD, I haven't known her for as long as you can imagine but I know she isn't the typical troubled kid you must've pictured for what I've told you about her. She wants to be depressed, that's another thing, but she doesn't know why. She'd probably strangle me if I started talking about her on here, she reminds me a bit of my mother with these things: both so obsessed with not being talked about. I remember she specifically told me not to name her in my book, the minute I told her I was intending on writing one, she's obviously very naive or just plain stupid to think I wouldn't. I don't usually do what people tell me to do; I even

93

sometimes do the contrary of what I'm supposed to, just to piss the hell out of them. I like pissing people off, not because I'm a *sonuvabitch* or anything, it is just that their reaction surprises the hell out of me, it really amuses me, and I realise how my morals have been shaken and principals beaten. It's hilarious; you should see how they get with these types of irrelevant stuff making them feel like you've ridiculed them, and people don't like feeling inferior to you; they don't like feeling anything at all. Andy always mocked me for the hanging around with those three, but sometimes I just took it as a sign of jealousy, he never really had anyone but Thobias, Lloyd and me.

I'm sorry, I feel like this is just getting too dramatic, and I don't want that. If there's one thing I can't stand, it's the typical melodrama that is created, and for what? For nothing, just to satisfy our immutable boredom. I can't stand many things; BD always said it was a problem if I had such small tolerance, but then again, so did she. I'm precisely talking about BD because I want to piss her off, I haven't really spoken much about her, she's a real someone this one. She's the image of music for this generation, many may have never seen that in her but it's one of her best qualities, not her seductive talking, long acrylic nails, or diva snares that keep you from approaching or her simple guise of promiscuity. Music; the knowledge of music of being able to listen to something and know if it's good or not, now that's a true flair, at least, the only one that matters. Without music, nothing of what I am doing right now would make sense, it'd feel empty, like something I can faintly see, and feel like I can grab but once I try it fades, and makes you feel hollow, like your body is a vast never-ending echo. And you can't move or hum to anything, you're lacking that essence that gives your life a different colour only seen in rhythm. Without music there wouldn't be silence too. The two most paradoxical sounds together provide the only survival for a dead instant lasting a lifetime.

Anyhow, after a long meditation, I've decided to snoop around the train now that they've finally chosen a good song to decorate the lonely red and blue alley. The song playing is *The Big Ship*, Brian Eno. I wouldn't be making such a big deal about it if they'd put any other song but this song is the type of song you want to listen to when you're walking through a blue and red carpet to shade the empty walls. Seriously, if you're not reading this paragraph whilst listening to this song, you haven't understood anything of what I've told you these last few pages till now. I felt a déjà vu of old Stanley's *The Shining* and little Danny Torrance cycling around in his tricycle in the infinite corridor of 2/2. I wasn't cycling, and the door 237 didn't stop me from walking once I went past it. Don't imagine my scene around corridors to be the same as Kubrick's idea of the same scene. Mine might not be as appealing as his for the fact that it'd be compared with his. I can feel the corridors getting smaller, soon they'll be preventing me from breathing; I'll be suffocating in prime colours and that's when I wonder if I have finally fallen in love. The music is provoking this illusory effect of the colours in the carpet to become stains in my iris, making my eyes look like a prism haze, you might be thinking 'how cool is that' but believe me when I tell you it's not, I don't even know where I'm walking to anymore. The easiest reasonable conclusion of why I felt like I'd just been shot would be that I get train-sick but that couldn't possibly be it because I've never gotten seasick to now get train-sick, but then again, it's quite impossible to get seasick in a rich kids' stinking yacht that only sails around the shore so daddy can keep an eye on it so it doesn't get wrecked.

This girl in my trigonometry class had one of those, I really can't remember her name, but then again, I wasn't invited so how the heck would I know, I'm not good with names anyways. From the moment you're born to the moment you die, you're condemned into living under the name someone else gave you without knowing the slightest thing about you, only that by pure genetics you belong to them and so they should be the ones to choose it, but no one belongs to anyone, especially to those that love you the most.

BD and Jean were invited. It's funny how they both had a different version of what had happened but that's just because they're very antithetic from one another so it didn't quite shock the hell out of me. I decided to believe BD's view of the tragedy only because she made it more comical to hear. Apparently, the girls' father busted her and the rest of the *sonuvabitches* who were drinking some funky booze they found hidden behind the bar. Provoked by a couple of aftershots, some of the bulky and soaring boys started throwing the majority of the bottles to the ground or even out the board. BD said they all looked like beasts and that I would've liked watching it, but I wouldn't have, it hurt me that she thought I would. It's the people who think they know you the best that are absolutely clueless of whom you really are precisely the ones that constantly repeat to you that they know you, as if they had to insure it to themselves not me. Anyways, a kid could've died there, but the father only called the police because of the damage, not for hurling in the air one of those quiet nerdy boys over into the sea. If it weren't because they threw him furtherer from the shore, he could've cracked his head open or fractured his fragile snake neck. I hated listening to that story so I don't understand why I'm even bothering writing it down. I bet you loved reading this bit of the book, reminded you a bit of all the load of *American Pie* movies you must've digested willingly or not. That day probably profited me more than anyone that went over there; I did the usual routine Andy always did with his older friends. It was the first time he let me hang around with him and his friends because he knew I was actually bummed all my friends were so eager of attending that upscale dump. He never liked me meeting his friends, but in a kind of protective way, he said they were all douches but it was fun to talk to them because they always had good arguments to discuss about and obviously, tremendous weed. Sometimes what people don't like to understand or just can't, is that you care about them, even if they don't give a damn about you. I actually don't know why I've told you this story as if it were relevant, I guess I feel like if I'd been there, it would've been different.

I'm trying to hold onto something so I won't feel so dizzy, or in a way, prevent myself from falling to the floor, but the thing with these train corridors is that you can't hold on anything unless it's someone's cabinet door, and that would disturb the hell out of them and probably get me thrown out because they'd get all delicate about it. The best idea would be to go back to my Satan's coven and allow paralysation to be my penal abuse. I would actually go back to the cabinet if I could, but just turning around seems the most impossible task I can overcome right now. I'm guided by the smell of the bar snacks, as my eyes are no longer a resourceful sense to indicate my following baby steps. The bar must not be that far away if I can smell it from where I'm woefully standing with quivering knees and a pale face, or maybe it's not even pale. I haven't looked at myself but I confide in my stomach's swirls that I'm a beryl bearing. It feels kind of kooky walking blindfolded without a fold in my eyes, anyone who would be looking at me must think either of two: I'm blind or I'm just wacked out. I would think I'm wacked out too, but only because I like thinking everybody's been moonstruck, then again, I deeply hope they haven't so they're not like me. It always breaks my heart meeting someone who reminds me of myself, I have to vilify them immediately. You must picture this strange child as the perfect description of me or that I have mental health issues but the truth is, not even I'm lucky enough to be described as one of those; saying I'm crazy all the time doesn't mean I am crazy, it's probably the best proof that I'm quite ordinary. The disappointing mediocre truth is that neither of both speculations is true. I must admit I've exaggerated my loss of sight, but then again, as I've said an abundance of times I like exaggerating everything, it makes my surroundings far more interesting that they've been gorgonized to be.

Seq. 14 Int. Different Cabinet in Train

I woke up to what felt like the incessant running wheel of a car, spinning ceaselessly inside my head with the motor cacophony included, I'd become a garage. I still feel the dizziness I had felt before, only less intensely. I am still rather confused, trying to figure out what happened if anything did happen. When you wake up, the way I've just woken up so suddenly, it takes a while for your eyes to adjust to any type of focus, everything seems blurry for the first few seconds and you notice this glistening achromatic blaze which is later destroyed by a constant blinking in order to get back my proper eyesight. I finally open my eyes. A little girl was staring at me; I'm saying little because she seems small enough to be considered little. Although I wouldn't rely much on my sight right now and its speculations, so I'm not really able to describe her to you. I guess you'll have to make up your mind of how she looks like or what size to measure her with. I just knew she was looking at me as if I were some sort of eerie creature gawking at her; I was about to speak when she stopped me and spoke for me.

"Don't speak, maybe you'll puke again," she warns me without hesitation as she quickly pulls a trash can from her right and places it in front of me just in case I did puke.

"I've puked?" I ask, trying to remember what had happened to me the past hour or so. Touching my head naïvely in despair as if that were going to recreate any remembrance of the latest event.

"Yes, in the middle of the hallway," she says with a disgusted expression. "Father picked you up and brought you to our cabinet," she elucidates joyfully as she kneels over to hand me a glass of water. I drink the water as if I'd been in drought all my life. I felt utterly observed by the girl; she made me so uncomfortable, it took me ages to finish that cup of water.

I feel much better than how I felt the instance I woke up; my head had surely stopped swirling like a farmer under the rain when its crops are growing. I gave her back the glass, they were all planned gestures and it was a rather perilous situation, which I was so exceedingly anxious to evade from the fastest as possible.

"I'm so tremendously sorry about that, but I'm feeling better. Thank you so much and everything but now I can go back to my cabinet," I say politely with my best phony smile with the secluded purpose of tricking her into thinking I was telling the truth and that, well, I did feel better even if I didn't, something I normally do to get someone off my back.

"No, Father is a doctor, he said it's best for you to stay laid down and not to do any sort of heavy movement until we arrive to Chicago," she orders still with the same innocent smile that eventually ends convincing me into not doing another sway movement because, deep down, I knew she's actually right.

"How long till we reach Chicago?" I ask keenly, completely changing the subject as I slowly sit properly.

"Two hours or so, by the way, my name is Marie, it's so nice to meet you!" she friendly introduces herself, launching her juvenile minuscule hand towards me so I would shake it.

"Nice to meet you, Marie," I say as I was shaking her hand. Unconsciously, we had been shaking each other's hand for quite a while now, that tends to happen when you've just met someone and you're both left completely alone to deal with the inconvenient situation by yourselves.

"What's your name?" she asks nervously.

"Uhm… My name's Connie," I lie.

"I love it!" she says in overexciting glee, her gleaming eyes illuminating her enthusiasm. I knew she was lying the moment she blurted those words out with that over-exaggerated ardour; it's a classic. The moment you meet somebody you've never met before, the first thing they'll ever say to you is the thing they most hate about you, if you're not the one who starts being cynical then you know what the person in front of you is the one planting that cynical seed to a cynic friendship grown between diverse events in which you most likely might continuously coincide.

"You think? I don't like it much myself…" I confess with a phony waning crescent smile, which didn't look like a smile next to her wide exposition of stainless teeth. The contour of her mouth was surrounded by melted chocolate.

"Why?" she said, intoning highly on the 'y' like she was singing. "It's really pretty! I love my name, it's like Jesus's mummy's name," she says.

"How old are you, kid?" I ask. I feel like my pronunciation had deliberately replaced Matthew McConaughey in *Dallas Buyers Club*.

"I'm eleven and three quarters because in exactly 56 days, it's my birthday and I'll be twelve," she recites mechanically but with a scent of melody just to complement her high-pitched voice.

"Do you always speak like that?" I ask irritated by how mechanic she just sounded, it looked like it had gotten her a hell of a long time to learn that by heart just to spit it out like that to look a hell of a smart kid before she forgot again.

"Speak like what?" she asks befuddled, looking at me as if I were the odd one of the two.

"Like you've been programmed to recite everything you know but haven't actually understood its significance or if it even makes sense, you know, like in school when you have to learn something and you read it out loud with not a clue of what it means but you're there reciting it word by word to make mummy proud," I say nervously and rapidly, unsure of whether she understood anything of the load of crap I'd just fired at her, thinking she'd have a clue of what I'd just said.

"I want to be an actress, I'm good at learning things by heart," she exclaims; it looked like she'd just pat her hand on her shoulder of how proud she was, only she didn't, saying it was enough of a pat in the back.

"How do you know what you want to do if you're only eleven? You don't have time to think about that crap, you shouldn't be thinking about all that, not now at least," I say, noticing my tone starting to sound intrusive aggressive instead of sweet and inspirational.

"You swear a lot, we aren't meant to swear," she accuses me, but still smiles. That annoyed the hell out of me, that cynical angelical smile trying to cover the bloodstains left on the sheets but still holding a bloody knife in her hand. I bet she couldn't stand me the same way I couldn't stand her. I was actually fine now; I'm sure I could just stand up and leave back to my cabinet. I felt like I was being held prisoner and her dad was sure taking a hell of a long time to come back. This kid was probably bored as hell wanting me to keep her company. I wouldn't mind it if she weren't so damn snobby, and holy and all, acting all grown up. I hated that; I particularly hated that on a kid, even more if they were a kid who was barely eleven.

I don't like basing my conclusions on appearances, but for what she was showing me, she looked lonely, the typical rich kid whose parents don't have time for and just bloat with expensive gifts that really aren't anything at the end of the day. I bet her dad isn't even a doctor, probably some really acclaimed well-known Hollywood plastic surgeon.

"When's your dad getting back?" I ask.

"I don't know, I think he went to have lunch at the VIP lounge," she brags.

"Why don't we go see him?" I suggest as I stand up slowly from my seat to head towards the door that was barely ten cm away from me but seemed to be on the other side of the other side.

"He's in a meeting, he doesn't like to be disturbed," she informs me, sounding a *helluvalot* like she were his secretary. "Why? Are you hungry? We can order something so they bring it here if you want!" she badges uneasily as she launches me back down on the seat, preventing me from reaching the door handle.

"No…uh, don't worry, I'm fine, but I think I can go to my cabinet now, Marie," I say, standing up again.

"No, wait!" she demurrers, blocking my way. "I'm really bored. My twin sister, Eleanor, was supposed to come on the trip as well so I wouldn't be that bored but she wasn't allowed in the end because she had this really important competition," she says as she takes a deep breath to regain the one she'd lost. She looks down at the end of her tiny toes in shame, trying to make me feel sorry for her. If her shame were mutated into water, we would've already drowned in it, not only us but also the whole train. I don't understand why she was acting so shameful; it looked like telling the truth for once, killed her.

"Well, I'm sure she'll win and tell you all about it. Do you ice skate too?" I ask, trying to hype her up again.

"No, I'm really bad at sports, I always fall and Eleanor laughs at me, but I'm really good at drawing," she says, still bowed down, I wasn't sure if she was trying to make me feel sorry for her or if she had gotten actually upset. You never know with these kids, they always want to be the centre of attention, it was a hell of a good chance to skit, she would take minutes to realise I'd left.

"Would you like to see some of my drawings?" she exults out of nowhere enthusiastically. She went from looking like a lost pup to an overjoyed playful one in two seconds.

"Yeah…sure…okay. I don't really have anything better to do," I splutter in distress. She was a poem with no structure, with no time;

she wasn't a poem but not being able to understand her when she understood herself made her one. If I had any idea of how to write poetry, maybe my sentences could be excused of not making any sense, that's why sometimes I wish I were considered a poet who doesn't write poetry.

She then starts digging inside her bag for all her drawings; apparently, she has a million in there because even though there were already about 50 on the table, she still dug for more papers. Her face wasn't her face anymore; it was a pink purse with girly stickers decorating its velvet fur, I would start describing the damn purse in the most outstanding vivid imagery as possible but what would that be for? I don't want to ruin your imagination with mine. I'll just say she disappeared in that bag and even though I could still see her, she wasn't there. It's like her drawings had absorbed her into the blank stainless spots she hadn't dared to use yet.

She got her head out with a couple of more drawings and lay them on the table so perfectly, it made me dubious whether she had OCD. The drawings weren't as crappy as I thought they'd be, it actually startled me how exceptional they were, I'm not saying they were drawn splendidly and accurately defined. She sure went out the line a thousand times but that's probably the reason why they looked so good. It wasn't surreal art either, she had a bit of Dali going on in there but it wasn't quite that which made them even more awe-inspiring. I felt like one of those really lousy art buyers with their expensive brand black eyewear they always have on so their physique fits their profession, and a cigarette or a pipe on their left hand as they inspect the masterpieces and do over-preposterous facial expressions to mark whether they like what they're looking at or they absolutely think it's dreadful. I had no clue about art, I know my dad's an artist and all, and I love art, don't get me wrong, I just don't understand it, it's just not my way of expressing what I see or feel, sounds rather cheesy written like that, but you know what I mean. You ought to fall in love once in a while if you want to understand art in a museum or just any type of art anywhere really, but art.

"Do you like them?" she asks, anxious and intrigued, as she can't stop looking at the drawings and then back at me, dehydrating for some type of approval from somebody, anybody, just to feel like she's achieved something or what she's done is valuable by the publics' ignorant eye.

"I'd say I love them but I don't," I start saying as I notice her facial expression drain of happiness again. "I think they're very

102

alternative and strikingly creative, and if I knew anything about what 'good art' is, it'd be easier for me to tell you how amazing they are in a way that doesn't seem like I'm being a phony about it."

"They're amazing," I finish up simply saying breathless even though I hadn't spoken.

Her facial expression metamorphosed again into exhilaration, she looks like a monitoring doll with a handle on the side of her head that was timed by a chronometer to change expression every five minutes and I must say it was really giving me cold feet. If I'm to speak honestly to you or to this piece of paper of which I've become prisoner, for an expanding instance, I saw this cabinet as the paper I was damned to continue writing in and she was the guard that prevented me from breaking away. How ironic it is to run away of wanting to run away from running away. What I'd just written made no sense whatsoever, but didn't change the fact that I was terrified of actually being a prisoner in myself but not from anybody else. A book is really a labyrinth once you get in it; not even the writer knows where it finishes. I mean maybe we don't even really want to get to the end of it anyways and I'm not saying this in some extravagant poetic metaphorical way which is probably how you've interpreted it once you've read it, but looking down at the words I've written, they seem to sum up to create an everlasting labyrinth, one you can't get out of as you read it and one I can't decipher how to finish. As writer and reader, we may not experience this the same way but we're both travellers of the same exuberant everlasting journey. If I'm honest with you, I'm well damn exhausted about this whole thing, I'm sure so are you. The concept of what love is, was etched by the wrong hands, and they weren't just a pair but a dozen and a dozen more—all those hands which never get distilled by the dirt of ego and the smell of self-interest. It has to be reinvented, someone has to have the guts to shower with not soap, but flowers, roses, any flower you could think of, even have a bath covered of them, and then sit down in front of their writing desk with water drooling from the points of their hair creating rivers in the hollows of their back and start typing, because you don't mould love, you don't create it, it is thrust upon you with flaming words as you write them unconsciously, as I have now. Love isn't flowers on Valentine's day, expensive diamonds or moderated I love yous, love is passion, it's not heaven, it's hell, it's not God, it's the devil, it's not sweet, it's spicy, it's not dead, it's alive, it's not cold, it's burning, and it burns like a rose in summer, that blooms constantly over the heat. Or we might as well stop harassing about other people's love and just get along with our own business and what it means to us, since it only affects you and nobody else.

"That's when you know you've found someone really special. When you can just shut the fuck up for a minute and comfortably share silence."

—QUENTIN TARANTINO
Pulp Fiction, 1995

Seq. 15 Int. Different Cabinet in Train II

We didn't talk for a while; she's just been doodling all this time. I just juggle my lost gaze between the translucent window at my left and the opaque door at my right, keeping me locked up. I must say though, I start to endure Marie's company to a point where I actually enjoy the sound of her scribbling blue pen on paper, and the tearing noise of the pages she constantly rived apart in distress when she finished something she didn't like, which was most of the time. I actually felt an urge of asking her why she's destroying everything she creates before having a chance to revel in it or, ask her to stop, but I didn't dare to; the simple reason of this being: I didn't want to be the one to say something vacant that could destroy the fullness we'd created, that consuming silence that rode around the room like Sagittarius between the paralysed stars that rhapsodise the night which slowly invade the empty landscape I'd been looking at from the window, with a leaky cloak of darkness. Our silence was one that I'd never heard before; it had stuck sounds in every of our hidden peeks now and then. Her eyes would rise from her cave of papers and my gaze would slide north every once in a while over the book she'd lent me. I was reading this book that only had pictures, it was called *The Cat in the Hat*. I found some parts of it really funny, but it didn't really interest, even entertain me that much. I wanted to ask if she had another book or if she could just let me go to my cabin and get some of the ones I'd brought with me. But then again, I couldn't really interrupt. Not often do we realise that it's our insecurities which push us to want to avoid silences like these, but then again, it's us who are weakened by its imperial impact on our social capacity to basically be part in a phony conversation just for the hell of it.

I fear her dad will suddenly come in through the door causing the entire outside riot to replace the sound of two injured heartbeats bloating in youth and an epileptic pen humming to Joy Division's, *Disorder*. Although, I must say her father was taking a hell of a long time to come back from that supposed meeting of his or whatever it was she said he was busy with. I can't help but get suspicious over the man who apparently found me. I don't even know the man and I already bloody hate him, but I am actually quite 'glad' he's taking such a long time. I imagine him using the word 'glad' as his rely on trying to express thoughts that haven't levelled up in his parvenu triangular head. I presumed all this because my surrounding has driven me to that judgement; the soft virginal tact the seats transmit once I leisurely thaw in them, of course, with the collaboration of the warmth trapped in the Greek-designed walls of the cabinet. I guess it sure must've cost him a fortune to earn a cabinet like this, at least compared to the one I can afford.

I'm not good at this, at being in silence. I'm not good at looking out the window without procrastinating about the whole absurd significance of my pathetic existence. I'm not good at many things; I'm not even good at writing. I'm good at talking about myself without even consciously knowing what I'm talking about, or for this matter, writing about. I just know I'm trying to fall asleep but I'm not able to, she hasn't stopped drawing. Before, I was fascinated, now, I'm ignorantly terrified because she hasn't ripped apart any more pieces of paper since I started to jot this paragraph on one of the papers she'd thrown before. The room isn't flooding anymore with paper snowballs, I won't suffocate after all and that kind of bothers me. I was already prepping a death speech or a suicidal note to leave pinned in the interior design of the surreal room in my head. The suicide note would be pinned in a leather booklet beside a white rose painted in rose staining the marble bureau, and I'd have *On the road*, *Peter Pan* and *The Catcher in the Rye* left beside it with many bookmarks on pages with underlined phrases in a vibrant red from the drained out pen that would be tilting at the left edge of the desk as if it, as well, had just said its last words with mine and was ready for whatever was coming for it once it lost its balance and finally fell on the solid ground that sustained all of those collapsed memories hidden on the metaphorically cracked walls. That's not how my room actually looks like, the cleaning lady my dad hired after my mum left made sure of that, she'd always change the order of my books which bothered me the most until I pinned her a message on the bookshelf warning 'KEEP OUT! There is nothing to clean here'. But that sure didn't stop her. She got on my nerves, she only lasted two weeks but only because she was deported for an apparently quite terrifying situation happening back at her hometown. I never asked her where she was from or what happened, we never really spoke, only because I never saw her, she usually came when my brother and I were supposedly at school. The only thing I knew about her was that she continuously assorted the order of my books, she just changed the structure of how they line up one beside the other in their perfect large to small sizes with its authors all buckled up in their territory. I don't know if she did it intentionally, but it bothered me as hell.

I don't want to talk about my room anymore, it's supposed to be a private sanctuary, although now it's just a room that's been raped by authority for research. The police or whoever my dad called to look for me must've gone in there and destroyed the whole place looking for a hint; adults are so naïve; children don't leave hints behind. I don't think much of what might be happening there, I think it's because nothing really is happening and if it were, I'd probably never know about it so I don't see why I'd think about it much really, it's not like it'd do me any good anyways. I'm just in this really uncomfortable position again and I'm waiting for the melatonin pills to kick in so I can finally stop fighting my eyelids on closing. I even feel the need to rebel against my own unconscious instincts just for the hell of it, if not, I'd feel like I'm betraying whom I think I should be. I live suppressed under this fake appearance everyone created for me back home and for some stupid reason, I'm sticking to it like I agreed, even though I don't, I know I don't. But that never really does mean anything to anyone, at least to me, it's stopped meaning anything—you know, knowing too much sometimes can feel like not knowing nothing at all just for all the continuous added doubt. I'm thinking as I'm writing on a paper napkin all these useless thoughts, I'm just doing this to fall asleep; I'm the one irritating Marie now. She'll get used to it, she's a kid, and unfortunately, they get used to everything until they turn 14 and realise what they've gotten used to is wrong. Sometimes not making sense makes me feel better, like the Zoloft for depression only I'm not depressed, not anymore at least.

Marie stops drawing and looks at me. I smile at her. She smiles back. She starts ordering all her drawings in a perfectly structured pile on one side. She stretches for a second and looks at me again. I grin uncomfortably and do the same. We both lay on our respective sides of the cabin. She fits perfectly, I don't, so I hunch and move a lot. She turns the light completely but the cabin's still lit up by the moon. Looking at the moon for a moment, I realised all those objects us poets scandalise about as if they were ours by giving them a voice, we monopolise them. The comparisons, the metaphors, all

108

exist thanks to everything that already exists before them and we are arrogant enough to believe that, that moons shine how it shine because we decide it to shine. It's a way of giving significance to things nobody would ever give significance to; it's a way of changing the perspectives of those who don't see it. You should've seen the moon, it was a crescent moon tonight and it was very pale, even so pale, Marie commented, "She looks sad." I smiled at that comment and closed my eyes, but before I looked at the moon one more time as I noticed it was following the train. In LA, the moon was always dirty and so were the stars. I look over to where Marie is lying and close my eyes. My back is itching so I begin to scratch it and keep on scratching it for a while. I stop because my arm hurts and is falling asleep, and I hate when that happens so I stop, although my back is still ailing. I turn around a couple of times to find a comfortable position, but I don't. "Can't you sleep?" asks Marie from her side of the cabin. I open my eyes and see her sinking slowly inside the pillow; all her particular characteristics are standing out misshapen, she looks like one of Saville's works.

"No, not really," I say as I change my position to lay my back on the windowpane.

"I haven't been diagnosed or anything, but I think I have insomnia," I confess, breathless, as a yawn interrupted my following sentence. "I'm…I'm taking melatonin now," I sigh as I turned and changed my position again so my legs aren't so crumbled one onto another.

"If you want, you can sleep where I'm sleeping," she offers kindly as she gets her pastel pink velvet blanket.

"No, don't worry, I'm comfortable here," I say, stopping her before she actually stands up and obliges me to actually end up changing places with her. The only difference with her seat and mine, is that she is smaller so she fits better; she could've fit perfectly in one of my dad's gigantic suitcases he keeps in the garage for when he had to travel continuously for a month or so.

"Well, we can talk if you want," she suggests as she accommodates herself to sit down. Her talking was actually driving me to want to forcedly go to sleep so I'd stop hearing her. She'd been too overly nice to me since we had met and it was starting to trigger my nerves. I felt bad about it, I just can't stand overly nice people and it just all feels too phony for me.

Weird thing these two: feel and think. They can never agree on anything and they come from the same place. I used to get irritated very easily when I was little, around twelve, my mum would constantly repeat the same question: How was school today? The usual question we all know and we've all been through a dozen times, but she really cared, she liked to know how I was getting along, but for some reason, it irritated the hell out of me. I'd be nice about it for one day a month until I stopped and just decided to ignore. It just bothered me; it bothered me how worried she always was. I don't like people thinking I'm having a rough time unless I actually am, or even then I find it a bit suspicious. If you're having a rough time, a real rough time, you don't talk about it or tell anybody because you're having such a rough time, you don't have the strength to really tell anyone anyways. That's why I never liked talking if I felt sick about something, but I wouldn't put a good face either. I didn't have to be cynically superficial about it and that's what started the complications. I'd just be too honest about everything and that'd provoke my mother because she was partly the same. As I grew up, we just argued more for meaningless things just so she could prove her authority and I could humiliate it.

"I'm actually starting to feel the melatonin kick in, but thanks," I friendlily tell her as I turn my back to her so she gets the hint that I am going to go to sleep, or try to anyways.

"My dad should be here shortly; I hope he doesn't mind you stayed over," she says.

"You told me I couldn't go to my cabinet because he wouldn't let me and now, right now, you're telling me that he doesn't even know I'm here?" I ask aggressively as I stand up from where I was laid.

"Don't get mad, I just thought you'd be better here," she starts saying with her sweet innocent voice.

"Well, I'm not. I've been wanting to go to my cabinet since we met!" I finally admit with a tone of despair.

"That's not very nice," she shrugs.

"Well, I'm not nice, kid. I stopped being nice when I grew up," I shot at her, immediately regretting having said those words.

"I hope that never happens to me then," she says. I notice she's starting to get mad too. I knew I'd overreacted but these things; they really annoy the hell out of me.

"It will, you can't do anything about it," I confirm, destroying any spice of belief she had left.

I get my things and go out the door that had seemed to be so impossible to be opened. I don't even turn around to look at her, I find it'll make everything look very dramatic and I want to avoid that. This time, the corridor is less clear due to the lack of light, but

I knew the direction I have to go in and the number I have to find. I look at a fixed point the whole way so I wouldn't get dizzy again. I walk as fast as I can so my body doesn't have time to collapse due to my trembling legs. I walk directly with precision and balance to where I really belong. The fact that she'd gotten me so mad increased my lack of concentration on the objective of the 20-step journey. I know it's selfish to think this, but I really wished she came running behind me and convinced me to stay. I like people doing that, because they never do that and I guess sometimes it'd be nice to know what it feels like, for once to know or feel what people feel when they're cared about. It's also naïve of me to say this, it's not like my family's never loved me, or my friends for that matter. I know they have. I'm not stupid enough to believe they haven't but that's not really the point. I think there's a difference between your friends loving you occasionally when it's most convenient, I'd say, and your parents loving you because they feel like they have to. I think maybe my mum felt like that because she just stopped loving me or she was tired of being forced into loving me only for a society's impression of a parental obligation and so she left. At least, she was honest, she could've been phony about it all her life but instead she left. I don't really hate her for it; I just think she could've taken my brother and her husband with her. I don't mind being alone, I really don't. The more I say those words, the more I realise I do, I do mind and I can't tell anybody.

I've never been into sports, I think that's why I get physically tired so easily, I've hardly walked and I'm already out of breath. I feel like I've just been shot or choked to death. I can feel my lungs begin to wrinkle. I'm a smoker, so that's maybe possibly it. The crazy shrink I went before, Katherine with a 'K' always told me I had so many problems because basically I didn't do sports. That was her goddamn solution, bloody sports. She said it'd clear my mind you know, be more worried about my physical appearance than all that 'nonsense talk' (she called it that) I had with myself. I really didn't like that guy; his name was George. So I asked my father to take me to Katherine with a 'K', she was apparently really good, or so BD said. I really never had someone with whom I could completely talk to, so at the start of my sessions with her, I'd talk non-stop you know, about everything. I didn't even have time to consider lying to her because of all the blabbing that was going on, like I'd taken a truth pill. I like telling people why I think I'm fucked up if it's under an extreme confidentiality between only two people. She was also a stranger so that made it easier. I once told her I killed someone and she damn well believed it, that stupid lady shrink could've gotten me in jail. She told my dad, and that's when I realised our sessions weren't so confidential after all, so I stopped telling her the truth and I just mocked her the whole time. So our time together was entertaining for me and irritating for her. I knew she hated me, she knew I knew and she also knew I hated her too, so we just tried to cope that one hour a day together so my dad would think I'm getting better if I was ever sick, and she'd be able to pay the rent. We were civilised after all, even with all that hate. What does that even mean? Hate. I hate hating. When I said my dad would think I'm getting better, I'm not saying I'm sick, he just thought I was sad about my mum and all, he made my brother go to a shrink too for a while, and so did he. To be completely honest with you, I actually miss Katherine with a 'K', and I mean she must have her story too. I think we all have a story, maybe she doesn't go to a shrink to tell them her problems and that upsets her. Do shrinks go to shrinks too? I think if I were a shrink, I'd go to many shrinks but with different identities, I'd never tell them I'm a shrink too and I'd just complain about all the problems all my patients confide me with as if they were my own to see what the solution was, if there really is one. Even if there was a goddam solution for anything, which I highly doubt to be honest, we have to stop relying on absurd solutions because they're just somebody else's propaganda.

Seq. 16 Int. My Cabinet

I finally find my cabinet; I am standing right in front of that wrecked internal frozen cramped door, staring at it with compassion. I feel sorry for it, I feel like I'd been out all night cheating and it killed me, but then again, it was just a bloody door. It doesn't have any feelings, it wasn't my mother, it couldn't start arguing with me and telling me off for arriving later than curfew; it was just a door that made me feel miserable, oh so miserable for being just a door. I went in and found everything in the same place I'd left it in, it's as if the process of time had been forgotten in this part of the wagon during my absence. I still haven't filled up my stomach the way I wanted to, so I am cold and hungry again. After all, we never really last in paradise, even the dead get bored in heaven. If I wanted to kill myself, I wouldn't do it, not because of what I was leaving behind but for what was coming was much worse, not being able to wake up from a nightmare is no fortune. Although I did think about killing myself, I think it's something we all think about often but do nothing about it because suicide is absurd, if you don't want to be here anymore, go somewhere else. Even after death, our name will be cursed, you can't even get rid of a reputation once you're dead, you start another one, whichever your case. Worst part of being dead is you're still alive. It'd be interesting to be forgotten once you die, your existence just simply fades out of every corner you've filled in someone's thoughts and the fear of oblivion would no longer be an issue because it'd be worse than inevitable, it wouldn't even be thought of, it'd just happen. I wish when my cousin died, that had happened, I wish he still wasn't alive without a physical presence; those are the worst, truly, knowing somebody is here but not being able to see them. I'm talking about death because I feel like somebody's died in here whilst I was gone and the worst part is, I fear it's me.

I start to regret leaving Marie all alone; I feel an urge of going back. Anyways, I'm doing the same thing I was doing there only here and alone. I'm sat in an uncomfortable position, looking out the window and just simply remembering, or who knows, slowly forgetting until the only thing left of who I am is my eccentric disturbing name, and soon that will be forgotten too and I'll just have to make one up. We can't forget who we are because we haven't had the chance to know what there is to forget; we aren't a memory. What I am, is just a wrecked teenager like the rest of the millions of wrecked teenagers out there with the same insignificant objective; dodge oblivion and be somebody to the eyes of everyone because, deep down, we know we are a nobody to our own but some worthless creation between the beat of a doomed heart and a drained epileptic brain in stupor. We just want to achieve greatness, scream 'I did it' to the world and prove everybody wrong. We just want to shine for some seconds, we want to gloat our arrogance, our ego and vanity. We want to see our photograph everywhere, our names being desired, we want, we always want to be the future of the future. We aren't dreamers any more, we are just the ones who created a concept they no longer believe in even if they say to do so. Take me, for example, I am an advertisement once this book is published, I really will just be another advertisement of another version of the stereotypical teenager. They'll kill me in the womb; I won't have time to breathe before I've been slaughtered by society, the good and bad. I'll decay and they'll succeed, this will be forgotten and so will I. I think you ought to be a somebody first in order to achieve being an absolute nobody. You can only be forgotten if you've been remembered first, you can only be seen if you've showed your face more than twice and so you can only disappear once you've danced all night.

I'm looking out of the window. All this procrastination is making me sick; it all just sounds very depressing. I want to smile but my face hurts, so I think about this one time I was in the sea looking at the sky. It was a beautiful day and I was floating, and I could hear light sounds under the water. I've always asked myself why the sea made those sounds, it used to creep me out but then I ended up appreciating it. Thinking of this I realise how pathetic I am for yelling at Marie, I want to go back there. I have nothing better to do, I just wanted my booklet to write on so I could show her my wine-stained poems and the broken pages muddled up in my bag. We could compare her broken pages with mine, we could do something, maybe exchange opinions on each other's dichotomy or similar way of taking advantage of the moment presented to us. I can't remember the number of her cabinet, probably because I never really bothered to know. I'm not sure if the numbers of steps I thought of are accurate to the actual distance to get there. I feel like I'm being too monotonous about the days, like I'm living some type of routine (the thing I'd blindfolding avoid), which I'm not. I don't want to bore you with the obvious, yes, I evidently must fall asleep in some minutes and then wake up. But I'm really not bothered to describe in great detail my nightly suppression and my awakening. I don't like writing about the complete obvious, about the scenes they cut out in the movies I watch. I'm falling asleep now. I am asleep.

I wish I knew what to write at this point, I thought of this paragraph as I fell asleep last night. I often do that you know, procrastinate endlessly until all those thoughts are supressed in a dream or a nightmare or whatever it is that happens in there when you're temporarily turned off, paralysed, disconnect to let the brain? Body? Both? Whatever it is we are, just rest from the awful pain of its enduring existence. It's hard to fall asleep when you're alone, I've always lived with that thought but now it's just empowered itself in the ranking of things I consider important list. Maybe that damn wrecked soul of Anthony was right, maybe I do just need to fall in love, and terribly hating how cliché this is going to sound, maybe love is the bloody answer for everything, I just don't know because I've never really found a lover in somebody. Sure, I loved Andy, my father, my uncle, even the bastard of my brother and my egocentric mother but that's mostly family, it's like it'd be consider rude not to love them, after all those things they apparently do for your good sake. So why not love them right? How heartbreaking would that be for them, for my mother? I might even have or do love Diane, BD and Jean, even Mike for that matter, but even though I chose to love them, there is a limit to how far my love goes for them, so in a way, it's not truly love. I could even love Marie if I tried, and Anthony, well, I could've even loved him if he hadn't disappeared. Either way, whether you love or you're loved or any of that goddamn cheap propaganda, we continually tell ourselves to stop us from wasting half our salaries on helpless pedantic shrinks with the best diplomas; you are basically alone and it sucks.

I'm bored of not finding anything to think of but that little girl sat there in bloom trying to acknowledge what just happened whilst drawing and erasing her pieces of paper that just appeared endlessly from that Mary Poppins bag of hers, like the only thing she needed was somebody's emptiness to draw on. That's when it hit me, she could run away with me to New York, she could do some little cute scribbles on the sides of my book so it wouldn't only be dark in it, but it'd have one of the deformed faces she draws without taking her hand of the paper. I observed her do it continuously before when I was with her, she'd start to draw a face and from there, she'd create an abundance of them, all the pages were covered in those faces. Some were thin and angry, and some were fat and happy or controverted in temperaments; only similarity was they were all bald with one Van Gogh ear, but they all had something different in them either way. She even outlined unique race features so there'd be a diversity of everyone. Thinking about all that made me realise, once again, I had to take her with me, I thought of kidnapping her for a second; I started to picture a kind of *Thelma and Louise* scene only we were both really just kids, and I don't have a licence yet…so the dream car wouldn't be on set for this sequel. I start getting all my things muddled up in the same mess some call a 'bag pack' and headed out that haunting cabinet. I walk steady at first; my respiration rate can't keep up with each heartbeat plunged through all my body. I feel water dripping over my forehead for a short while, terrified it is because I am nervous, soon I realise it's just the damn air conditioner over my head being satirical. I evidently look through the cabinet windows as you well know I don't remember her number, only that it was for sure located in the first-class section up at the front, near the cafeteria. It's ironic how I just spontaneously decide to take this kid with me that I barely could stand a few minutes ago and that I just met out of nowhere to make them my companion to New York.

I can hear her infantile cheeky voice shouting at someone from three cabinets south from where I am. That's when it changed, you know, the race between my heartbeat and my respiration rate; heartbeat went slower as my respiration increased provoking me the illusion of an asthma attack. I got closer to the shivering cabinet, in discretion and absolute silence. I feel like some type of ultimate FBI spy centimetres away from catching its delinquent. I am about to knock on the same door that had held me captive for so long before, until I hear his voice. It had never been registered in the sound department on the left wing of my brain, so I couldn't recognise it, but I didn't have to recognise it to know it was her mythological father who suddenly in the most unexpected way decided to appear to ruin my aspirations. I'm saying mythological because I doubted about his existence for a while back then. I am anxious to see what he looks like, I want to see if he has slept with my mum or if he's currently sleeping with her, or if he wants to get married to her or get her knocked-up so she'd have the chance to raise a decent child for once. I hope it's a girl if they have one, and I hope they give her a nicer name than mine, and that she looks pretty. I hope she was everything I never could've been for her, but I hope she wasn't everything she had been to me. This is the part in the book where you feel compassion for the lousy character I've exposed as a better or worse version of myself. I mean, by now, I think we've all realised this isn't about the story that builds up the bloody book but the character profiles that are in it.

I just want to go in that damn cabinet, stomp in like the head teacher of my school used to do in the middle of any class. She'd just go in with her chin up feeling so damn powerful, with that smirk in her smile, and we'd all have to stand up and say in a choir 'Good morning' or 'Good Afternoon'. Why can't I go in and do the same? He isn't going to say anything to me, he doesn't know me, and well, he'll recognise me because, apparently, he's the one who found me drowning in my own overloaded anxiety or undiagnosed claustrophobia. I take a quick glance from a small corner on the side of the window shield in the door, he actually has a resemblance to Anthony, only he is much younger and looks like a proper businessman on a business trip. He is sat down but I deduce from his shoes that he is a tall man; he has a brunette beard that connects with his Elvis Presley sideburns hiding his ears, not to hide them but to camouflage his attention for conversations. I couldn't quite catch a glimpse of his eyes; due to his Tom Ford pastel black eyewear that I'd recognise anywhere because all the snobby art buyers my dad works with wear them whenever they come around his studio. He had a big nose to balance the weight of the glasses; he did have an inevitable slight of resemblance to Gary Oldman when he interpreted Norman Stansfield in *Leon: The Professional*. His voice scraping his glands as he speaks making his words sound rough and worn out either from being used too much or being kept inside for so long, either way his voice terrifies me. I soon realise I can't just stand there peeping like a stalker for the rest of the 30 or 40 minutes left till we arrive to Chicago. I stand up silently and trace my steps backwards the same way a drawing traces the lines that makes itself for creation. I did this so I can repeat my entrance only with resonant steps in order for them to hear me coming, so when I do my entrance, they won't be too alarmed. I do as I've just said and head to the door handle twisting it to the right so it'd let me through, wondering what they saw from the inside as that handle twirled slowly. There was silence.

I slowly come in. They're both already looking at me at the same time, Marie in anger and her father in confusion.

"Who are you?" Marie's father asks, as I close the door behind me. As for Marie, she doesn't say a word, she just looks at me so astounded and perplexed that I can't decipher whether she is happy or exasperated to see me again. As for me, I take my time to properly digest the situation before doing any further action I might regret.

"I'm—I'm the girl who apparently fainted in the corridor some while back yesterday evening, and you picked me and brought me to your cabin with your daughter or so this is the story she's told me…of you being a doctor and all," I say insecurely, frozen in the same position he'd left me in after asking me who I was. I knew the colour of his eyes now, no eyes had ever glared at me so deeply before, it was inevitable not to notice the colourless light in them that gave them such a clear sad blue, they kind of absorbed any hint of nervousness I had, leaving me completely static.

At first, he looks down, then looks at Marie, then looks up to the ceiling, and comes back to stare back into my eyes and smiles showing half of his cleansed teeth. I grin back unsure of how to react.

"Oh yes, yes of course! I was telling Marie off for leaving you out of her sight. But now that you are here, it doesn't matter. Please do sit down," he says, offering me a seat beside Marie.

"Uh, thank you," I say as I sit beside her uncomfortably, she still has the same lost gaze she had when I came in. I could feel she was angry and I felt terribly sorry for it. "She didn't leave me out of her sight by the way, I just really needed to go get my things in my cabinet," I say nervously.

"But you are empty-handed," he points out. Now I just look like an imbecile and maybe got Marie in bigger trouble than she was.

"Well, yes, I decided to leave everything there, and come say sorry to Marie for having a fit at her and I'm really sorry," I rephrase at a high speed. I tend to do that.

"Did she upset you in any way?" he asks, as his tone goes all scrubby again and his eyes fixate on his daughter; leaving her motionless like she was a defenceless insect in his spider web.

"Oh God, no, all she's been is wonderful to me, I just got a little stressed you know, I really wanted to go back to my things," I say, looking back at Marie to see if her broken face had summoned an unwanted smile, but it hadn't, she just bluffed at me. I guess she wouldn't dare come with me to New York now even if I begged her.

"I understand, in that case, Marie, forgive me for not believing you," he says.

'For believing her?' I think to myself. What kind of parent needs proof to believe their child unless, of course, he wasn't her father? I really don't like him, I know he's been all but nice to me till now, but I know when someone is being phony with me, I mean after all those years of cynical friendships and parties, I should've learnt something out of them, other than to write about them. He was like this guy from the advertisements that's got this clean superficial smile after he explains the most useless of things that he knows are useless but he's got to win his life somehow, so he'll just do these advertisements everybody hates as he dreams about, one day, ending in Hollywood.

"What's your name, dear?" he asks.

"Uh…oh damn, I forgot to ask y—" but he cuts me off before I can finish my sentence like some future-teller.

"Alexander Elijah Crawford," he says as he lounges his hand towards me to give me his card, when I thought he was going to shake my hand. I feel like I'd just live one of those déjà-vus people are constantly blabbering about when they try to convince themselves they're not living a routine; it's just a 'déjà-vu' in a French accent, just to make them sound fancier. I look down at the silver card with his full name in roman capital letters marking the difference of hierarchy between him and his co-workers down below in a smaller font by the name of his company 'Crawford & Co' how ultimately original, and at the lowest of all that crap was his business contact number and the address of his work building.

"A pleasure," I say, with an unsecure cynical smile as I continue to stare at the useless piece of card I am involuntarily holding in my hand.

"Mine, dear! So are you travelling for pleasure or work?" he keenly asks, which I find absolutely absurd.

"Dad, she's seventeen," Marie suddenly blurts out, rolling her eyes. She reminded me of my brother for an instance. She sounded so mad, I was afraid of turning and looking at her. I felt miserable right now; I was too intimidated by a look that avoided mine through a spectrum of pride. I don't like being ignored, which sounds rather self-absorbed but it's the truth. I felt abandoned and humiliated with my face towards the wall in a classroom full of children that kept pointing at me and laughing, and a teacher that taught either way. This little girl had been my anchor for a while, I know I've said to hate her guts and I have, I really have. I just have to admit somewhere that I was lying; I just need to write it down because I'd like to remember sometime that there's no such thing as two strangers in a train.

"Oh, what are you doing travelling alone?" he asks amused, interrupting my thoughts, which, for once, I'm glad are being interrupted.

"I'm going to visit my grandmother in Chicago," I lie. I didn't want him to know the truth: that I was running away and all, that tends to freak out people, especially if the 'people' I'm referring to are the typical lousy perfect 'American Dream' parents, like the one's pictured in Arthur Miller's play, *All My Sons*. He'd probably would've done either of two: call the cops to call my family or forced me into staying with them and tagging along to their plans until I was sent home. I really didn't need either of both those options to happen nor, for that matter, want for any of them to, so I just decide to lie. I hinted that Marie noticed I was lying, but it didn't really freak me out. I knew she wasn't going to say anything for the grin she gave me. The fact that she even gave me a smirk tranquilised all the previous negative thoughts I'd had before.

"Well, I hope you have a wonderful time, whereabouts does she live?" he asks. He was really starting to get on my nerves with all those specific questions, what did he care where my grandmother lived? Is he going to come visit her or something? I have no idea how to pull out this one, I know nothing about Chicago, so how am I supposed to just say some random place she supposed to live in?

"She told me earlier her grandmother lived around the East Village," Marie interrupts again. I stop being frozen. I look down embarrassed. I look up again and catch her eyes looking at me, and even though it wasn't a physical vision, she smiled.

"What a wonderful neighbourhood! I hope you have a great time, is she coming to pick you up?" he interrogates.

"Oh, no. She's too old for that, I mean, since my grandfather died and all, she hasn't been out of the house lately so I'm probably going to grab a cab or bus," I lie trying to sound more convincingly than before.

"If you need a ride, we can take you," he offers delighted. I feared he'd do that since we'd started the conversation, and for the reaction on Marie's face, so was she.

"What are you doing in Chicago, if I may ask?" I ask, hoping to change the subject with the purpose of his previous proposal fading his mind.

"Well, I had some business to do, and Marie accompanied me as I hardly see her and her sister due to all the business trips I'm constantly in. But this trip is only pleasure, and spending time with my little pumpkin and get her all the things she wants," he says, giving a big smile to his daughter who didn't quite agree with him.

"Well then, I hope you have a wonderful time too!" I say, not knowing what else to say, I actually was hoping he'd just shut up instead of bringing up more useless small talk.

"We are staying at The Langham on 330 North Wabash Avenue if you need anything. How long are you staying?" he asks.

"Just for a couple of days and you?" I ask back even though I wasn't interested about what he'd answer.

"A week or so, we can't stay too long or Marie will miss her sister too much and her mother, Joanne, will get hysterical at me," he said, with a following cynical laughter, as if what he'd just said was some Woody Allen spontaneous cracking joke at a conventional party. He actually reminded me of the talkative man in the queue to the cinema from *Annie Hall*, yes, the one Woody had a fit with.

"Why didn't Eleanor tag along too?" I ask.

"She had some dancing nonsense of hers. I've told her a thousand times that's not going to get her anywhere, she's meant to carry on my business and so does Marie," he says. "That's why my wife left me you know, she says I'm all about work, but if it weren't for my work, she'd have never married me and the girls wouldn't be able to go to the school they go to or even live around the safe neighbourhood they do. I gave everything for that woman, and her happiness and my little girls, I just want them to be happy. I just want to leave a respected legacy to my little pumpkins!" he says, starting to sound a *helluvalot* like an actor interpreting the role of a father.

I look over at Marie this time, she looked as lost and petrified as I was with the crap he was pulling out to entertain us. I wanted to tell him to shut up so badly, but I didn't want to leave Marie alone with him, I was actually hoping that he'd leave me alone with her, so I could ask her about New York. I mean she may be mad but if I were her, I'd rather do anything than stay with this ape. I just decided to go along with it; it isn't the first time I was faking liking someone anyways. Sometimes, it's just best to listen to them because once you tell these types of people to be quiet, you've written the death sentence for your funeral.

"Oh, I'm sorry to hear that," I say, hoping it'd be the end of that phony conversation. I mean you ought to be blind and deaf not to notice the bore you're being to everyone else around you.

"It's okay, I'm lucky I met this wonderful woman who is pregnant with my child which I hope will be more receptive to all the hard work I do to give him the best of the best," he says. That just froze me; I wasn't capable of faking another compassionate facial expression after that, I just stayed emotionlessly frigid. Not because what he said was insane, I mean he'd said a lot of insane crap since we met and I hadn't frozen like this before, but just the haunting idea that 'wonderful pregnant woman with his child' was my mother. I didn't dare ask her name or to even follow on with the conversation, I just knew I had to go to the bathroom.

"If you'll please excuse me, I have to go to the bathroom," I say as I stand up to head out the door.

"Of course, please, Marie, go with her, it'll be easier to find the bathroom," he says kindly as he did a hand gesture indicating to the left side of the corridor. "Do you want me to order something to eat in the meantime? You girls must be starving!" he later adds before we leave. I was about to say it wasn't necessary and that I was quite capable of going to the restrooms on my own, but then I realised if she came with me, I could actually talk to her naturally without this old man peeking an ear at our conversation.

"I'd like some French fries, Daddy, and Bernice here… What would you like?" she asks me, before we completely leave the room. I felt in between two parallel dimensions, as if the line separating the corridor from the cabin had halved my body and if my face was symmetrical, I could even dare describe myself as two reflections of the same person. You can see me now; my face being gently separated by a thin black line you can't really identify because your perspective is so precise.

"I'm good, maybe a water will be just fine!" I say.

"Very good then!" he exclaims joyfully as he pulls his wallet out.

We leave the room and start walking away from the cabin in silence.

"Why am I trying to become what I don't want to be...when all I want is out there, waiting for me the minute I say I know who I am."

—ARTHUR MILLER
Death of a Salesman, 1949

Seq. 17 Ext. Chicago

We're arriving to Chicago faster than I expected, after so many consecutive hours to get here, finally being here just made them feel like meaningless seconds. I am laid back in my seat watching the countryside caterpillar transform into a beautiful metropolitan butterfly. I was going to miss the sensation of being locked in such a small compartment; I fear I'll have agoraphobia once I come out to the open space. Once I get used to something, it's hard for me to change it or get used to something else, it usually takes me a while to accept things are not going to be the same or the way I'd imagine them to be, that's why my friends always said I was so stubborn and impatient. Although I think it's something that happens to everybody and in a way, it troubles me. I complain about not having a particular change in my life most of the time but when that change is about to happen, I regret ever wishing for it, or even if I didn't even want things to change and they do. When Diane left and when my mother left, it didn't impact me as much, it was a change I knew was going to happen before it did; I grew up expecting it, so before the change even had a chance to occur, I had already accustomed myself to live without them. I know it sounds pathetic, unnecessary, depressing and it's not really what I want you to think, but then again, you ought to think whatever you want as much as you can, since you can. When I first started writing this novel or whatever it is, I knew your critique will eventually intimidate me, what you're thinking right now is already triggering me. You know how I feel and how I think in this exact moment. I don't want people thinking I have mummy issues or parental issues, because I don't. She left because I made her leave. I was waiting for it to come anxiously and sometimes I feel so guilty for thinking about it. I'm not going to get dramatic, I'm tired of writing about it but you know what was unexpected? Thobias leaving was a bullet gone wrong but still creating a wound on a left shoulder.

I've never really bothered talking about Thobias before, because I don't feel like I should and I don't want you to assume things like; he probably is 'the guy' of the novel, or the responsible for this being considered to the eyes of some a 'love story' or a 'romantic novel' but you're, they're wrong. It wasn't like that, things aren't always like that with everyone, although I'm going to be honest; I really wish it had been like that for once, with him. He left with his parents to live in South Carolina or New Jersey; I can't really remember where it was the family run off to or even why they left LA. Those are the types of questions I try to avoid making, not only because they're uncomfortable and annoying, because probably so many other people have asked them before me, but simply because I don't see the point. I rather it stays as a mystery my whole life so I can remember it and not forget it. He used to get along with Andy, they were about the same age, and even though they didn't go to the same school and got to know each other, because of me; they were friends, the type of friendship where you don't need to worry or overthink about whether you are friends or not, you just basically kind of unconsciously agree on liking similar stuff and being able to share it with one another without shame. They were both into the same music; the surfing was a concrete topic of discussion between them and probably the most important cause of their friendship because it was the only thing they ever really did when they saw each other: surf and talk about new music discoveries. I wonder if he even knows about what happened to Andy, I think he would've cared to know. I sometimes regret not calling him and telling him what happened, and even maybe after, asking him about how he was doing and if he was planning on coming back…but then again, at the time I convinced myself my uncle had told him everything over the phone or something, maybe even invited him to the funeral to which he never turned up.

I'd consider start talking about who Thobias was for me and how we met, and all that nonsense bullshit people are normally interested in when it comes to these types of things, but I'm not comfortable doing so, I don't even think it'd be the right thing to do and I also don't want to give you false hopes of a wonderful story, when it was actually pretty basic. So I actually have no idea why I've even started to write a second paragraph about him. Remember how I previously just said the voyage seemed like meaningless seconds, well, I withdraw it, as I am completely wrong. I suppose I'm just very anxious or I get very anxious when I'm waiting for something that is about to be given to me with hesitation; it's like the feeling a kid gets when he sees the wrapped up presents under the tree waiting to be opened but you can't open them until the morning of the 25th.

In the meantime of my lonely desperation, Marie is drawing again and her father, well, he is snoring and very loudly, and to be honest, it quite ruined the whole scene I had in mind for my arrival to my objective. Although I still have to make one last stop, and I still haven't finished the goddamn book and I'm afraid I might not finish it in time for New York. Although, it's not like I'm naïve enough to believe that once I arrive there, I'll just head to the *New York Times* and get a 5-star review on this completely absurd novel. I wish sometimes I were still naïve enough to believe everything I dreamed had mere possibilities of becoming real. I have to admit what is haunting my thoughts since I realised I'm near being in Chicago; I have to find some cheap motel near the train station to arrive in time for the 11 o'clock train to New York and I suppose in some moment I should eat something, I haven't eaten since I left my brother's breakfast in the dining room at home. I feel like I can still smell it at times, it is a way of receiving nostalgia without being conscious, I was even feeling at all nostalgic. The smell felt like hidden hints I had left on the way, so if I ever needed the way back, I'd find it just like Hansel and Gretel.

Marie's and my conversation hadn't gone well when we went to the bathroom because I supposedly had to pee, when, really, I just wanted to have a break from the interrogatory her father was giving me. I didn't get to ask her if she wanted to join me, not because I didn't have the chance or the guts or any crap like that, but because I knew she didn't want to come and I didn't want her to feel like she had to. I didn't want to feel refused either. She said, "I'm sorry my dad can be really annoying sometimes but only because he cares, he's good," and that just broke my heart. That comment had been echoing in my head since it came out of her innocent mouth. She liked that bastard, how could anyone like him whether he was her father or not, I detested him, not only because of this uncontrolled blabbering tongue but by how phony he'd forced me to sound. I even had to start being who I had nightmares of becoming only to appear 'polite' towards an authority figure like himself.

I sense her father starting to wake up so I immediately fake being asleep until the loudspeaker on the train can 'wake me up' and I can finally get as far away from him as possible. I've left Marie a little letter hidden in her pocket so she'd remember me. It's important to leave traces on the people you'd like to be remembered by, because unless you do, they won't. I feel like I've been boring the hell out of you, to be sincere, I've bored the hell out of myself too. This wasn't my intention from the start, I actually came with different intentions other than seeming like a little arrogant brat who has no idea of what she's talking about, but I'm not going to apologise—if I continued, it's because I've enjoyed saying all those things I've written and describing all those things I've done, and maybe, deep down, so have you. Even I'm a narcissistic bastard, probably the most narcissistic of them all and here I am trying to cover all that reality in a fort of words after words. Now, truth be told, faking being asleep is more annoying than I thought it'd be, so I fake waking up before the man living inside the speaker has a chance to do so. Alexander smiles at me as he settles down in his seat; he gives Marie a petty kiss on her forehead and the end of her nose, and in response, she gives him a little giggle as she keeps her hand and eyes on the paper. Then he looks at me and gives a little sigh of despair as a hint, so that I'd incite a conversation. I ignore it.

"You've slept quite a while," he says.

"So have you," I say smiling, I even dared a little giggle escape my mouth just to keep up with the act I was trying to pull out.

"Indeed, and what a well nap that was! Haven't slept like that in ages," he says, before his yawn caught up with him trying to vocalise.

I just smile, I mean it's not like I can really say anything at this point to change the conversation's boring subject without getting a reproach afterwards.

"These cabins are truly marvellous; don't you think?" he rhetorically asks as he admires the decorations that surround it. "Yes, they are," he affirms to himself.

"Yes, sir, they're wonderful," I lie, without taking my eyes off of him.

"You're lucky Marie liked you so much, I couldn't even dream of staying where you were, dear," he says. That was rude, but I think he didn't even notice, people like him are so adapted to saying things like this without being told anything about them that they just keep on doing it so naturally, it even doesn't seem rude anymore, making it appear as if it'd be rude not to say things like that.

"I suppose…" I say, with the typical "ha…ha…ha," uncomfortable phony laugh.

"Do you know *The Great Gatsby*? A classic! Maybe you haven't gotten there yet but in my time, it was a wonder! All my Columbia colleagues and I dreamt of being like him. Are you familiar with F Scott Fitzgerald?" he asks, all in one exhilarant breath.

"I've read the book, although my personal favourite is *This Side of Paradise*," I declare.

"Oh—I don't quite know that one!" he hesitates, frowning his eyebrows as if that were a tactic that'd give him the answer. Then he looks down and back at me avoiding my literary challenge, "Anyways, I've ended a real Gatsby myself, don't you reckon?" he gloats about himself and whatever wonders he has done to the world that have paid off his Long Island West Egg mansion.

I'm not bothered to answer after that, there's just simply nothing else to say. I didn't know how to keep up on a conversation like those only because anytime anyone tried to have one of those, I deliberately turned the opposite way. He actually doesn't speak after that; he just looks out the window or reads the newspaper he was holding over the right knee of his crossed legs. His foot would often slightly dance from side to side showing enough of his socks so the Ralph Lauren brand logo at one corner was exposed. Marie was amnesic to what was going on, she just sat there as she had done for as long as I had known her, she often too looked out the window as if she were drawing a detailed landscape of what was seen over the translucent mirror, even though the horizon wasn't one of Turner's brushstrokes. She sometimes caught me staring at her and gave me a gentle innocent glimpse, and got into doing what she was doing before she felt my eyes upon her.

This setting could've been repeated for ages if it weren't for the feeling of the train decelerating and the rattle of the people standing up from their seats to get their belongings. It's as if, suddenly, the train had awakened, and all of those once vacant sinister corridors were now boosting with flesh and stinky breaths. The train had been given back its vitality once paralysed, the irony of this I found completely hilarious. I'd been roaming the train for the past hours as if it only concerned me whether we were ever going to arrive to Chicago or not and now my arrogance laughed at me. The train had passengers. I was beginning to become anxious, they were all piling up like bricks on a wall all over the train with the same anxiety I had to get out, for instance, I stopped recognising my hands. We could've been mistaken for a herd of sheep if it weren't for our facial distinguishing features which, I must say, at the end of the day mean nothing. But here we were in an interrupted silence of movements; objects falling to the ground, and the constant inhale and exhale of the person breathing behind. I felt so lonely between this mass, until

Marie held my hand, I don't know why she did that, maybe to make sure she didn't get lost on the way out of this flock as her father was a couple of heads behind us and it was probably the safest thing she could do: hold the hand of an adult. I gave her my hand till I realised this and took it away violently, so she grabbed part of my jacket, I mean it wasn't as if she were some small minion or something, she was close to the same height as me so she reached to get a hold of me without having to grip my skin tightly to feel secure. We stood there for some minutes until the doors finally opened, and the masses began to evacuate the entrails of the train as every step we made unlocked the streets and avenues of the city to let us through. When the doors opened, all our lungs took a breath in unison and our heart raced for more. I was finally in Chicago's Union Station; if it weren't because Marie still had hold of the denim tomboyish jacket I was wearing; I'd be already running from this underground labyrinth of the improved replica of New Orleans.

Seq. 18 Ext. Chicago

I wish I could fast-forward everything; I want to skip off this coming day, but I can't. Unfortunately, time is the only thing that we still haven't dared to control even though we should rebel against it as a law imposed and not an inevitable subject. If I'd been given force enough to reach the skies when I was innocent a child, I could reach now and fast forward the clock or even stop it. No matter whatever consequence it would have upon us, Lewis Carol made that happen when he wrote *Alice Through the Looking Glass* and I wish I could too, just by getting through the end of this book before I get through the end of this day. I have been distracted, I haven't finished and I have a countdown trembling behind my spine as I feel the words' shadows crawl upon me, before I arrive to New York tomorrow night. If I dare make it that far and prevent doubt of making me look backwards like Orpheus did condemning Eurydice to an eternal damnation in hell.

Marie will soon be gone and so will her father, and I will be alone again. We are escorting one another out to the clear glass door, although it must be my paranoia but I feel like her father just won't let me go alone. I will miss her company for the first few hours, like I missed Anthony's company until I met her. I stop missing once I start forgetting and I start forgetting because I've found a replacement. To be honest, I never thought oblivion to be so mechanical until now.

"Will you miss me?" asks Marie as we walk towards the exit. I was hoping we were going to skip this to be honest.

"Will you miss me?" I ask her, avoiding having to answer. I knew I couldn't lie to her but I also knew if I didn't, I'd regret it.

"Yes, very much!" she exclaims as she slightly tilts towards me to give me a deformed hug.

"I'll miss you too," I lie as I embrace her whilst we continue to walk. I wasn't sure I lied though, although it comforted me for a second to think I did.

Those were the last things we said, the goodbye summarised in a distant wave of hands and I was surprised her father didn't say anything else to me. I was expecting a huge farewell scandal out of a small meeting, and I had never been so glad to be wrong. They left in their Porsche cayenne whilst I faked to walk to the taxi stop until they left. Once the car was out of sight, I headed over to the bus stop down the opposite road, not knowing on which bus to get in. The only thing I knew was that I wanted to get to the centre of Chicago as soon as possible, I needed the music, the background conversations and the lights whether they're artificial or not; I needed interaction with something other than myself.

I don't know anybody in Chicago, I don't have any suggestions of where to go or what'd be a good place to eat, I don't have to be worried of the feedback I'll have to give like whether I like it or not. I don't have to think about being honest or lying for conventional reasons, or worry about buying gifts. I'm not looked over, nobody knows me and they don't want to know me, they'll look at me the same way I'll look at them; either they're in the middle of the way of a lost gaze, or just happen to trip over in my sight, I can look at them, and not want anything from them but to step away and let me continue my walk. I can notice things like this: I can clarify the different colour tones in everyone, the different colour patterns in their clothes, the different colour constructions in their eyes and the different dyes in their hair. I don't have a reference, anybody to whom compare them with, I can let them be what they are. I can just look at them and they can look back at me with just a vacancy of recognition.

It feels nice to be in a bus packed with people standing up and sitting down, holding babies, reading books, listening to music, talking to one another; just doing things to keep them hectic. I describe this as 'nice' because it is pure, it doesn't need a complex synonym to be a greater scene than what it is, it is simply nice in its minimalistic way. I feel the warmth of the woman beside me and the breeze from the little baby in front of me, breathing desperately as it stares at me from his mother's shoulder trying to reach out to me with its little hands. I turn around and look out of the window; I can slightly hear Sonic Youth's, *Incinerate* playing in the boy's headphones behind me; I start to think of how his ears can cope with that loud tremor without deafening him and wish I could be doing the same. I can see the different types of cars cross our bus with people or even animals in them; I start to wonder where they are headed. Which leads me back to my reality, where am I heading? I don't know what bus stop to get down in. I look for a familiar face in the crowd to follow their steps in trust without knowing them, as if they were going to lead me somewhere. It was difficult to distinguish any racial singularity; they were either too similar or too different but I couldn't find anybody who I felt I could trust in order to get down at the same bus stop they would. It's not that I'm not independent or scared of getting lost, after all I already am, I'd just like some sort of anchor in this city so I can be able to move in it like a bed of roses in summer instead of a bunch of fallen leaves in autumn. I feel like I've spoken too much, it is quite terrifying how you're still reading this.

I found him. The person I'd get down with, I found him. Yes, it's a 'him' and not a 'her', and I can't really distinguish his age as he is quite far away from where I'm standing surrounded with other people, making it impossible for me to have a clear image of his face. And you must be wondering now, then why trust someone you can't really see? Well, he happens to have a particular tick that he's kept on doing since we left the station that reminds me to my Uncle Lloyd. You must think that's really messed up, and I'm not going to start explaining myself. I think that's enough to trust him, I'm just waiting for him to do his move and get out of here. He won't stop laughing too and he's looked at me twice whilst I looked at him, which only puts me ill at ease. I only looked at him so much just to make sure he was still here, and that I hadn't missed my stop. These desperate thoughts make me feel like a worried mother for her child playing in the park alone. Although I feel uncomfortable depending on this unknown person, I decide to translocate my gaze elsewhere once in a while, I don't want him to come over and accuse me of intimidation or stalking. The bus was beginning to evacuate as masses of people went down continuously, but he didn't so I didn't either.

I feel like if this book was given an analysis from a feminist perspective of any sort, this'd be outrageous, a woman depending on a man? I am saying this because during my literature exams, it was all we'd do. I hate the fact that even literature, even thoughts, even ideas which are supposed to grant our freedom, have to be classified, they have to have a meaning, a reason behind them some sort of explanation so it makes sense to the ignorant; so the ideas can be destroyed and mechanised. That's why I don't believe in poetry anymore, something like that is supposed to be pure and liberal, something that you understand because you find it beautiful, not something you have to understand, in order to find it beautiful, in order to like it. This is what, in my opinion, has incited the death of individuality. I can't even imagine what they'd say about this book, but really, what would anyone say? Not even its own writer has conscience of its genre and its characters or the storyline it follows. To be honest, I'm still under the doubt of whether this book is fully fiction, if it's got any heroes or villains or if there even is an antagonist and a protagonist, I suppose I should be the protagonist of this novel, but what scares me is not knowing who's the villain, or even worse, knowing it's me.

All this is probably because I don't want it categorised under some lousy genre, but I really don't have a clear conscience of what this is. I do think the critics are fundamental in our world, a necessity as they help put in contact worlds that disclaim one another completely, the one of the poet and the reader. And well, a critic, as Baudelaire once said, has to be passionate, politic and personal. I know they'll have something to say about this, or even worse, they'll have nothing. You must be exhausted I've been referring to you up until now and probably further on too, as either 'you', 'we', 'them' and 'us' constantly, depriving you from what you feel to know as your individuality as your own, as what makes you different from everybody else. The hell do I know you, I haven't even met you. You might've been one of the people in the bus with me for all that I care; you could be my old teacher, my childhood crush or a classmate.

I am young, I am naïve, I am a writer—do those things have anything to do with the fact that I what I am trying to say won't always agree with what is said? Maybe, but it applies the same to the artists—young and old, to the musicians—young and old, and to the poets and writers—young and old or dead. There is money for those who can't afford an imagination so they can waste it on eradicating it. They want to make us feel like we depend on them, like we need them in order to get through, in order to be known, in order to reach fame or be a public voice. Can't we just write to be free and to liberate those imprisoned by the lurid haze in their eyes and ears? I don't want to confuse you; if you wanted to be confused, you'd go to a therapist, not buy this, whatever it's supposed to be.

I've got the sensation a revolutionary democrat might have felt before starting to talk like this, or writing his speech, even sometimes talking about things like these makes me feel stupid of how much it infuriates me, the anguish of whether what I'm saying will ruin me or not. I am worried that you read me as I am and not as I intend to appear: a shallow angry teenager. I am pathetic though,

I really am—I've let society consume me in order to abandon those who love me, for what, for a childish dream, a blinded vision, an ignorant success, to reach pride for myself? Even exaggerating my thoughts and pains like Shakespeare in his plays, I still feel like I've said nothing yet, nor for me or you. I am just moaning like a foolish adult with the taxes he has to pay, and whatever it is I am moaning about is absurd. But then again, what we moan about has the same importance as what pains us and what we love, because only we will know what it is to feel that type of pain. The only things that are truly ours are the ones that once we share them only we can make sense to them.

I'd apologise for writing, but as I've still got a fixed hawk vision on my prey, I won't. I don't usually get distracted easily, not even with my thoughts when it concerns an objective that shouldn't be bypassed. This is one of the last stops, I can feel it as well as I can feel the panic, the sheer panic I thought I'd never feel, it was the panic I wasn't capable of feeling but to my surprise, I was now. I was getting down the bus for so was he; I try to get down last so he wouldn't spot me and assume I was following him. So I do my actions discretely, for what I'd slightly read in a tabloid we were in the Loop of Chicago. I begin to compare it with New York's Soho or the meatpacking district, so in that way, I can feel more familiar with it. The loop was packed with tourists as well as shops and restaurants, and probably nightclubs, only the sun was still gloating its brightness to sanction them to shine. There was music in the streets; I could hear it reflect on every angle of the buildings, and be spawn as vapour from every vent on the ground, accumulating each and every naked citizen in their showers, alone or with their lovers.

I start walking down the street the bus had left me at, already losing sight of the reason I had ended up here. I feel like I've just arrived to Dante's purgatory, Chicago was my intersection between hell and heaven if I believed in such things like being some pilgrim in search of a destiny through the guidance of a superior, intellectual divine soul, and all that crap they feed you after you've done your communion or before, the only good thing about all that sermon is the angel's wing, which is really just bread but it has some divinity in it, I'll tell you that—or it's just the Pope's special recipe. I mean the whole concept of divinity and God is all propaganda. But the hell do I know about this matter, right? I've only read the children's edition Bible, and it really was because of the pictures. I know, I'm a hypocrite. I'm sorry I always start talking about things I don't know about, it's just sometimes my arrogance feels playful, but hopefully, you've understood where I'm trying to get to. This whole religion montage is something I'd rather not get too into depth in as a distraction of what further step to take in this metropolitan aura I've gotten myself into.

I stop thinking and put my headphones on. I look for my iPod as I've left my phone in LA. I didn't like that phone and I'm glad I didn't bring it with me. You know sometimes phones can be really annoying; they replace memories with their screens but you already knew that. I really hope you're not reading this from one too. I search for a song in my iPod, I don't know what I'd like to listen to and that bothers me because normally I do. I look down my different playlists, I know I could shuffle but I find it exhausting, I'd be fast-forwarding all day. I take my headphones off and decide to put them on again when I know what it is I'd like to listen to. In the meantime, I am walking, the streets are dirty and I think I've passed at least four homeless men sat in one corner of the street asking for money. I wish I could've given them a coin but I'm pretty broke and homeless myself. I look around, there are blonde heads and brunette heads, there're even bold heads. They make me feel like a giant as if I were looking down at them and they all look the same, I am staring down at Picasso's drawing of a city from a high tower; all cubic. I try to look forward instead of up whilst I'm walking, although the clouds are distracting. They keep covering my steps and I am starting to get nervous. I am walking down the street, I have an urge of crossing to the opposite road to see if anything will change, and I do so but nothing changes. I start to think again and decide what song I'd like to listen to. I pull out my iPod from my jacket again and plug in the headphones, which I then put in. I look for the song I have in mind, I find it and *Everybody's Talking* from this really good film you ought to see, *Midnight Cowboy* starts playing. Now walking down the street is different and I feel like I've been here before.

"If people bring so much courage to this world, the world has to kill them to break them, so, of course, it kills them. The world breaks every one and afterward many are strong at the broken places. But those that will not break, it kills. It kills the very good, and the very gentle and the very brave impartially. If you are none of these, you can be sure it will kill you too but there will be no special hurry."

—Ernst Hemmingway
A Farewell to Arms, 1929

Seq. 19 Int. Coffee Shop

I am sitting down on a bench in the middle of the street. My legs got tired of walking and to be honest, my bag is starting to degenerate my spine. I feel exhausted, and I think it was about time I felt this way. I am looking out to the nothingness, which in this case is covered in buildings that constantly reflect a fractured image of what is behind me and what is approaching me. The buildings are also covered in announcing logos all over the place, advertising themselves. I notice some are better than others and I see how competitive they are. I'm really just looking; I'm not even looking for something to distract me or find anything that will attract my attention. My vision is vague; my eyes are open because I don't want my contact lenses to freeze. I knew I should've brought another pair but I forgot, my mother always told me to bring an extra pack with me just in case. I'm tired of looking like a drooling bulldog so I open my bag to see if I can find something I'd like to read. I look in my bag and understand why it is so heavy, I brought too many books, but there's never really 'too many books'. You ought to read, you really do, if you don't, all your drawings will be just images you can't run away from and nobody likes a cuffed artist to a childhood memory. You have to read, if it's the last thing you do, read, read as much as you can, read for reading, not for anything else, read to know all those people you'll never personally greet at sophisticated phony dinners but will know, just by reading who they'd like to be under the names of the characters in their books. You have to be someone else many times to be your own someone someday. Ideas don't suddenly appear and vanish through generations, they stay and they are modified, even completely change but there'll always be a hint of somebody else's first thought in them and what you do with them is what will make them yours.

I've pulled out Kafka's *Metamorphosis* but I think that book's too intense to read right now so I put it back inside again. I want to go to Barns and Novels now but I must admit finding anything here seems quite impossible. I really have nothing better to do anyways, it's not like I'd like to sit down in this bench until the next morning. Plus, I've been sat down for most of my journey so I certainly don't want that to be the case again here. I am just so tired, the bags under my eyes are heavier than my imagination; I feel like they're pulling my face down making me look like a Tim Burton illustration. I am thankful for not crossing any flat mirrors yet. For some reason, I feel like I can't think, I can only write constantly and it's exhausting. I want to stop because I'm not saying anything I'd like to read. I'm still sat down, I feel like I should go eat something before I start looking for Barns and Novels. I hope I don't have to get the metro; I don't want to forget I'm supposed to get the train again tomorrow morning. I feel like the train trips' been all a dream and this is reality, I am actually here and I am actually not there, and I am beginning to feel really good about it.

I'd really like to take you through this exhausting day, I feel like a hangover jock found in the middle of someone's garden after a house party. I was told that happened once, I pretty much think it's happened to most jocks but I'm not one to stereotype. The fact that I say that so many times makes me think I might be one. Anyhow, the only thing I know is I have to eat, and find Barns and Novels, although the whole Barns and Novels is really a whim because I don't really need to go, but then again, it's a good place to start to know where to go. I stand up from the bench slowly because my body is fighting against me, as it doesn't want to move. I pull myself together and walk towards one of the fast foods that clog the streets with their abundance. I think it might be illegal so I begin to head over to a coffee shop instead. I'm not headed to Starbucks; I don't like it probably because everybody only goes to take pictures of the drink instead of actually drinking it so that really makes me think the coffee might be really bad. I walk past a Starbucks, not even glancing at it as an option and continue walking downtown to see if I find anything. I cross thousands of stores and fancy restaurants I wish I could afford but I'm glad I can't. I bump into a lot of people walking in masses either in a Segway or a skateboard, nobody says sorry they just keep walking, and I don't say sorry either and keep walking. I can't really see the sky by now, and it's not because the skyscrapers are too tall, because they're not, this isn't New York, but because there's a cloud of sadness cloaking it, I feel like God's taking the mickey out of my current situation. We hardly ever have those in LA, that's why people are always so tanned and shiny and well, bronzing is most of the time on sale now. I've camouflaged myself in the mass because I no longer see my hands. I'm walking slowly and calmly, with no hurries of getting anywhere, to be honest, I am enjoying this silence and commotion as '*Alive, Empire of the sun*' starts playing, and I close my eyes and open them immediately because I feel like I'm in a commercial or a movie of any sort. I feel like I'm smiling even though my mouth isn't moving or even open, my teeth are glowing. I want to change the song but I can't because I actually like it, and it's really the most antithetical song that could be playing on right now when everyone around me seems to be strolling to their grave, not that kid though, he's jumping all around the space that's been torn away from him. I'm giving you all this talk to distract you from the fact that I haven't found a decent coffee shop yet, and I should probably walk backwards and just sit at Starbucks like another fellow American would do. You'll probably think I'm about to find the coffee shop of my dreams with one more step and I wish you were right, I really do, but there's nothing one step forward. I turn around and start walking uptown. I spot a little coffee shop between two beautiful extravagant restaurants that are squashing it. It doesn't look nice, but it looks lonely and sometimes lonely is what you need.

We all knew this had to happen; it's not like I'm really going to end up in Starbucks, sooner or later, the little special coffee shop had to appear. I cross the road running without looking both ways to make sure a car wasn't coming; I hear a couple of honks so I think I should've looked. I'm in front of the coffee shop under the name of 'Coffee Shop' and a big large coffee door. I find it funny and go in. It's dark inside, the lights seem to have been put down to create ambience but it's just too dark because the local only has two big windows, which have been covered in graffiti from the outside. I still don't feel regretful for coming in here so I sit at one of the tables and look around. The place is decorated with wood as if to create the illusion that you're in a woodcutter's home. The place is also filled with logo stickers stuck all over the place; I also notice a couple of posters in one corner of the room. The posters are from bands like RHCP, Nirvana, Joy Division, Cream, The Animals, Sex Pistols, and there's also a couple of Queen and even Frank Zappa. I look around the room again in search of the waitress but I only find more waiting costumers like me. I head over to the counter to grab a menu and at least have an idea of what I'd like to have. I feel like coming in here might've been a bad idea after all. As I approach the counter, Al Green's, *Tired of Being Alone* starts playing and so I turn around and spot this boy at the end of the space plugging in the speakers to his laptop. I want to head over there and ask him if he

139

knows who's in charge, but I don't. The song suddenly changes to *Have You Seen Her Face*; I hadn't heard that song since this little prom dance we had at school to celebrate the end of our sophomore hell. I went with Diane to that, you were supposed to go with a male partner and I remember we actually got told off for not doing as we're told. I never really liked The Byrds to be honest, but that song I really liked, although it isn't one of my favourites.

"Can I get you anything?" a voice near me says.

I turn my head back to the counter, dislocating my vision from the music playing on the other side to this refined face staring at me from behind the counter.

"Hey, yes, I was just looking at the menu," I say.

"Alright, well, when you know, I'm here," he says.

"Okay, thank you," I say as I start looking at the menu leaflet.

Nothing seems really appealing; I'm saying this because photos are attached to this thing and I know I shouldn't judge a book by its cover but I'm really OCD when it comes to food. I want to leave before paying for something I won't like, and it's not like I've got the money to pay for something I won't eat. I'm quite limited to be honest, and I still need to save some money for the book I'll buy in Barns and Novels. You must've noticed by now, I like being precise which is really contradictory with my personality but I really like planning everything ahead even though I am spontaneous. Either way, I think I'm going to head out of this gloomy place.

"I'll have a glass of tap water please," I say.

The guy at the counter fills a glass with water and brings it over to me.

"Thanks!" I say.

"You want to use the bathroom too?" he asks.

"Urm…no, thank you," I say confused. I then understand he's just pissed because I'm not really paying for anything so I start searching for a tip jar. I don't find one.

"Do you have a tip jar?" I ask.

"What do you think we are, a charity?" he asks.

"No…uh, I just—" I try to finish saying but he cuts me off.

"Look, drink your water and leave. It's alright, this place is getting demolished by Saturday anyways," he says, looking down.

"Oh…I…uh, I'm so sorry to hear that," I say.

"It's alright, kid," he says, scratching his growing beard. "It's not your fault."

I finish my water and *The Chain* starts playing, I want to ask him who was it that played this song.

"Who's this song from, I know it's *The Chain* but I can't remember who sang it," I say.

"Oh, Fleetwood Mac, one of the greatest," he says as he cleans the counter with a damp white sheet.

"I like the music you play here," I say as I start packing my things again.

"At least, someone appreciates it, I've been working on this playlist for a month now," he says.

I want to leave but I also really want to finish listening to this song, so I fake taking longer to pack my bag. He doesn't really notice me anyways as to care, I look up at him and he's miming to the song moving like Slash did in one of the Guns n Roses concert.

"I could give you a copy if you want," he says.

"For how much?" I ask, regretting having asked that.

"What do you mean?" he asks confused, and then seems to get what I meant because he says, "Music doesn't have a price, and if you've got taste like I think you do, you earned it free. It's your right to listen to music, especially good music."

I nod nervously ashamed of being such an idiot and slightly laugh to cover up my tracks.

"Well then, it'd be great to have it," I say smiling. I can feel how the song is slowly reaching to its end and *Jungle Jazz* begins to play.

"Kool & The Gang, know them?" he asks as he starts walking towards his laptop on the other side of the room, and I turn around on my seat following his steps.

"Yeah," I say, followed by an improvised nod and a foolish smile. I feel like I should get going but he just went through the trouble of giving me his playlist so I stay sat there looking over to the dark spot he's working at.

"Is cassette alright with you?" he asks from his side of the room. I don't want to shout back so I move to where he is.

"Sorry, what did you say?" I ask.

"Is cassette alright with you?" he asks again as he looks for something other than the cassette he's holding in his hand.

"Well, I don't really have a cassette player," I say ashamed.

"It's alright, I'll give you the address of a friend of mine and he'll give you one. He's got plenty!" he exclaims as he does a movement with his hands, which seem to mime an explosion followed by a noise of a bomb made with his mouth.

"I don't think I can—" I start to say.

"It's alright, he won't charge you, we don't like selling things that people should have as a necessity. Believe me, and I ain't wise or anything, and probably know shit but I know one or two things and those are," he pauses what he is doing to look at me and says, "1. You could perfectly survive a week, even two without food but not without music, you'd go nuts, and 2. Don't ever say no to things that are given to you for free." He then scratches his hair and slides it backwards. He has sort of long dark hair, looking like a retired surfer, his highlights have lost the sun's caring.

We sit there as he prepares the playlist, once it's done, we head to the counter and he grabs a worn-out yellow post-it stuck to the table and asks me for a pen. I say I don't have one, so he heads over to the other tables and asks the people if they have a pen but they say they don't so he comes back and looks for a pen again. He kneels down and pops his head out again, and says he found one on the floor. He writes down the address of his friend under the name of 'Marcel Cassette Guy', and turns the post-it around and writes another little note, which I can't really read. He gives it to me. I find this to be a good opportunity to ask him where Barns & Nobel is.

"Here you go, don't get lost, it's right around the corner," he says.

"Thank you," I say, followed by an uncertain trembling voice that asks, "So um…do you know where Barns and Novels is?"

"What's that?" he asks.

"It's a bookstore," I say.

"I have no idea, kid, maybe Marcel can help you," he says.

"Well, thanks then," I say, with a shy laugh and head over to the door.

"Wait, kid, it'll be faster if you go from the back door," he says. "Follow me, babe."

It feels strange being called babe. He walks towards the back door and I follow him like I've never wanted to follow anyone; with the fear that if I didn't, I'd be lost, a fatal dependency. He opens the door and leads me the way as he points the directions with his fingers. I thank him once again and leave his little coffee shop, but right before I leave, '*Charlie Don't Surf*' starts playing, and I turn around and find him winking at me as he shouts, "The Clash is in there too! Oh and, kid, tell him Jovi sent you," and slams the door behind me. I start walking my way out of this dark alley packed with old cardboard boxes and smell of trash. I see a dead rat with flies around it on my left so I move towards the right to avoid getting closer to that.

Seq. 20 Int. The Apartment

We all, especially at this age, reach a point where we hate society, but I think it comes as a consequence of hating ourselves first. We bore what we love and we fight against what we want for what we already have. We live wanting to be allowed to be free, but there's the problem, we shouldn't think you have to be allowed to be free, you should just do what you want to do, there is no authority upon yourself but yourself. I am saying this because I got it all wrong, I've been thinking about it since the bartender threw me out the backdoor with a cassette full of good music. I hope it's good music; I really liked what he was playing in there. It's been a long time since I haven't been surprised by the music at some bar or a club in any case, or even a party where you're supposed to be able to play whatever you want. I go around the corner from his bar, and read the address he wrote down under the name of 'Marcel Cassette Guy'. I start walking, searching for the number 36 on a building door or on the wall near a door. I notice a guy in a black hoodie looking down at his feet; he isn't that far away from the coffee shop's back door so I head in his direction, avoiding looking at the numbers on the wall. I presume he is either 'Marcel Cassette guy' or a friend of his. Jovi was right, the direction was literally only five steps away from his local and even though I felt like I should be suspicious about all this random kindness, I am not. The guy in the black hoodie still hasn't noticed me as I start walking over to where he's standing, it bothers me not to be able to see his face under the hoodie or whatever it is he is looking down as he fidgets with his hands.

"Marcel?" I ask timidly as I stand in front of him.

He is immune to my approach and ignores my call, still looking down and fidgeting with dice. "Marcel?" I say again, louder, hoping this time he'll look up and just answer a basic no or yes. He doesn't react once again so I feel the urge of just giving him a gentle push, I start to wonder if he is wearing headphones and that's why he can't hear me. I guess I ought to try it one more time, although it doesn't really give me a life changer if he doesn't answer, after all, I didn't want the cassette or the cassette player in the first place. It had all been just a beautiful coincidence to fulfil my lack of entertainment.

"M—" I begin saying but his scraped voice cuts me off as he says, "I heard ya, just wait a minute." I stand in silence considering it so rude for what could be counted as five minutes; I start counting ten sheep, then 20 cows and so on to distract myself as I stand there looking at this guy's kneeled head covered by a hoodie.

He stops fidgeting and looks up at me for a slight second, but I don't have time enough to distinguish the construction of his face.

"Aright, how do you know my brother's name?" he says, looking to the sides and then down again, once again, not giving me time to see his face.

"I was at this coffee shop and—" I begin saying but once again, I'm cut off by his pedant voice.

"Hey, listen, I asked you a question, not your legacy," he says, cracking up silently.

"Jovi told me you had cassettes," I say.

I don't have time to process his complete change of climax as right after saying Jovi, he launches over me and gives me a tight hug with a condescending smile that I notice he has sin tattooed all over his upper lip, he holds me from my arm and leads me through the door under the number 36.

"You could've said that earlier! I'm sorry if I sounded rough, I've been having a bad day and all, you know you never really know who to trust and all, especially around this neighbourhood," he says as he walks in front of me opening different doors of different sizes to let me come through and then locking them behind me. "I'm Marcel's brother, my name's Elliot. So tell me how come old Jovi sends you over here asking for my brother?" he asks. I look at him perplexed without saying a word, wondering if he has time to breathe in the middle of his sentences. "You a good friend of old Jovi's or what?"

I don't answer I just keep walking behind him worrying of where I'm headed, feeling a tremendous eager of going back to the coffee shop and killing that guy Jovi. Although I was rather consumed by Elliot's interest in having a conversation, and it wasn't his fault if he was as clueless as I was on the whole situation so might as well take advantage of it.

"Oh…um…no, Jovi and I barely met some minutes ago because I went in his coffee shop and I liked his music, and then he went all crazy about me having to have a copy of his music so he sent me all the way over here so your brother would give me a cassette player to be able to listen to the music he gave me. It's really confusing," I say breathless, rolling my eyes.

"And so she speaks, what's your name again? It's not cassette, is it?" he mocks as he continues guiding me up some snail stairs with a red carpet murdered with holes and stacked with khaki spots. I must say the building is beautiful from the inside even though it looks like a shithole from the outside, like an old palace in ruins under water, only this one was under a pile of dusted bricks and cement but it didn't lose its royalty once you were inside.

"I can't tell you my name," I say.

"That's not fair, I told you mine," he says.

"It's not your real name, you just said yourself you have trust issues, why give your name to a stranger?" I ask with audacity.

"I knew Elliot didn't suit me, it's too upper east side, right? Although there are a couple of musicians named Elliot, maybe that's why I thought it'd be convincing," he says, before starting to walk up the stairs again, so he could have time to properly vocalise out of his breathless voice. You could notice he was a heavy smoker, he sounded like my dad when my mum left. He couldn't even walk down to the grocery store without breathing properly; they put him in hospitalisation once because he fainted on the way once, I remember I was worried sick of whether he had lung cancer.

"So you're a musician?" I ask keenly as I follow him up the stairs again. I was beginning to wonder how many stairs this building could actually have, it wasn't like it were some New York skyscraper or something, but it sure looked infinite and I sure as hell wish he wasn't taking me all the way up to the penthouse for some stupid cassette player.

He stops walking, and with one leg on one step and the other on a step below, he faintly turns around so only the point of his nose and the movement of his mouth can be identified, and he says, "I'm not only a musician, I'm a drug dealer," and then gives a slight turn wide enough so I can see the idiotic smirk on his face. He turns around back again and says, "I'm kidding, princess, I'm strictly only a musician who doesn't know how to write songs, so basically I'm a failure that works when my niece has a birthday and my sister is just trying to be a good sister, and hires me and my brother to play at her daughter's party, so her rich husband can pay us a fortune because he doesn't know we are related to his wife and that we are not professionals, and she can compensate for casting us out of her life after our mother—" He stops looks up to the ceiling and prays silently until he breaks and says, "Rest in peace, Julianne." He resumes his hike up the bleeding stairs, which are waiting to crack in any second and drive us to the ground like an aeroplane on fire would. I never thought of my death being so chaotic and erotic at the same time, now that I've written those words, reading them I have to say I probably have.

"Jovi's girl, you speak too much, seriously, I'm going to ask you to be quiet for a while so I can have my time to think," he says, in sarcasm.

"I'm not Jovi's girl," I reproach.

"Well then, tell me your name," he says.

"Why don't you tell me your name and then I'll consider it," I answer back.

"Okay fine, if you're so keen to know my name, it's Clive," he says confidently, although I don't exactly believe him.

"I'll consider it," I simply answer. "Where are you taking me, Clive?" I ask, with a higher tone at the end of 'Clive' so he knows I'm mocking him.

"I'm taking you to Marcel so he can give you the damn cassette player," he says as he looks down and starts saying in a lower voice. "I've told him millions of times to just open a little shop downtown where it's easier, but no, he has to go all vintage on me, and tell me he'll have more costumers if he's incognito which I find completely stupid and irrational, and what I don't understand is why the hell do I even have to be in charge of his lousy costumers guiding them to him as if I worked for him, and he just waits up there on his goddamn throne for *Christ's sake*," he complains without stopping to have time to vocalise in order for me to understand what he's saying. I knew most of the time he was talking, he wasn't talking to me, he just wanted his brother to hear him from wherever he was hiding because he wasn't capable of saying it to his face.

"So yes, Cassette chick, to answer your damn question, a couple more stairs are awaiting for us before we get to him," he says, breathless again this time. I was hoping he didn't die on me in the middle of this, *how'dyacallit*...constant Hamlet monologue?

"Okay thanks, Clive, hey isn't it weird you're called Clive and not Geoffrey or something?" I mock him hoping he'll get where I'm headed at with the comment.

"Why would I be called Geoffrey—" he starts saying but doesn't finish his sentence because he understands immediately where I was going.

"Don't you ever think I'm Marcel's butler or sideman, or whatever because you're wrong," he says madly, and then distinctly says to himself, loud enough for me to hear, "I'm going to kill that *sonuvabitch* making me look like his pussy."

We went up a couple of more stairs, there weren't so many if you looked at them from the last floor, there were about five floors in total, only the whole romantic snail staircase made the journey seem endless, and Clive's talking made it even longer. We walked in silence towards the door, Clive in front of me still silently complaining to himself as he looked for the keys in one of his pockets. He found them not inside of his pockets but inside his trousers, which repelled me from ever getting touch of those keys even if they are the only way out of here. He opens the door and goes inside as I follow impressed by his oh so chivalry.

"You like what you see?" he asks as he takes off the damn hoodie and exposes his face. He wasn't that ugly, at least I didn't see him ugly enough to have to cover his face under a black hoodie all the time. I wasn't sure then if he was asking if I liked his face or the apartment/shop whatever it was they defined it by.

"Yes, it looks nice," I simply said, referring to his face and the apartment in one so there wasn't any confusion.

"I know, I designed most of it myself. I studied architecture and art before giving up because nobody liked it, which led me to wanting to domain the world with the bad music I make," he says, with a mischievous laugh.

I grin and say, "Well, I think you did a good job, normally, art teachers don't know what they're talking about when they say they don't like something."

I wasn't lying, the place looked great, it was stuffed with posters all over the walls from bands I knew which made me feel less freaked out about being there and I liked that it was minimalist, the furniture wasn't a big deal, they just had the essentials of commodity: a sofa, a desk, a kitchen hiding somewhere and two beds on two different sides of the place. It was also packed with books that literature was hanging off the ceiling as well as a millennium of vinyls all stashed one over the other, making it look like a column holding up the ceiling from falling down. The place was not only being devoured by art in all its senses but it was colourful in a place so dark, I mean the only light coming in the room was from the smallest window I'd ever seen, they didn't even have views but their interior design. The walls were all white except the kitchen wall that was melting red roses of such a red carnal colour and literally not figuratively, you could really smell the paint as fresh. Its whole ensemble was quite cannibalistic, but I didn't say anything, I just smiled at Clive as he showed me around as a way of killing time till his brother appeared.

We sit down in their black sofa with space only for two and as we sit there, I look around finding all types of instruments hidden between the chaotic turmoil I saw as order.

"Marcel's showering at our neighbour's," Clive says, looking down at his phone as he writes down a text I can't read. He looks up at me peeping and says, "Yeah, I told him you're here and he'll be up in a second. You see, our water system got cut off a couple of days ago because I fucked the janitor's wife in the janitor's closet after she brought him homemade cookies to work, so he got really mad about it, which I don't understand because it's really his fault if his wife is looking for pleasure elsewhere. Anyways, he'll put it back on when the Landlord comes back from Michigan." He explains although I wasn't really paying attention, I just felt his words and voice as a background echo, the same thing I used to do when people in LA spoke to me about circumstances in their life that I had no interest in. He wasn't even talking about himself; he was talking about the janitor and his landlord. I just looked at him and smiled. He looks down at his phone again and in a low voice says, "Fuck," as he looks up and bites his lip.

"Marcel said Jovi doesn't want you to pay for the damn cassette player," he says as he sequentially looks down again and murmurs another silent 'fuck'.

"Oh, it's okay, I can pay—" but he cuts me off before I can say anything else.

"No, Jovi said you're not getting charged so Marcel isn't going to charge you," he says angrily.

He starts fidgeting and soon I begin fidgeting with a bracelet I had in my hand, I fidget carefully not to break it. We are both in silence insulting each other in every smile we share to try make the situation less awkward. I hear a low knock on the door and I wonder if it's another costumer but Clive doesn't move, so I assume it must be Marcel. The knock gets louder and a girly scream shrieks, "MARC, come out, I know you're in there." I look at Clive but he doesn't do anything, so I don't do anything. We hear a couple of more fist punches on the door followed by the same insufferable shrieks like the ones we heard before where the girly voice was asking for Marcel. We look at each other and I'm incited to ask Clive who she is.

"She's Olivia, this girl he's seeing or not seeing. They fight a lot, but her sister is hot so I told Marcel to stay with her a while longer just so I can finally have a threesome with both of them. I think he told her when he was going to break up, or get back with her, so that's maybe why she's so pissed off," he says.

"That makes sense, although it doesn't really," I say confusedly, averting my gaze from him.

"What do you mean, C-S?" he asks. It takes me longer to answer because I don't understand why he is referring to me by that name.

"Seriously, don't call me C-S," I say.

"I need to call you something... C-S," he says.

"All right Geoffrey, call me C-S," I answer back trying to annoy him. He breathes heavily inside and out, and then looks at me again as if he'd just come out from a therapist session as a new man.

"So, why does it make sense but it doesn't?" he asks.

"Well, I get that she feels insulted and all, but why come back banging on his door after he said that, and I don't really understand the big deal about a *ménage-a-trois*," I say.

"A ména-what?" he asks.

"A threesome in French," I say.

"Oh right, yeah me neither, but Olivia is a feisty one and she's probably more pissed by the fact that Marcel doesn't want to have a relationship with her," he says.

"And why doesn't he?" I ask.

"Well, she's beautiful, I can testify to that but my brother doesn't really care about your species' feelings and all, he's more about desire in the moment kind of guy," he says prideful. I laugh discretely at how ridiculous that just sounded, but I give him a kind smirk so the pedestal he has his brother on doesn't fall on his head and make his life worse than it already is.

"Last time I checked, Marcel Junior, we are the same species," I say.

"You say that because you've never been in love," he says sighing as he looks up to the ceiling in disdain.

"I bet you haven't either," I answer back.

"True, but at least I know what I'm talking about," he says.

"And why wouldn't I?" I ask.

"Because you can't talk about what you don't believe in, and I do," he says shrugging leaving me confused as hell.

I bet this absurd conversation could've gone for years if it weren't because the door suddenly bashes open and is closed so rapidly we don't even have time to identify who just came in. My

149

best guess at this point was it was the psychotic girlfriend Clive was so desperately to have sex with.

To my glee and Clive's disappointment, it was his brother, or that's what I conclude, I mean they do have some facial similarities that could proclaim them related. He was handsome, I'll give you that but he was too over the top of himself, at least that's the impression he looks like he wants to give. I dream of the moment in which he gives me the damn cassette and I can flee out of this crack hole before they think I am some Olivia doppelgänger, and I sure as hell aren't interested in being mixed up with these two guys, I also have to find Barns and Novels.

"You must be Jovi's girl," Marcel says as he approaches me after throwing his jacket over the desk and falling to the floor. He grabs my hand and kisses it.

"Yes, but no, I'm just here for the cassette player," I say, smiling uncomfortably as I distance my hand from his repellent lips.

"Sure, I know, come over to my room and I'll show you the choices," he says

"Oh, it's fine, I trust you can pick one I'll like," I say, and it's not like there must be a grand variety of cassette player designs or something.

"Don't be shy, what's your name again?" he asks. I expected Clive to say in the background, "She's not going to tell you."

Right after thinking it, it's exactly what he does, so I turn around look at him then look back at Marcel and say, "Ronnie," even though it's not my name.

"Beautiful—well, I'll go bring you one out now," he says.

John stands up and heads over to his room, and disappears behind a curtain on the right wing of the apartment.

I sit down again beside Clive who doesn't look too happy and I say, "It's not my real name," he laughs as a result and gives me a kind wink, for a moment I feel like Clive has gained a couple of kilos between the time of John arriving and I sitting down beside him again. I feel like he's slowly being swollen into a helium balloon, and I can't help but imagine Harry Potter's step-aunt every time I look at his face. I try not to laugh or freak out, so I stay mobilised like another minimalist furniture decorating their household. Soon after, Marcel comes out holding the cassette player in his hand and throwing it over at me. I miraculously grab it in the air, the farewell is quicker than I expected as they say goodbye, and just ask me politely to close every door behind me and not talk to any strangers until I've reached a ten-metre radius from their

150

apartment. I do so, I leave the apartment and rush down those bloody stairs, literally bloody and head out the million doors they asked me to close behind me until I finally reach the streets of Chicago. I look around to figure a way to get out of here without having to go through Jovi's coffee shop again. I spot a small corridor a little further up from number 36 leading back to where I was before. I put on the cassette Jovi gave me with all his music inside Marcel's transparent cassette player, I plug my headphones and start walking as *Sultans of Swing* starts playing, and I try to remember the last time I listened to Dire Straits with my dad driving in his old red Saab in the freeway from Los Angeles to San Francisco.

"I never saw the morning until I stayed up all night,
I never saw the sunlight until you turned out the light,
I never saw my hometown until I stayed away too long,
I never heard the melody until I needed the song.

I never saw the white line until I was leaving you behind,
I never knew I needed you until I was caught up in a blind night,
I never spoke I love you until I cursed you in vain,
I never felt my heartstrings until I nearly went insane.

I never saw the east coast until I moved to the west,
I never saw the moonlight until it shone and I felt depressed,
I never saw your heart until someone was trying to steal it away,
I never saw your tears until they rolled down your face."

—Tom Waits
San Diego Serenade, 1974

Seq. 21 Ext. Streets
Without Names

I could say what I've repeatedly said since I arrived to Chicago, and that would be to tell you that I'm walking which I am but I'm sure we don't have to waltz around the fact that I'm walking again without knowing where to as I've said countless of times before, so I think it'd be a good idea to skip that bit. It's still daytime and that tranquilises me, because even though I want to make you think I have it all under control and I'm not scared, I feel like I can't really lie to you, and I am terrified. I'm walking so much because I feel night-time catching up with the end of my ankles, like the shadow I can't get rid of when I look at the ground and see it covers most of the space I'm walking in. It's someone that just won't leave me alone, like a stalker I share a bed with without allegedly knowing, an intruder that is stepped on every time I move and yet wants to continue following. I have stomped on its face, even on his feet but there is a sort of sadness in its walk, a sort of sadness I can't get rid of and one I like to stare at. I can't stop procrastinating now that the sun will be replaced by a moon not bright enough to play its part, even covered by its pierced dark prince skin that sheds scopes of fading light. I know they're dying and so I'll walk blindfolded through these unknown streets without liquor in my hand terrified of being what I am; sober. I don't want to make a big deal out of it, if you think about it, there're just a couple of hours until day-time will rise again, but then again, a couple of hours aren't just a couple of hours. The funny thing is, it's only 8 PM and in summer that means the sun will stay longer, but still that doesn't forget about tonight's night.

I don't want to bore you anymore with the nonsense talk of these fatal fears, I can't let myself be beaten by them now and it'd be useless and ridiculous. If I knew how to write poetry, this book wouldn't exist because even though it is creating an improvised satire about the 21st Century, I am a lover of words that tangle in the beauty of their vowels unaccounted for how ridiculous and humiliating they may sound in XIX where beauty is summarised into a small flask full of impurities sold as pure. We don't release enough passion, we aren't led by our desires and that's why we are the visual image of corruption, we are Poussins' modern representation of *Rape of the Sabine Woman*, only we'd be raping not only Sabine but each other in any figurative and literal way. I feel like I have suddenly begun to sound like a preacher (someone who I certainly don't want to be associated with or even confused for) at least that's what I feel. The old romantic poets are doing this to me; Charles Baudelaire, Goethe, Pushkin, Blake, Oscar Wilde and Allan Poe are responsible for this delusional state of my recognition of the absence of beauty in everything I look at.

I mean you can judge me, I've told you thousands of times to do so already, I even feel like I have begged for you to do so, I need someone to tell me the truth they wouldn't want to hear, I need someone to notice, to realise that what I'm saying, I am not saying for anyone else but myself, I am only trying to convince myself that I could be able to do this. I am not regretful of choices I have made but I am still one of the most condemned people I will ever have the pleasure to meet, but still so I must say my wounds have been covered by these pages like bandages, I feel like I'm even offending literature by proclaiming my book as such. My book I say, as if it were really mine, I have only written what tears me away at night even sometimes at day, like this one time I was reading Houellebecq. I am simply using all this 'my book' nonsense as an excuse to unburden myself. Being published is additive, it's an impression wanting to be made, it's camouflaged as a way of proving myself to you and how contradictory it is to say that I don't care what you think about me, but then again here, I am like an idiot trying to prove something I already am.

I think it is quite obvious I am stuck at this point, I'm thinking of maybe going over to a park where the green leaves can serve as mirrors of a child's lost imagination, I need a way to expire this sensation that has damned my every thought to relinquish its aspirations in my soul. I don't really believe that being surrounded by nature is going to inspire me in any way, I know many writers have often said in their interviews that they like going over to a quiet private place where the only sound loud enough to hear at times is their heartbeat depending on the love poem they're trying to write, or on an unrequited love from a pedantic temporary muse. My dad used to tell me this as well, he always told me that he needed to get away from civilisation and hideaway for a couple of days near the sea or in the hidden depths of a forest, and that used to be hard for him, to find a place like that in Los Angeles, that's why he was locked up in his studio most of the time, I guess he found nature between the cracks in the cement walls that hid all an artist will never be ready to expose. Either way, I feel like I am out of options, so I start looking for a park somewhere, although it should be a small park submerging the city, not like New York's central park, which is more of a tourist attraction than a park anymore. I am hustling through the people coming towards me in the streets, rarely have I noticed someone going in the opposite direction as me.

I am narrating the story of youth impersonated in this body I've been given, these facial features that are meant to distinguish me from the rest, they're meant to look at me but yet they can't because if they would, I would stop being a face. I can't help but stroke it as one would their lover's in bed and for a slight weak moment, I have this urge of telling you how I look like because I feel like if I never do, you'll see me as a broken mirror in a home decorator store being replaced for a fixed one. I continue walking straight, I have this sensation of walking on a ball that keeps rolling down the street and this only incites me to walk faster. I see everyone and everything as colourful Christmas lights, every blue tank top is a blue light bulb and every face is a fainting bokeh. I wonder what my face must look like from the outside, whether my tongue is sticking out or my eyes are popping out. I begin to slow down the moment I realise this, the moment I realise I am wasting my time by moving too fast and I stop and look around to see where I am. I notice a taxi stop a couple feet away from me, so I head towards the first one in line and hop in without asking if it was available. I close the door behind me and sit down near the window behind the driver; I can slightly see his rebellious eyebrows on the rear-view mirror.

"Where to miss?" asks the driver.

"Urm…could you take me to the nearest park," I say.

"I'm going to need directions, ma'am," he says in an irked tone.

"I can't really give you one," I say as I shrug, trying to somehow make him feel pity for me. "I just arrived."

"Alright then, you tell me when to stop," he says as I notice him roll his eyes through the rear-view mirror, and probably murmur to himself the typical moan adults make once they've come across an indecisive teenager. He puts the chronometer on and drives. He was quite laconic for that matter, but I liked him that way.

"Thank you," I say softly, not wanting to piss him off.

I look out the window longing for something that looks more like New York, but my eyes are getting tired and they can't seem to spot any green places around the area. I want to ask the driver if he has a map, a compass, any contraption that can guide these delinquent eyes that steal the views as a breeze of lashes slowly seal the world away from me: I sometimes feel like I'm in a luxurious resort in the Bahamas every time I blink, my eyelashes serve as palm trees. If it weren't because the driver spoke something I didn't exactly hear, I would've blacked out.

"Is this okay?" he asks.

I look out the window and spot a small vacant park a couple of blocks from where he was intending on leaving me. I nod and look for my money.

"It'll be ten dollars," he says.

I hand him the cash trying to daunt him so he might not pick all of it, and without another word to each other, I exit the cab and contemplate as it drives away. I look around for a while, searching for the name of the street because I know I'll regret not doing so when it's midnight. I know I told you I wanted to try out the whole meditating thing in the park like my dad said, and that probably being in such a peaceful space is what I need but I don't feel like heading over to that damn park in the end, I'm afraid if I sit in one of its benches, I'll never stand up from it again. You could guess what I do in the end, but it's so obvious you wouldn't have to go through the trouble of guessing when I'm about to tell you that I'm already walking headed to that little spot of green in this squared ground palette surrounded by this tempest of loud noises and obstructed spaces encaged in metallic artefacts. The park isn't that far away once I begin walking towards it, and although I'd love to tell you all about my little stroll to get there, I'm not. I sit down in the bench I spotted when I was eight feet away from getting to the park, and I begin to pull out rambled pages from my bag to write on them. I get out one of the pens on the front pocket because they're easier to find and I just sit there waiting, waiting for them to be filled as I know the sooner or later I'll begin to scribble:

*I like being with **people** because I feel like my problems diminish, they even stop being **problems** because the problems of those around me seem to me to be extremely more interesting and it takes away the burden of having to think about mine, over-think even to such extreme that I feel like I don't have any problems anymore. **What are problems anyways?***

*And here I am, alone thinking about too many problems that aren't problems but annoying thoughts. Maybe it's because I stop thinking, and I summarise all my senses into only listening and observing…in this way, humiliating my **conscience** and its' **disobedient impulses.***

*I love saying I'm **selfish**; it's really a trick for those around me, I always **play games** with them like a little **spoilt** girl, I have to play in order to be distracted, and not cry and shout. I've always wanted to be selfish, and I know in a way I am because, well, we all are, but I'm not the right quantity amount of selfish, as I'd like to be. When I think about my **dream**, I immediately think of how my dream will **affect everybody** else—I base myself too much in that, but it's not that I'm selfish or egocentric, I think it basically means I am insecure. **Nobody cares about it**, but I can't stop thinking that maybe it will matter, maybe someone will **fall in love** with me, or will consider a different aspect of me to consider or they'll feel proud of me. So, I basically go from what the **dream** would means to me, to what it would mean or impose to everyone else as a **priority** and how they'll **fucking** react.*

WE CAN'T BE **SAVAGES**
WE CAN'T WRITE

*(**Love** is considered **cruel** when we realise that we aren't talking about **love**, but about ourselves)*
WE ARE THE SUBJECT!!!

*If I had a **girl rock band** like Joan Jett and 'The Runaways', there'd be more **women** and less scared girls—*

*It'd be the **21ˢᵗ century** resurrection the first time where we could gloat about having a historical and **intellectual development** more important than damn technology. It'd be a **generation** in which the pureness of a tear would be noticed as well as the sound of an uncontrolled laughter—*
*Oh, it'd be a justice **camouflaged** by the atrezo they have loaded in **paradise**.*

*If I want to be a **fucking good writer**, I'd stop worrying about being good and concentrate more on whether I like what I write more than its designated public. I don't want to base it in* *illustrations* that aren't *mine* when everybody should have their own, and I want to see everything from where nobody's looking, because I'd like to be able to look at myself in the mirror and not see any of you.

> *liar*
> *person*

Being a **hypocrite** doesn't have to be considered something negative that could **hurt** or even more like a **default** or worse a reason to back away from an **association** with **someone**. Being a hypocrite is being honest because we all are, **denying** it to somebody already makes you a hypocrite. The **word** is always there. There are words that haunt us, and meanings we overlook.

There are things I **write**, and I write them so fast because I **acknowledgingly** don't want them to make **sense**, I don't want to look up and completely understand what I've written because it'd **hurt**. I want to get it off my **skin**, ripping it off, that's how it all ends up in these rambled **pages**, they are the result of **my serpent skin.**

Because of my **lack** of consideration, I have **become somebody** I haven't met and can't compare to.

Who is my **real image?**

Which is the **voice** that chaperons and that figure that holds it, always covered by **attire** that destroys her.

I want to know, and I **fear** I never will.

I am **sadness** wrapped in forced laughter like—**Venetian** carnival mask at a masquerade ball in which the stare is concentrated but the smile courted by red **lipstick** stands out more. And I **waltz** around the dancing floor with a fear of falling down— it's a **virtue** for my rampant feelings to be walking faced to the floor.

> I don't want that my **feelings**
> *ideas*
> *thoughts*

distract you from your own ones, I mean I want to **influence** my reader, not monopolise/ (robotise?) him/it.

I mean it's the only reason why I didn't want to publish this book in the first place, don't think I'm writing this as pure narcissism or that I can actually be that **naïve** to think that what I write will influence you whatsoever. I'm just **advertising** it out of *experience—it's just an **ATTENTION SIGN** like the ones they have at the '**Rolling Stones**' concerts*

*I don't want you to **use** me, or **blame** me as a getaway from yourselves, I am not a **drug**; this book wasn't written to rip its pages as **moderation** to sniff some coke or roll a joint. Although if you do, do it with love.*

***Fuck Fuck!**—I want to write **poetry**, I want to write something that doesn't feel so **mechanical**.*

*Something that feels **spontaneous**—but thought through, because words have a back **spine**, they've got their own **personality** and depending on how you use them, they could **crack, or even worse they'd bend too much**.*

Short story short (really, the shortest story)
*An **inspiration** has drowned itself and any ounce of **creativity** left in it is nothing but the last bubbles of the sea.*

*This is the moment where I realise I'm sat on a bench and I can't hardly read what I'm **writing** anymore because it's too **dark** and these **letters** are covering the **blankness** once impregnated on these pages, making it impossible to **recognise** these **past conceptions**. I want to stop, but now I know I can't because I **need** to **punish** these papers one more time.*

The love they all talk about, isn't the same love I think about. I don't know if any of you have ever been in love, or if you are right now, or if you have and hated it, but all I can say in all its pain and glory, understandment and confusion, and highway of stages of pure happiness, of pure anything really—even stages of hate in-between—that I wouldn't change the feeling, but the person I am feeling it for. Ever.

An improvised poem
***Youth** was **invincible** for a while,*
*It couldn't be **tamed** by materials and futuristic games.*

*It was the **liberty** parents envied,*
*A **revolution** that wanted more than their **desires**,*
*They were the **generation** that freed each other and every **rainbow possibility**,*
*And when it **rains**, and I look out of the window,*
*The **streets** are lonely packed with **blind** people,*

*There are no more **children** to wreck*
                *their **truths** and **limits.***
*They are all in **silence** for I hear only the **tears** of an angry rain,*
As no one but me notices it,
As I have this urge of going down there to the
                       drained *streets,*
*And **scream**; scream as loud as I can,*
*To sense the **noise** in my palm as everyone*
                around me puts their headphones on.
*The **sound** is drowning me beneath a **water** not so deep,*
*And everybody's **drowning** with me,*
*I am in a dark room of **gluttony** and **greed.***
*I step over everybody's **abstractions** as they lie*
                       under *my feet,*
*Light isn't a **resource** when senses be mistook.*

*Regretful **cries** from past come up to my window sometimes,*
I sit in a corner facing a white wall,
*And I **scribble imagination** in little faces instead of words,*
*Now **nobody** sees me because I **destroyed** them all.*

And after wearing my hand out in all these white strips of paper slowly being sunk down by the black ink of my pen, I make of them ruins no antique monument has ever seen and walk towards the nearest rubbish bin, for I can't find a lake to shove them in. I stand up from the bench which once had been bright green and now has lost its entire colour; I find it sad but refreshing. It'd been a long time since I'd walked the streets of a rambling city surviving against the tempest that is the night, I was anxious to head back to the hustle and for some unknowledgeable reason, I feel impatient of going to a Jazz club even though I have no money, but who needs money when they have taste for music? I can dive myself in any of these bars without a dime to buy myself a drink, and get drunk with the sound of the saxophone whispering its pains to my ear, I could even go down to any metro and roam its allies finding dead musicians in hobo's bodies. I already feel like a drunken sailor and I haven't even gotten to the good part of Chicago yet, I haven't found Barns and Novels, and I sure don't know where to find a Jazz club, the good thing of moaning about things I can't find is that I have all night to look for them. My thoughts are drained by the overload that was pouring a heart out instead of my brain on those pieces of paper no one will ever read because my arrogance has driven them insane.

Seq. 22 Int. Jazz Club

Chicago isn't only about the millennium park bean, also known as the Cloud Gate. Although now, at night, it's more beautiful than it's ever looked on all those pictures some of my classmates showed off about at school, it deformed the lights of the city into dancing fireworks aiming at our lost souls in the night. I'm not really going to get around how I ended up here, under Kapoor's gigantic bean which only seemed to stretch sideways instead of upwards like old Jack's did. I'm still in the Loop if you're wondering and the park I went to was the Millennium Park, only I ended at one of those ends no one really goes to anymore because it still preserves the vitality the mother of all the sons planted in our gardens, the one's that create forests in our homes. I just know this now because I read it on this pamphlet I found on the floor near the sculpture instructing the whole history of the Cloud Gate. This park is more like a nature park caged by a variety of callous metals, caging it like a wild animal, restricting nature to the basic design some architect decided to make for it.

I'd like to introduce you to Chicago now, I know I haven't done it properly yet but it's really just been because we haven't been introduced to each other either. I mean I can't even get the names of the streets right when I'm asking for directions and that's basically because I don't even know where I'm headed at. I can hear my steps on the cement that is the sidewalk as if I were wearing Astaire's claque shoes—that's when I realise how desperate I am for the scene of some jazz, and I know I've said this before but I need to find a local that escorts music, real music, the one everyone abandoned a couple years ago for some superficial money-maker teenagers singing the same love songs with a different letter composition, but if you were to analyse each and every pop hit in the last year, you'd realise they're all saying the same things, with the same voice and represented by the same production companies, the only thing that parcels them is who's making more money for being the best of the worst. You really can't disagree with me on this one, even if you feel that one of those pop stars has changed your lives or some crap like that, you know they haven't. I mean only because they're saying what you wish some lousy panned boy in your school would say to you, doesn't mean they're any good, they're commercial only trying to buy your love, not caress it.

I moved around Chicago that night, I headed to the South Loop when I felt the North had nothing else to offer after I'd gone by the border of the Chicago River which just caught up with me in the Near North Side. I'd heard before that it's the only river that flows backwards so I thought I wanted to take a look at that, even though at night, there wasn't anything to notice because, for once, no light was bright enough to clear the hollow inside a river. The moment I threw some raw pages I had in my bag, the effect made me reconsider and patronise this river for driving all that which I might've felt somewhere that contradicts all forces. I found it romantic not knowing where all those words would end, bypassing the fact that they'd eventually disperse and that science would take its course, and nobody would ever be able to read them, they'd be completely disintegrating as if they'd never been written, and they'd just been an accident that flew away and flooded in the wrong river. I found it quite maudlin even for me to be thinking about this as I threw more pages in, not even caring about the damage they could eventually bring if I continued. I was bored as hell, I felt like I'd been walking all of Western Avenue all night *ad nauseam* and it wasn't even ten o'clock, or at least that's what I reckoned. The city itself isn't romantic, I don't believe in romance if provoked by a materialistic erection. I am saying this after have only seen what someone lost would see; attractions to feel identified with the unknown space encountered, that in my case is Chicago for me. The smells were threatening, humiliating any perverse faeces of any sort, they were contradicting depending on where you strolled. The sensations I felt were entrancing, like I'd been put under a spell as the scars in the vehicles that raced beside me hypnotised my shoelaces to coil behind.

That's when I met her, on the pavement on the other side of the road from where I was standing near the river. I noticed her faintly before I crossed the road, but the same way I noticed half of the people around her. I was walking with my head down when the crossroad figure of a man walking turned green over to the other side. I hadn't really noticed her though; I was too exhausted to, but eventually, I did because she made sure someone noticed her when she wanted. I don't remember much of what I saw until I saw her and her playful devilish smile which contradicted all herself. I hadn't met her then, I'd just seen her and not even my prejudices were up to standard to what she later represented. I remember once I was on the other side to start walking uptown because before in the park, I ran into a woman who instructed me how to get to Barns and Novels, and advised me that they were going to close soon, so with that in my mind, I ended up where I was. She stopped me, like any devil would, before sending a fraud priest to hell disguised in a choirboy's ensemble. She asked me where I was going, I don't remember her exact words but I reminisce they were something like that, I had ignored her at first, not on purpose though I just hadn't considered she was talking to me and I was too busy repeating the directions the old lady gave me over in my head, like wooden horses in the merry-go-round of La Rochelle.

I'm initially writing this in the past tense because I find it easier to write about it now than last night. I didn't know then I'd be feeling this way and it would've been a waste to tell you my superstitions without having dealt with them before, I also didn't have much time to sit down and pour my thoughts out if my glass was continuously being served with French burgundy wine draped by a corset that read *Châteauneuf-du-Pape Pierre Andre* in a strawberry red, as its subtle flavour. She's staring back at me as I'm writing these words, from the other end of the sofa covered in a borrowed blanket reading *On the road* which she pulled out from my bag a couple of minutes ago to entertain herself. She moaned I wasn't paying enough attention to her, and now she's with Sal and Dean driving through route 66 not for entertainment because I notice her underlining and she's working, and I don't say anything and continue typing all of these letters racing one another to see which one makes it to the full stop first. You don't need instructions right now; this isn't a manual on how to read and especially not a map as where to know where we are at this point, this really is the only opportunity I'm giving you of knowing who the person behind these typing hands is.

I'd never met someone like her, during my seventeen years, I've met plenty of people, but this time, she is surprisingly someone I'd never come across with—she's the shooting star we all wish to all the other stars. I mean no one has ever stopped me in the streets and asked me where I was headed, and later on insist on taking me out for a spicy margarita. I denied the first two times, and explained to her that I had to go to Barns and Novels. She told me she would take me there herself personally tomorrow morning, but right now, I had to try a spicy margarita if it was the last thing I did in Chicago. I remembered on one of those trips my parents and I did to New York a couple of winters ago, they used to take my brother and I to this bar named Bar Six on 6th Avenue. I'd always wanted to try one. I hadn't told her too much about myself you know—she didn't ask either and so neither did I, but she sat me down on the terrace of this tapas restaurant, and ordered a couple of things in Spanish which I didn't understand, but nodded every time the waitress asked me something, most of the time she just wanted to refill our glasses. I guess this was her way of convincing me to go drink a spicy margarita with her. I felt crooked, as if I'd been a spectator of my own Truman show, it made me mad—irate for that matter, it made me not want to sit with her and smile. I felt like she pitied me, like she felt she had something great to offer to someone so misplaced. It was strange, spontaneous and distracting at first, it's always odd when someone you've never seen stops you in the street and insists on having a drink with you—we normally interpret it as a perversion. It's beautiful and frail if read in a Scott Fitzgerald novel but sceptical and tempting if devoted personally to you. She started talking about herself, where she came from, how old she was, what she was doing and her name, all those things she thought I might've been interested in but I didn't care about one bit. That's when I started noticing the drawing of her face, between the blabbering she was giving me I had time to actually know who she was, where she came from and all that nonsense she was giving me in such hyperbolic detail to sound convincing. I met her by paying attention right where she was distracting me from looking. She had a bony structured face as if her cheekbones had been grinded with a spear in order to carve her face just for her, like one of Policleto's sculptures portraying mythological goddesses such as Athena and Aphrodite combined. But it wasn't at all the shape of her face that made her who she was, she had these brown dark eyes as if they were trying to cover an image, which brought out a semicolon on the edges, the same way tears do, only she had no trace of any. Her stare was magnetic, it really ate me up because even though it wasn't pure like she wanted it to seem, it was that moonless night she kept for herself every time she blinked her eyes, which started dominating me. You have to understand this one thing: It's not that eyes are a poet's favourite thing to romanticise about, but you have to understand if a poet looks into your eyes, it's precisely because they're not eyes.

I remember in slight episodes how after a couple of small plates covered by different types of foods she constantly forced me to try, we left leaving a two-dollar bill tip. We walked around the streets, she held with a leash talking about politics as she moaned and demurred of the injustice of our inability to vote. She told me how she wanted to study medicine but wasn't ready to surrender herself to anyone that wasn't herself even if it was her vocational desire. She spoke about freedom and how she was tired of Chicago, she mentioned Europe, constantly dreaming about Spain. Her dreams shaped cities like Madrid and Barcelona, and men with dark eyes and brutal spikes in their faces that trembled lines as they joined their hair. She explained how being a model was an accident and it'd never been what she wanted, in fact, she repeatedly condescended superficiality and the importance this generation has given to false images, I could see how much that matter had touched her so I didn't dare ask how she'd become a model—sometimes it's easier to ignore details that'll sink in someone's skin, not like wounds but worse, as unbearable memories. We then went on about literature and art; we stargazed about going to visit the MoMa and the interior isolated world that resided in The New Museum, we imagined walking up the Met steps to visit Greece and Egypt at a lower cost, even past travel to the Renaissance. I asked her to come with me but she told me that right now wasn't the right time to leave Chicago because she'd recently fallen in love and even though I wanted her to so desperately to accompany me, I understood without ever understanding who'd give New York up for love. She then rambled on about her brother and how she'd forgotten she had arranged to see him tonight. She told me he lived in New York, and worked in Wall Street like all the wolves that howled with fine women and expensive alcohol, as well as covered their fur with a full moon that felt like silk and fur. She spoke very highly of him, and how close they'd been since little kids—she hurried me out of the alleys that'd so fondly adopted us, we were orphans not of our parents, but of our past lovers who'd arranged to create cities like these to compensate their rejections.

We went to look for a cab and headed to ermm…uh-mmm, Hubbard St, I think it was, she told the taxi driver in her faint angelical tone. That's where she had told her brother to meet her, in the ride she explained that they should've been twins, only he came out one week earlier—I wondered how that happened for I found it strange. She derived from the subject with no hesitation so I didn't ask anything more, she then went on about how we were going to her favourite Jazz Club in the city and that if I loved Jazz the way I told her I did, I was going to love it there. We talked about Bepop

165

and Charlie Parker as we waited to be let inside, behind a cue of retired brokers and their wives, ads of Cartier. I felt fortunate to have met someone so eager to show me all I was missing out on because of introversion. She lived at a pace not many could be able to keep up with, she was a madwoman in a madman world, the *New Yorker* could've given a review about her without having to read her, showing her off with the most ace adjectives in red salient bans to describe her; 'She's brilliant', 'An outraging delicacy of Satan herself', 'Mesmerising', 'An Dynosian vision' and so on, covered all over the newspapers. I remember once in the Jazz club, which ironically was called 'Andy's Jazz Club'—I remember concretely this because I thought about it for a while, I didn't talk about Andy with her. It was a night to talk about what gave us life, not what tore it away. We were sat at the bar in those uncomfortable high stools and she'd ordered two glasses of the French wine I told you about before, and she'd not quit staring right into my eyes when we spoke. We started speaking about what I was doing in Chicago and all the lousy things you already know, I felt like she enjoyed interrogating me, and for the first time, I liked having a chance to answer. Once in a while maybe, she'd wrap her hair behind her ears as if tucking it into bed, or she'd turn her head sideways to see her surrounding like an instinctive animal before clawing its prey to not let it run away, and even then I felt like she was still only looking at me. Not in a romantic, seductive way—not at all, not even in a menacing way either, she just simply made me feel like she was interested not only in what my mouth had to say, but what I could say without it. She sort of reminded me of the stewardess I told you about in the train. They both had a similar particular incandescence of pureness revolving on the sidewalk of their faces, only hers hadn't been conceived, she enthralled it through the darkness that hankered inside her.

She gave me a sense of life I had always rejected as fictional due to all those desperate idiotic cries of attention that built up that false happiness that tangoed on the screens around me. In her, I sensed that happiness my family, concretely my father, had always denied me with, and with which I had so gladly collaborated to make real. She had madness in her, a madness to be alive in every breath she could take as if the next was going to escape from her. It was something that pulled her to the edge of a suspicious adrenaline I so envied. After a drink or two, she had me talking about my dreams and what I felt in that exact instant gifted by a lustrous rune of a burgundy wine. She even got me talking about love, and what, in any world, it would mean to me. Some might've thought we were wild at that point, that we portrayed the typical arrogant behaviour of feminine hormonal teenagers who only cared about themselves and their overrated felicity under the influence of alcohol. We were two girls screaming and swaying, hustling, jittering whirling, boogieing and rocking with passion in every one of our desultory gestures, we were the jazz in a New Orleans railway station. We were those shooting stars people kiss under, not knowing it's just two waltzing girls drunk on wine.

We had an advantage: we could not give a damn about the world and everything would be okay because differently to them, we haven't restricted ourselves because that's what maturity is underlined for a 'perfected condition'; 'a person who has attained the age of maturity as specified by law'. We aren't children anymore, and being adults isn't choice, because once you've seen the world, once you've read as many books as you possibly can and you've actually enjoyed them in order to read them again, once you've humiliated all your dreams by accomplishing them, and you've seen the world with texture and not from your grandparents' binoculars that you found stashed in a basement—you have a choice of living still only independently to prove yourself you can do both. It's not about parents, or teachers or even the law and government anymore, it's about what makes you mad and grips you to the bone in a way you have to hold yourself because temptation has been defeated by desirous instincts, you recognise the lust is there even if you turn your back the other way. Not many people this century can recognise anything anymore, not even the fingerprints traced on their clothes. The lust to live is the only sin you'd been sent to heaven for, and that night, we were two sinners in heaven.

I met her wearing red, a summer red dress, considering it was winter, she was a pebble of caviar on a white dish. It covered her breasts enough so they didn't become a playboy campaign ad and it covered her legs to a length she'd be able to attend a Victorian royal wedding, enough to be Shakespeare's Viola. She had long legs, although you couldn't see them through the dress, it was too opaque to but it fitted her as if it'd been designed thinking of her, sometimes the best muses in the fashion industry are perceived the moment they fall asleep. She was elegant because that's the impression she wanted to give; she had a complexity that brought up a resemblance with Gia Carangi. I never said she was beautiful because sometimes saying something like that out loud can condensate all the beauty out. Some might've thought she was the devil that night—only she

167

knew where to hide her Venetian masks too good, she never left herself out of sight. She wore a red flamboyant lipstick (which you might've guessed considering the portfolio I'm giving you of her) that lit her in a way no cigarette with a lighter in hand of a black suit could've ever achieved, she wasn't fire or the sun or any cliché comment contouring the glow she brought upon herself. She simply had a gripping darkness that marked her insane, like a wolf deprived from the moon she wasn't deprived of anything. She didn't need any moons because she wasn't restricted to any lunar philosophy, a night that loathed in the depths of a hollowed sea used to cover herself from the lies of what happiness looks like: a fondant of white chocolate, a casket crowded with competing shades of pink roses and a sunrise. She portrayed a madness of happiness I had never seen pictured in any lousy magazine. It's not that she had light in her or darkness, it simply was she didn't need to be compared with such superficial bearings, because once you lust for life the way she did, you become simply what you want to be and she did that. That's why not even me with my attempt of a poetic description of what she made me feel is enough, you ought to meet her to know what she is. We ended up in our lingerie at a strip club after that, at least that's what the Polaroids on the table in front of us steer.

Truth is, we became really good friends, in one night, I had the best night in a city I'd never been with a woman I'd only seen in dreams that weren't mine under the influence of a red velvet wine I'd never tasted—but was explained to never taste again but listen to instead, like a vacant seashell disowned by the sea at shore where a million cries are confused for a Chopin crescendo. I saw colours I'd never mixed in art school and they produced hallucinations no drug could ever attain to. The jazz didn't play around us, but with us, as the saxophone's notes embraced us, seduced us like a snake does its prey tangling us in the jungle of blues. The night felt like a year at last regained jubilation, for I had just stepped my foot in hell flown by divinity herself. I had finally caught up with my desires as well as endorsed the madness of living. To be honest, for the first time, I felt like I could look at that distorted face usually provoked by the watery mosaic in my eyes every time I tried to stare at her. I could look at her with the same courage I had last night and tell her what I want to hear. It's my eyes that have a certain glow after I pull them from the toilet seat, for the first time, I can see autumn in them and the redness surrounding my eyes doesn't blame tears or discontent but proof of having choked by rejected food too late, by someone who's famishing for an image that belongs to her. The truth is she held my hair last night when I felt the world upon me in slices of epicurean covet, and in that bathroom at the strip club in our lingerie, the lightning focused on the scratched amaranthine cast that made the in between of the bathroom tiles flood with the stains my eyes had lost, once gotten it all out from my chest to a stranger I'd just met. I remember we sat there for a while, with the bathroom door closed and a queue of a dozen ladies eager to do the same thing, pounding on the door so we heard they were waiting, like cries from lost souls driven by the current of the river Styx.

We didn't move from there, we hadn't been spiked or drugged or any possible thing you might be thinking of right now as an excuse to what we did, what I did, but the thing is, there isn't. For the first time, the most romantic place for me, that I could think of right now was that bathroom with its lightning and my new friend hugging me as we unburdened anything we had in mind due to the influence of the innovating tender alcohol. I didn't regret ending up there, I'd been wanting to get my clothes off ever since I got on the train from Los Angeles, I've always felt of nudity as a dominance instead of a vulnerability. We had many conversations that night as intellectuals from different generations and backgrounds, the only difference we had with those who didn't end their nights half-naked in bathrooms like this was that we didn't need a title to feel like ones, we weren't as superficial as all those intellectuals who make it their life mission to be considered as so in the most snooty way as possible to enter a high society elite of some kind—who's only motivation is being read as an 'intellectual'.

We had so many conversations, we ended up walking with the sunrise as our candy-coloured shadow trying to find her apartment in one of the streets we hadn't gotten lost in, and that's really where we found it and how we ended where we are. It's curious though, that half of that night I had written on napkins from a borrowed pen from the bartender who apparently was friends with her. She made it obvious she had read all of my notes as they'd been partially covered with her red lip smack signature all over them, completely humiliating the ink. The napkin also had the initials of Andy's Jazz Club entitled at the top and bottom of the small squared personalised wipe. Either way, spontaneity like that can only and should really only be explained to an audience like that, if not what is left of it but a solitary fantasy. Not even a writer writing to entrance its reader in a tremendous murder that is a lie, is capable of living up to such expectations that the truth can sometimes handle without being planned. Don't be alarmed at how rushed I've began to write, I just feel there are so many things I want to say, to write down, and once you're in the city, you become the city and so do the pages once they're crumbled up as skylines that need no defined contoured lines.

"…I stumbled after as I've been doing all my life after people who interest me, because the only people for me are the mad ones, the ones who are mad to live, mad to talk, mad to be saved, desirous of everything at the same time, the ones who never yawn or say a commonplace thing, but burn, burn, burn like fabulous yellow roman candles exploding like spiders across the stars and in the middle you see the blue centre light pop and everybody goes 'Awww!' "

—Jack Kerouac
On the Road, 1957

Seq. 23 Ext. Chicago Union Station

"I've got to get a cab to Chicago Union Station," I say as I put down my laptop and look at her, that's still reading *On the Road* with eyes tempted to never part from its written lining.

"Uh…yeah, sure," she says, with no sign of interest.

I start looking around for some appropriate clothes that won't bring me too much attention as the ones I'm wearing now, which really only involve a transparent white blouse her brother probably lent me.

"Can I borrow something from your wardrobe?" I ask, headed towards the wardrobe which I honestly don't even know if actually belongs to her, as well as this place. It's like a baronial palace in ruins, decorated with expensive attire to cover its aging, like it'd been given Botox.

"Sure, get anything you want—but why are you in such a hurry?" she asks, amused but still shows no sign of interest as to what is going on around her.

"I have that train to catch I told you about," I say as I put on one of her shirts and grab one of her skirts because I find no trousers between the disaster of amounted smelly socks and dirty underwear, as well as smudged dresses and colourful blouses all shattered around the room like the sun's light through the bay windows.

"Oh yeah, you're still going to New York?" she asks as she inclines her head backwards to look at me upside down from where she's seated.

"Well, where do you expect me to go?" I say ironically.

"I don't know, yesterday you were so on about going to Barns and Novels because you needed to buy a book," she says. "And I promised to take you there, remember?"

"I know, it's just eight am and I've got the train at noon; I don't even know where we are right now!" I shriek of complaint and exhaustion.

"Well, now that you say so," she says, inclined to become alarmed. "It's eight am?" she asks in a rave. "I've got to get running to the interview with the model agent I told you about last night, the one with the dorky glasses," she says, striking out of the sofa as the book she was reading fly's over my head and she starts racing through the room for something to cover all those red bluish bruises she refers to as 'experimental art tattoos'.

"You're going to do great," I say as I lie down on the Chesterfield sofa again.

"That's if I get in time, thank you so much for waking me up," she says, in slender arouse. "I'm loving the book by the way, who would've ever thought I'd fall in love with a writer and enjoy reading at the same time," she says, with the devilish smirk she'd give the bartender last night so he'd give us a discount of some sort, because I can't remember wasting a lot of money. I barely got any anyways. I just look at her as I snuggle to find a comfortable pose to fall asleep in again, trying to remember if it was her that bribed the bartender or I that bribed her brother in order to get all those free drinks.

"Weren't you the one that was hustling like a businessman a second ago?" she asks, confused at my brake to evacuate as she throws the damp towel she used last night to sterile the makeup off her face.

"I realised, I've actually got till noon," I say. "At what time does your interview finish?" I ask her as I contemplate her exhilarant rushing. She asks me if I'd like a coffee as she dashes in front of me like a children's cartoon applying all the basic make up she neglected when we arrived last night, to look natural and seem undamaged. Covering any sign of last night in her under eyes, luring her cheek bones with glows of bronze that don't belong to her and a blush shade on her lips humiliating any rosewood wine had ever swam in them first. She'd miraculously envisaged an actress in her first day of shooting after a rough night with her producer at his office.

"I'll be back at noon or later," she says, wrapping her face into a birthday present.

"I'll be waiting," I say, and I mean it. I didn't need New York anymore, I already found it. If New York isn't New York when I arrive, after meeting her it simply means I can either never come back again or bring her with me so it'd be the same. I try to remember where her brother left, I try to even remember his face— but fail consistently to do so.

"Listen to me, I don't want to see you here when I get back," she says, trying to get me to look at her to approve of the seriousness in her tone, but I just lay down admiring her dedication to herself before donating herself to companies that plotted to obtain her self-doubt, if you were lucky enough to find any in her. She was a confident woman who was mad to be alive in such restricted conditions. I fell asleep with a light kiss on my forehead to not blemish the colour away from her lips, and I saw her body slowly exit silently with movement, as if she'd just had a run in with someone she quite didn't feel like to salute. She soon became blurry curved lines merging into a black closing door, and I laid there alone looking for a boy I wanted to dream of in order to remember. I felt like last night had been a Hunter S Thomson novel such as *Fear and Loathing in Las Vegas*.

My interview finishes at 13.00 because the bloody model agent wants to have lunch with me to talk about the specifics; I think I got it this time! I don't want to see you here laid down in a soundless sleep when I get back. I'm not going to be the one buying you another train ticket. Once you've published all those pages I found in your bag—and you've told the world all about me from my lip smack signatures on Andy's' Jazz Club napkins—I'll come meet you in New York for some coffee, even though I know you don't like coffee you will at this place. I'm sorry this fax can't be longer—I've got to hurry; they want to get some more shots!

Lilou

I never told her my name, but as I've said countless of times, questions always arise with unresolved identities, and that's what I was: an unresolved identity, an unidentified dream and an unrecognisable vision. The fax machine's noise is what woke me up, I was sure she'd done it on purpose on right the appropriate time, so I'd have the advantage of the growling and qualm that'd keep me longer in there, before I'd walk out of that apartment or hotel bedroom. I still hadn't quite deciphered where we'd ended. I felt refreshed for once, which really surprised me given the posterior circumstances of a heavy headache due to all the wine ingested and the endearing dancing, and endless last night promenade of having to keep my body up to pace with the taught mechanism my legs had been instructed of whatever the circumstance to always place one leg in front of the other to keep me walking, even at times when I believed it not to be possible. Thinking about it now, sat down in the chesterfield sofa I've grown so fond of, I realise she reminded me of myself, it was as if she was put here to remind me of who I really am, not only a figure who craves and lives off writing, the wonders and cataclysm that surround me but everything else. The urge to burn, shatter, scream, whirl and waltz. Do what you have to do but make sure you go mad about it, and puke it to the world, that's the only thing you owe anybody, yourself, to explode abstractions such as love and pain, and all those factors that complete oneself, or so say the physicians, whether it's Freud about dreams and desires or Maslow and Jung, even the philosophers like Schopenhauer, Chomsky and Nietzsche. I mean even Dali, Ernst, Picasso and Kush weren't surreal artists, they were real artists. They saw us before we saw ourselves. Happiness isn't something delirious, passion is, passion to fly to the moon in the first rocket and actually believe to find cheese up there in order bring back down, to find a rose in the brightness of a star and rip each petal with one simple question 'Does she love me, does she not?' I feel like I should be scribbling all of these thoughts on her walls instead of in the pages my laptop later executes once no more space is left. Everything had always seemed so ordinary, especially if you believe it is, the most triggering story, the most gravitating characters are those who create themselves on their own in a novel written by someone who isn't them. I've always felt as if every event in my life was somewhat backed up by a bullet point like in one of those lists where you mark your future plans, your favourite movies, your favourite books, who you've kissed all in an order standardised by a dead man. I just had to get all the clouds from my head and drain them into a rain that'll cover those pages, which soon will be out of order.

I know I'm typing like a madman, and you're probably shaking, maybe you feel like it's hard to catch up with what I'm saying or feeling at this point but I mean this is how things happen in the hustling cities, taxis don't stop for all of us waiting, people don't mind if you're trying to sleep in the subway, they've got to get their conference call ready, coffee shops aren't empty at seven in the morning and the streets stuffed with people are reconsidered to be not streets but boiling bubbles in an Italian saucepan cooking pasta because even in the kitchens, the sweat floods through the pipes like wasted water from costumers who didn't chug it all up. Everything goes fast because there is really no time in cities like these; their watches are pointed at each hour with adrenaline. Maybe you feel like I'm rushing my voyage now with what I'm writing, making it all sound exhilarating. I just can't stop. I've been dining Eva's red apple, which I stole from a street market stand, and now I can't tell you what I'm doing without making it sound unprofessional or unrealistic. I'm also not adapted to this lifestyle in order to keep up with it, before I left her home, I painted my lips same shade she did and left a trace mark on the fax she sent me so she'd know I received it when she got back. I didn't have to say anything else; we would meet. I'm just infatuated by the fact that I'm ambling down another unknown street looking for a cab to take me to Chicago Union Station. Whilst I try to gain the consciousness that fired itself the moment I ignored it last night, I am hustling now. I should be asking for directions but my gut tells me I'm wandering in the right direction where for the first time my lack of orientation isn't an issue but an advantage.

So here I was headed, once again, to an aim I was unsure I actually wanted to achieve, I was pointing at a diana hoping I'd miss. Trembling sweat went down the edges of my head, pouring faintly, but pouring. It was all my imagination that led me to these extents of probation, I knew somehow along the way I'd forget why I left in the first place. I was glad I was conscious about these facts, but I was torn apart by how I wish they hadn't been proven. I wanted to stay and I wanted to leave, I've never felt like this anywhere. The trip from Chicago to New York was estimated to last another 15 hours, I wasn't sure I could survive without shambling in remorse for a place to call mine. I know how this may sound and how you may be exhausted of hearing me complain so much about situations I've knowingly provoked—but you can't image the apathy I feel right now to go anywhere really. If I were to stay, I doubt I would go back to Lilou's apartment anyway, I'd just dwell like I did yesterday before I tripped over with her heartbeat attached to the origins of the ground. I want to remember more about last night, and even though I try and I try, I can't. It's all a sugar rush. I get in the cab I called with my hanging hand in heights of the road and requested to go to the station after all this absurd procrastination. As I look out of the window for the first time without letting my exhaustion distract me, I recognise the city, and the sliding images of the people walking, running, holding their children's hands so they don't run off to the middle of the road, the one's on their phone and the other's drinking coffee or trying to maintain a balance between the excess of bags in both their hands from shops like Versace and Gucci. I recognise the stores and the restaurants, and the hallowed night clubs dimmed by the light of day, as well as the cars dashing past my taxi—everyone going somewhere, even the buildings and all the economic materialism are a motion. She was a movement, our camaraderie a kinetic reaction. I realise I recognise it all because I saw it in her eyes last night when we spoke about fugitives and the Beat Generation as well as the Lost one, about becoming our heroes, and being the modern version of a Bonnie and Clyde only with different principals. This was ours, and we were the ongoing. We are supposed to humiliate those who've chained us to the idea that there's a possibility of such a thing as failure. I'll run and run towards the fire before soaking in split tears that don't belong to me, our tears never belong to us or to those who initiated them—our tears are the only sign of freedom we get but we have pictured as weakness. I was in the Chicago Union Station once again, only this time, I was completely alone—without Marie or her father, who I'd completely forgotten about. I hoped she was okay and doing well. I also thought about Anthony, I remember him because he'd been a reverie difficult to admit. Here I was, here we are and here it's all going to stop going very far.

This wasn't a spiritual prep talk; you know me too well to know that by now. At least, I hope you do. You know what happens when I ramble on so much about what's on my mind; it basically is that I'm trying to distract myself once again from taking a step. Oh, how tired am I of always doing the same thing to you, of making you think I don't care when I actually do, that everything I am hiding is simple: I love madness but I don't want to seem insane in the sense of a psychotic fever or a raven in my head. Yesterday, I realised this, and I know I've said I realised a lot of things since last night which makes everything seem stenographed in advance as if I was making it up, but it's true that once you meet someone—once you fall in love with something other than love and yourself, you begin to grow a notion of your surrounding that you would've never spotted if you hadn't left your guard down. I'm not only talking about Lilou at this point—I know you think I am, because I've led you onto thinking so, that's what I'm trying to remember from last night so I can actually write it down as reality and not some plenary fiction.

Seq. 24 Int. Another Train

I didn't want to be there when she came back. I did have inclinatory thoughts of contradicting her whole fax and surprising her, but I knew she wouldn't have considered it an act of love because if I actually loved her as much as I've said I do—I would've left because her believing in me should've been enough as to simply go. I knew she'd come visit me in New York, at least I hope so. I need more money so probably when I got to New York, I'd have to look up this old friend of mine I met when my family and I went in December. See if maybe he'd help me get a loose job and find me some cheap place to stay. I was sprawling all these ideas because I wanted to install myself there, I was planning on staying there all my life. I know how I said I would come back to LA, but I know I'm not. Not only because the voyage would be exhausting and the destination wouldn't be as lucrative but because I'd already left. Zeus didn't put eyes in our backs because he knew there wasn't anything to see once you turned your back. If I was going anywhere that wasn't New York, it'd probably be Canada or I'd probably consider taking Lilou to Spain, I've never been to Spain. Maybe we could even go around Europe, go to Paris and track down Hemmingway and Fitzgerald's abiding steps. I'd always have to stay low on the radar, just in case my father or even Uncle Lloyd came looking for me, or even worse, my mother, although I'm not too worried about them.

Here I was again, chained down murmuring about dreams to a reflection smashed by outsider catalogued views. As typically in a train that has no doors, my words are interrupted by a garrulous woman on the other side telling her friend on the phone about her chronologically planned schemes, and here I was trying not to get too caught up by those incredulous spoiled anecdotes. I no longer had one of those safe cabins I'd had the privilege of travelling in to come to Chicago. I was covered by plebeian couture not over my selfless body but clinging around the space that so gallantly wanted to haggard this ego. I couldn't think of anyone but myself right now, my vanity was astute as to interfere in one of my most fragile moments. I have been writing unceasingly since I began this route home and now I can't imagine a moment where I'll be able to stop. Who am I to say what we need and what it is we desire, the same as all of you, I am a nobody telling her story, but we're all interested in each other's stories—it makes us feel less lonely. Here I am, here this whole book is writing itself to tell you stories about me, because at the end of the day, when you've got nothing, the only thing you can think about is being told a story—because it's the only thing that can warm you in a cold like this. Yes—I am that girl, the one with not a care in the world that waltz across the skies, fantasising she's a wonder and explodes as a snowflake once the night dies. It might not be the adequate time to tell you this, but it never really is the adequate time to tell anybody anything anymore, there's always going to be a haphazard intrusion no one can back off. We all like reading something we can empathise with, someone in there we can espy or desire—that's why in this book, in these pieces of paper smeared with all my rhapsodies out of tune, I want you to recognise with the reality of your desires, to pipe dream awake.

I can feel this peculiar passion in me, one I've never felt before. I know how this is going to sound but I've evolved, I've grown—I've changed. I've found my Monsignor Darcy in the rails of this train, in the voices of my characters who've appeared to greet me, in the letters I've written with all my hateful repressions and all my love for beauty, in the temperaments of my soul, in the music and the wine, I might even be an oenophile now…in the singularities of life which have applauded at each step of mine. I feel, I feel oh, so alive that I could run to the city and leave the train behind. But these are just the words who compel one another when they know I can't do it myself. I sometimes feel like I am too mad to be loved by one, I mean after all, Alice did leave the mad hatter for the conformism of a reality that expected her. I even feel it's impossible for me to love someone, to even have a mere recognition of what loving someone means and imposes—I love too much, not only people but pains, places and gestures. I'm too much in love with the idea of love and my mad soul as the world around me to love someone without it being an infatuation or a momentarily obsession even as a convenience of their soul for my inspiration, and it all always goes back to where we all hide at night when we hear the moon howling for despair or the rivers colliding in the parks, for the necessity of being caressed by someone other than your skin. I'm sorry if I always end up in the same topic, that topic we all like talking about at fanciful dinners or over the phone when we should be busy doing other things, and I'm sorry I can't stop gripping at it as my own, as if it only depended on me, where the 'whether to be or not to be' is really just to love or not to love, that is the question. Truth is, we're always asking so many questions, I mean how is love a question or an answer—I didn't know our emotions were taking SATS without our permission, I'm sure mine would fail. I only know that in love, you will never agree and that is what will make it stronger, only if you can accept the love you are giving will never be the same love you'll receive but it will still be love. It sounds easy but it's not, I bet it's not. Unfortunately we have been created to destroy and love is our salvation, and when we feel we are nearly saved in one way or another we distance ourselves from that love, to auto-destroy ourselves again, because it is the only thing we really know how to do.

Here is where I leave my bold pen; every time I look at it, it reminds me about LA, I remember my father and Lloyd, and all the adults who were ever significant in my life in order to be talking about them this instant. I leave the pen on the desk and close the booklet I've been writing in because I don't seem to feel inspired, but that doesn't stop the urge of having to write everything down. I want to concentrate on the views outdoors as well as on the noise indoors—the woman snoring after hanging up the phone, the old man thronged reading Noam Chomsky as he falls asleep, and snorts in order to breathe properly, the officer going around asking for tickets and the family of three furtive children shrieking, jolting from one side to the other, all trembling in hype around as their mother tries to clasp them to the seat and keep them quiet, because she feels embarrassed that we're all looking at her when she shouldn't. They're not disturbing me. I leer out of the window again, only this time, I intend on fixating my mind in the construction of the window glass—I always wondered if this looking glass could take me elsewhere if my imagination hadn't been stolen by the nearing adulthood. I didn't know what the route was going to be back home, what places it was going to go through, not even if there'd be any stops or the estimated time till I got there. I just knew that when I got there, I would and that was about it, it'd be my American movie where I'd be at Central Station probably doing a couple of turns to adjust to the vitality of the aureate sun-flowered space around me, probably glare at the clock in the middle a couple of times, as I'd accept time for the first time. I didn't want to imagine my arrival too much, I knew I could get my hopes up and I didn't want to. I was tempted in this instant to approach somebody and ask them how long the ride was going to take, or even if we were going to go through Michigan, I don't know why but I wanted to go through London and Ontario—for some reason, I felt like I'd be able to see the Niagara Falls from this same window if we were ever to go through London. I felt my lips mouthing what I was thinking, I couldn't prevent it—I had to ask someone.

You might've thought I would've asked someone after all, but I didn't, the reasons being because, for once, I didn't want to talk to anyone, I didn't need someone talking back to me. I just wanted to fall asleep, at least for a while and remember at least not only yesterday's hallucinatory glares but find the detailed ones. I couldn't help but ask myself continuously if I had fallen in love, had I lost all my imagination to someone's soul I couldn't even phantom about? Was inspiration taking advantage of my vulnerability for a personage I furnished with all my senses, had I been undertaken by the principles of somebody else, was I drained out from my mind by someone else's madness? I just look out the window continuously asking myself the same rhetorical questions, hoping they'll serve as a helpful resource. I darned the moment I decided not to go to Barns and Novels, I could've bought something for this ride, although sticking my hands in my pockets now I realise I couldn't have bought the goddamn book anyways, and I'd never steal a book. I should read, I should write I tell myself; it's killing me not to be able to do so. I feel how I am nearing the city even if little time has passed, or so I feel. I look out the window once more, only this time, I don't move my eyes around, I leave my mind blank, my eyes blank, and just sit there glaring, staring, gaping and beaming to the stage that is out there maybe as an emerald's hidden forest; a sweating field piled with wheat and corn, or a vacancy with railways that are stalled, even, maybe, if we were to go through London, Ontario, a bridge to Niagara the closest thing to Elysium—would be the one holding the train's misanthropic composure and drive it somewhere else instead of New York. That wouldn't be ideal, not for me.

I have to survive this book on my own, there's nobody else writing it with me, there's nobody I want to write it about, the only inspiration I have is nothingness, it's the blank white page, that white damn blank page I always talk about, the only one that can make me feel less miserable when I realise I am alone. I am angry now, and I thought feeling at least an emotion would contribute as a medium to cover all these pages. The thing is, I think I've told you everything there really is to know. I can't continue rambling like I have for the last past hour—I reckon it's been an hour. I really have no idea of anything at this point, I just don't want you to think I'm troubled or anything, or fantasise about why I ran away—I mean I might've never told the truth before this book, the thing is, unfortunately, there isn't really a reason. I mean if I were you, I would've questioned myself about it for a while and then accept that what I am writing is, in fact, the only truth there really is to anything. I'd never dare speak these words to someone, I'd never let those I love anywhere near this book—I'd never want them to pity me the same way I pity myself, I wouldn't be able to cope with myself if they knew how deeply hurt I am by them, how they're the main character of all the novel, and how that main character is presented through my own voice is what frightens me. I know I am about to be succumbed into a dream, but I only admit this on paper, for I don't want my consciousness to think I agree on falling asleep, if I accidently whisper it to it.

And the truth is, who in their goddamn mind would be interested in reading what a renegade rebel from the state of California is screaming, not in capital letters because that would draw too much attention, but in minuscule letters so she can be slowly perceived and understood, and not be felt as an outrageous threatening earthquake, as the reaction and screams of a bloody teenage girl in a full moon, *Literally bloody.* Why would anyone, not only care but dare read, what they've been hiding away from all their lives? It's a rhetoric question, so you don't have to worry about me leaving some space under this brick for you to answer it, although maybe you should: only carving your answer with a gentle whisper to the mirror from which the steam will soon condense, the moment you let the words gale in sleepy sound waves that once felt in the mirror, clouds crack.

I'm stuck again.

"He adored New York City. He idolised it all out of proportion...no, make that: he—he romanticised it all out of proportion. Yeah. To him, no matter what the season was, this was still a town that existed in black and white, and pulsated to the great tunes of George Gershwin.

Uh, no let me start this over.

'Chapter 1.

He was too romantic about Manhattan, as he was about everything else. He thrived on the hustle bustle of the crowds and the traffic. To him, New York meant beautiful women and street smart guys who seemed to know all the angles...'

Ah, corny, too corny for my taste. Can we...can we try and make it more profound?

'Chapter 1.

He adored New York City. For him, it was a metaphor for the decay of contemporary culture. The same lack of individual integrity that caused so many people to take the easy way out was rapidly turning the town of his dreams in...'

No, that's going to be too preachy. I mean, you know, let's face it, I want to sell some books here.

'Chapter 1.

He adored New York City, although to him it was a metaphor for the decay of contemporary culture. How hard it was to exist in a society desensitised by drugs, loud music, television, crime, garbage...'

Too angry, I don't want to be angry.

183

'**Chapter 1**.
He was as tough and romantic as the city he loved. Behind his black-rimmed glasses was the coiled sexual power of a jungle cat.'

I love this.

'New York was his town, and it always would be."

—Woody Allen
Manhattan, 1979

Seq. 25 Ext. Views of a City

Closely, I felt how I was getting there. I felt it in the ink that raced down the pages and the velocity of the city I'd just woken up to, only I was upset I hadn't dreamed anything—I think it might've been for my lack of sleep, or the conditions I'd just slept in, with my head looking down as all the blood concentrated in my brain and my neck twisted, in order for it to be difficult to decide what way I was looking at. My legs crooked, as my arms. I must've been very exhausted to actually be able to sleep at all. One thing I know is that I'd slept a hell of a long time to be able to see Manhattan rise in front of me. I deduce we must be going through New Jersey. My mother loved New Jersey; she said the city was too loud and if we ever were to move from Los Angeles, it'd be to New Jersey—maybe she's here, in one of the compound grey houses we've just passed by. I have a strange sense of longing, stabbing me in the chest and even though I hate to say things like these, my heart hurts, like it was looking desperately for a gasp of air, as if it'd changed roles with my lungs and for a vast ephemeral second, I had this urge of crying. It's been very long since I cried, and as I feel my agitated heart ache, I visualise how it must look as an image projected in front of me to bear, and I feel tears trying to carve through the crystals in my eyes, dying to get out, but I just won't let them even if I'm also dying for them to get out of the imprisoned state I've got them in. I feel like I can't breathe for a couple of seconds, and even though I'm trying my best to tell you how I'm feeling at this given moment so you can not only read it and think, 'what must be going on' or 'what a nut job, she's so exaggerating' or even how 'she's got anxiety for sure' or whatever your criteria can provide. I don't feel like I'm drowning, it's more like I've been put in my grave, and I am slowly being buried and I can't do anything about it. The thing is, I really want to cry *goddamit* and I can't.

Sometimes I feel like I moan too much and truth is I do, and that's not part of the plan if there ever really is a plan. Sometimes I confuse my book with that waiting room surrounded by people that don't have problems who go to someone to give them some. Sometimes going to the shrink is like going to the supermarket, problems are very often confused with food—they both fill you when you've got nothing to do, when you realise you're alone. Regrettably, I went to the shrink as I've told you before, all because my dear father thought I'd gone insane, but if being insane is a problem, then I think we have a problem. Don't get confused, I apologise for misinterpreting that sometimes I write what I think and other times what I say, and even though it doesn't look like it, there's a great difference. I am not weak; maybe sometimes I get scared that I am, especially when I am alone and I become it—how ironic. I'm just fed up and exhausted, of not being in New York already, sometimes I feel like this voyage has sprung features on me that I'm not familiarised with, I wonder if I'm a bastard child; I doubt it though, I'm as impatient as my mother. The thing is, that I'm about to taste Manhattan instant I arrive to Grand Central Station, even writing those words becomes moonlike craters in my skin. I'm like a little girl that wants her lollipop, that lollipop is sugar when you're a kid, when you're an adolescent, it's sex, and when you're old enough to pay for drinks with your real id and you live a so-called stabilised lifestyle as described in the magazines like *People*, the lollipop is your favourite city, in my case, New York— the candy that tastes, smells, looks, and even sometimes, if you come close and listen, sounds like a Tom Waits in a Coppola. I don't want you to think I need something from you whether it's love or attention, I'm not the outcast kid or the troubled kid or the kid who lost her cousin, the kid whose mother left—I'm not that kid. I'm the kid you don't pity, the kid that doesn't want to feel pitied, because really what is there to pity? I am in New York. You do realise by now I have actually gone mentally mad, for the first time, I'll admit, I think I've lost myself instead of finding me, and even though this might've looked like a soul-searching expedition where I'd find my soul and conscience in some bar in the city, in the eyes of a stranger from the other side of the metro, even under a stone in a park, or worse, down in the sewers where most of our dreams are flushed through a toilet seat—because let's be honest, the place where we dream the most is where we're not supposed to. Now talking about this, I don't remember the last time I went to the bathroom. Either way, I've been doing nothing of those things I'm supposed to do because, well, it's my instinctive way of survival the three great needs: water, food and going to the bathroom. All of this is interrupted by the man in the red coat and the snarling face under the red cap coming towards me from behind, only I see his reflection and get ready for what might be me being thrown out of this train.

"Your ticket, young lady," he demanded in a dominant almost threatening voice as if he'd been the stunt man of some mobster before ending up here. I liked the term he used to refer to me, 'young lady,' it was different from 'kid' or 'babe' as Jovi called me. I could hear him snort in my ear like an angry raging bull, and I really had not a clue where I'd left the goddamn ticket.

"One second, sir," I hesitated as I looked in my bag slowly to irritate him, I knew how my hesitation was leaving me axiomatic.

"You have it or not, kid?" he asked. And there all my illusions went back to hell; he'd just called me kid. I felt like punching him in the face, I've never punched anyone in the face.

"Yeah, can you just wait a minute," I say stressed.

"I ain't got minutes to wait, kid, so I'll do another round in a few minutes—hope you found it by then," he adverts me.

He walks away and I start looking all over my bag for the damn ticket I never bought. I guess I should think fast at this point, I don't think I'd like to be thrown out, I know it's hard to believe they still do this, but, unfortunately, they do. I knew I should've bought the damn ticket, I know I said I did and that I had everything planned but when do you actually say you have everything planned when you don't? All the time, because it's damn normal. The world seems strange from where I'm sitting, and I haven't even seen a quarter of it to know what it really looks like. This is probably my witty chapter, where I tell you all these optimistic things about how miserable your lives are, how miserable my life is and how exceptionally wonderful it is to admit such atrocity that it no longer is miserable but a representation of sagacity. I thought about my girl in Chicago and the brother I didn't remember, I thought about Diane, BD and Jean, and Marie and Andy, especially Andy—I even thought about Anthony, and well, I had to turn on a dramatic song now because the moment was beginning to feel so hasty, so I play *With or Without you* and do that thing of staring out of a window and I really try, I promise I do, I try exceptionally hard to remember them. What I do see is how good I look on the reflection of the window, and there is where I see them, not in my memory—what is that anyways? But I see them in the itch of light in one corner of an eye, between my lips where a smile rises out of wrinkle even though physically I'm not smiling. It's odd how the people we meet become pieces of you, through everything I've seen youth, madness, sex, corruption and solitude—not in order, this isn't a shopping list.

I actually wanted to talk more about sex, but I can't, I mean—I couldn't, and what could I say about it that you don't already know? I mean I guarantee we've all watched porn and had sex already; the most romantic thing about sex is that its emotional under cover but once it's unveiled, once the sheets aren't there anymore, it's gone and that's the only romantic thing about it, it's the facility it has to disappear, to become so fugacious until it's repeated again still under the belief that maybe this time, it'll stick around for a while, the idea of it, the emotionality in it won't only happen in the intimate playground of the darkest shadows of the nights, it'll be there too afterwards—I guess you might've wanted a love story and the truth is, I would've too, they always say the heart wants what it wants; well, I say mine's really horny at this point, I'm not going to be so delicate. Great loves like the ones you all wish for don't last a lifetime, they're ephemeral. Great loves are only great because they're precisely fleeting and Icarian, if they lasted longer, they'd become good, then okay and then they'd vanish like a spoonful of chocolate brownie in a sweating gawking mouth. I'd never want that for us, that's why I'm burning what is left before it goes out in flames by expensive matches we can't afford, and they're so expensive, they're more flammable, meaning the only way to stop it would be with a thunder of rain that'll drown everyone around us, maybe even us. I'd like to live a little longer. A great love like ours can only last two days, two weeks or two months—and if we're lucky, maybe even two years. And that'll be it, you will never be able to marry me because I don't believe in marriage—I'll want to continue rolling under the fires that launch up to the sky at night and you'll want to join me, but I know, you see, someday in between all that you'll want to stop and take a break on top of a rock or under the shade, and drink some wine and forget you ever saw it in me. And you'll break my heart and I can't let you break my heart. I'll continue strolling, and if you do so too, maybe we'll meet again and you'll fall in love with me again—I know I won't because I'll already be. And that is what love really is for someone who's never been in love, a lie. This isn't at all specific, I know I'm probably thinking of someone and even though I'd love to tell you who it is, I can't because I don't remember. That's what I've been trying to tell you, that's the blurry scene of my Chicago mid*winter* night dream.

And yes, there probably, most certainly is something poetic in what I want to say and maybe that doesn't prove my feelings as real but as delusional as some mere infatuation because what does a writer like me really know about love? Everything written on paper is not an act of love but a manipulation, why I'm manipulating I don't know yet—it may be because I'm looking for provocation, not a sexual one, don't worry I don't like getting strangers to bed, unless it's a stranger that knows how to stop being one. I just know, the moment I truly fall in love, and get back to this paragraph and read it, I'll laugh at myself for how naïve I was of thinking that I'd rather light a fire for anyone else, even for only myself, but him.

Now, I should be worrying about the ticket, but I can't, because I know I don't have it so it's not like I can really look for something that's not there anymore, I just have to hide somewhere. I think of the bathroom, but I know I'll have to come out someday. Let's forget for a second I am in this train, let's forget I've written 139 pages by now and let's forget that this isn't an autobiography, let's interpret it as a movie I'm about to fast forward, for I can't stand any longer to be supressed in the same narrative. I finally am in New York. You must be thinking I'm starting to give up, my chapters are shorter, my sentences are railing away and sincerely I am exhausted.

Seq. 26 Ext. The Big Apple

Let's start from the beginning. After everything that I've just written, all these pages, all these paragraphs, and sentences and words that are just continuously piling one over the other as if this book would become an orgy of Ts and Us, and all their cousins. All these pages that have incited a temptation of slitting your throats and squirm with your blood over these pages or on the other hand maybe, imbibe an antique memorable French wine's stepped on tears, down your throat, whilst you slice textures of Serrano ham and goat cheese, and apply them on a board which you later take to your room or to the terrace, where you accommodate and continue reading whilst you take a bite of this and a bite of that, and then a couple of sequential sips from the aphrodisiac wine—personally, that's what I would do. All of this gourmet imagery is making me feel tremendously edacious, and I feel like getting drunk on cheap booze from someplace down the streams of the city.

I did what I said I wasn't going to do, *goddammit*, I am a scoundrel! I never keep my word, not even when, supposedly, it'll pay the rent if I do, I'll have glory or even be able to afford an apartment in Manhattan that corners with the showcase of Victoria Secret or Calvin Klein, just in case some models saunter by. The thing is, that I've talked too much about my life and with too much detail, solidarity, somehow, has caught up with my principles, leaving me stripped. This time, I've really done it, I've really given you characters to taste, given you the chance to feast upon miseries that don't belong to you. But anyways, all of that doesn't matter anymore, I am in New York, finally, I am in the city, to which's only fit description it needs is the one it gives itself once you're in it, once you see it. What am I going to tell you! I am not an advert of some travelling agency; I'm just a teenager writing a book with my left hand, the right one's only good to hold the water pistol under my escritoire, just in case some stupidity goes through my mind and I have to shoot a neuron before it seduces the rest, and we all know what happens if a pretentious conceited guy (yeah, I think guy's alright) seduces all of the women; they completely faze and do everything he wants. If you're one of those, I'm not trying to offend you for that matter, I actually don't think I am, and anyways, the instant you read this, you'll deny it, even though your friends always tell you so but they probably do so too. Well, and if you're a boy and you're reading this, I salute you from the other side of the computer which has suddenly been illuminated with a video chat petition. If it weren't because I'm wearing my reading glasses, I'd answer just so I could hang up sequential seconds after.

I feel like I'm deviating, what do you think? Yes, you, the one that is neither a gigolo nor a mid-20th century wife. Do you think I should continue writing or are your eyes slowly shutting down, are your parents calling you down for dinner, or is your teacher about to catch you reading me when you should be paying attention to the verbs in French explained on the board? I wonder where you are, you might be in Tokyo or in some shared dorm in London or Berlin—I ask myself. I am intrigued to know from which television canal I'm heard from, in what bookstores have you found me or under which florid wrapping have they gifted me in. The truth is, I'm dying of disgust; it's assumed I shouldn't be doing this, because, well, I'm supposed to want you to read this book so you boost me some self-esteem with a couple of ovations via twitter, even though I don't have twitter or any of these social media applications you download so your phones are given the organs that incite anxiety in you every time you stare down at them and they're not boosting with red numbers in their corners. You can always find me in these pages though, maybe I say something interesting that deserves one of those 'retweets' that you are so fond of to feel more familiarised with your situations because other people can post about them.

The train stopped a while ago, I'm just waiting to come out of the bathroom without getting caught by the ticket guard. I hope the train doesn't depart before I have a chance to get out. I've been crammed here the two past hours if to say so and I am not exaggerating, unfortunately, I've been a fool. I should've bought the goddamn tickets. I am bothered, for as I try to silently and discretely get out of this bathroom, I am beginning to question love again and I think I understand why by being so detached with its theories, I am so attached to creating my own about it. Slowly, love will become love when it falls in love with another abstraction than itself, because I don't know what it is; if it's masturbation or incest but somehow love ends up always with love and that never works out. If love were all the things we say it is, then why do I feel it's got a lover we don't know about, and that's why we always question about what it is, which, to be honest, is complete bullshit, you should start getting on with your lives maybe that'd be the answer. Simple: love is a bankrupt prostitute on every corner of the streets that slowly combine to reform the myriad long avenues to which I'll soon be spotted sauntering in, glumly. I was impatient of surrendering in the black and white lines that drew the highways that intervened with the city, forcing people like me to stop at traffic lights once it turned red, when we're all restless to just keep on walking, it's not loud disconcerting sounds and neon lights which give you epilepsy, it's the red light of traffic light right across the street. Walking in New York feels nothing like walking, it's more as if you were floating, as if somehow you weren't only in control of yourself but the space around you; the world was drowned and we were walking on water. I was imagining my serenade as I evacuated the station. Grand Central is to where everybody arrives, as no one leaves; it's the only station where I haven't encountered masses and masses of herds of animals fighting to get into compartment wagons where they might not fit, I can't sense desperation unless it's from the opening doors directing to Teju Cole's *Open City*, and Capote's *Diamond Iceberg Floating in River Water*. I wonder now, as I make my way out of the golden puzzle towards the last piece, what will New York be to me or even if I'll ever be anything to New York, my dearest Manhattan?

I pause to take some minutes to think about it, I'm always talking about minutes and seconds holding me back, after proclaiming myself to be driven by my animal instincts, to be driven by a mustang desire. I was in E 41st street, the one who's neighbourhood is built from promotions and famous beagles I've never had a chance to taste, because I don't really like them, although now I'm feeling tempted of going over to 'Zucker's Beagles' and buying a bunch, if I can find any money on me I think that's what I'll do. Do you want a story now? Do you want me to write the adventures of Tom Sawyer in my handwriting? Or can I eat my beagle and walk around for a while? I want to get lost in the city where I trace a childhood with my fingers on the walls of every building, it's drawn in there with bricks and lucid glass, in the pavement on the floor, in the chewing gums stuck to it and the spilled drinks on the sides of the road, in the hot dog stands every five feet and the smell of onions the second you start going down the metro's staircase, it's odd but New York is like any place in the world, only that unlike every place, it has a resemblance with the past of a kid. I think it might be the first time I admit my insanity, my fear of never being able to be loved by my so-called madness has evaded, it has left no trace—no wounds or scars in the sidewalk of my soul, it simply has decided to retire, but it's gotta hell of a pension heading down its way. I thought it'd be easier to see the city as a person but it's not, I can only see it as a quixotic reflection of my impulsive ambitions, and I no longer feel alone or as if there was some force obliging me to be here, that there was any resemblance of my parents, of the people I'd been given without having the opportunity of denying their existence, nothing was produced without my consent and nobody was indebted in noticing me, in having to notice, and I had a chance of creating what I wanted to create out of myself. I felt as if the kid that had once lived in California, that had been raised by a surrounding she'd always neglected with influences that'd been conceived, where I didn't have the word in anything, where I was just merely the features of my mother and the attitude of my father, 'oh look she has her mother's eyes' or 'she's as creative as her father', there is always a conjugation, a comparison a subtle identification with somebody else that isn't me. I was never my own version. That's why you'll never get to describe me, I'll never show you my face smuggled in lousy adjectives because it is not my face, I didn't have the opportunity to choose my avatar, and here I feel I do. I am no longer anyone's recognition, I have finally become a somebody without a name.

I don't owe you anything, you don't owe me anything, and if you're reading this book is because probably somehow you felt intrigued or you had nothing better to do and you thought it might give you insight on aspects of your life you hadn't considered. I know, with books, you're supposed to learn something, and as hell do I know what you learned with this mess, with these pages one behind the other to which you keep scrolling through, scanning each and every word, maybe even devouring a couple, starting to feel a sense of parageusia, to find yourself realising there is nothing here, just my identity, the real one. The one that has no lies, no games, no rules, it is simply a personage I've created to shake my hand with and say goodbye. I walk around for a while looking for a cabin or walking in circles to see if maybe in that way I can grow the guts to ask somebody to lend me their phone in order to call this guy who could help me get installed. The truth is, I don't even know if he still lives here, his label is a Nick, we met when I came with my parents to New York because he was the son of these friends my parents had and we all went out for dinner once. We didn't speak much; he was all the time playing this killer game on his phone and didn't seem much interested in talking to my brother or me. He was older than me, a couple years older; I knew he could hook me up with something because before he left with his parents, he told my brother and me that if we ever needed anything, we should hook him up because he gets around. I still had the number he gave me in this paper he'd written it in and that I'd saved all this time. I took it with me just in case, I even remember doubting of whether getting a hold of it or not, because I was unsure of whether I could trust him. Calling him is a sign of desperation, and the fact that I'm feeling desperate taunts me, but I doubt I'll be meeting another Lilou in New York, or that I'll end up sleeping at an apartment or a hotel room so, as much as it bruises the scopes in my heart, I have to stop being a dreamer in order to survive. I walk uptown with the hope I'll bump into someone who could lend me their phone, although one of my senses is inciting me in stealing it if I ever get handed one, and I want to prevent that from happening, the only place where I wouldn't want to be a fugitive in is New York, I wouldn't be able to run away. With that in mind, I wander in the space around me, fixating my eyes not on what is happening or the people crossing by me, but a telephone box, not like the ones in London that's why here they're so hard to find. I had actually hoped it would start snowing, or that it'd be already snowing when I got here, I think I was so lost because it wasn't.

"We are all alone, born alone, die alone, and—in spite of true romance magazines—we shall all someday look back on our lives and see that, in spite of our company, we were alone the whole way. I do not say lonely—at least, not all the time—but essentially, and finally, alone. This is what makes your self-respect so important, and I don't see how you can respect yourself if you must look in the hearts and minds of others for your happiness."

—Hunter S. Thompson
The Proud Highway, 1997

Seq. 27 Ext. Manhattan

I'd like to try this again. I've only spent 30 minutes in New York, and the only thing I've done is take deep breaths and look around, trying to assimilate the fact that I'm here and I've done it alone. You're probably tired of reading this, it's just that I don't know what to do now but keep on writing, I feel like it patches everything up. I feel writing patches me up, it helps me take it all in, the tears seem like a racing car that mistook its road, and my aching heart humiliates any sort of pain with the different texture straps that my words sow to it in shades of red—sometimes I flood my heart with wine too. And even though all this sounded a little like a soliloquy from a melodramatic play like *Hamlet*, I'm not in pain, unless its new definition has been stolen and replaced. I've found a telephone cabin, only I'm doubting if whether I should or shouldn't call Nick my New York acquaintance, quite frankly, I doubt he even remembers me or he'd be willing to help without calling my father behind my back and telling him. I don't quite trust anybody, but I doubt I ever have. I look at the number in anxiety and look at the phone hanging, and do nothing but leave it there hanging as I walk away and throw the paper in the closest bin. I felt like I was cheating in an exam test if I did end up calling, me being the test cheated on by myself.

I just felt that if I were to call him and he'd picked up the phone things would've gotten complicated, we would've had to arrange a meeting place, and we would've have to spend a couple of hours together sorting everything out, I would've had to sign some papers so the moment I had money, I could've given it back to him which meant we would have to arrange another meeting in some months, we would've probably argued about mere details like where he was going to hook me up and with who, and I'd probably would've objected the first couple of times, because he'd suggest jobs I wouldn't be capable to do, and that would take me a lot of time from my writing and he'd probably find me a motel on the other side of New York instead of agree on someplace in between. I just feel if I were to call him and he actually did pick up, I'd have no getaway because someone would know my name, and that I am here. I didn't want anyone to know I was in New York, not even New York. Not because I was undercover, or I was scared somebody would find me, like my parents or my uncle, but because I just wanted to exist without a background. You know what I'm talking about, we've discussed it a couple of times earlier on, so I don't think there's any need of me repeating myself constantly. I never really met my father and I know this may come up as irrelevant at this point, but I've just come to acknowledge this fact. I have never met my father, at least not the way you have, under lectures and conversations at the dinner table, or spontaneous gifts after a long business trip or the allowance or even negligence of letting you do everything you want. I met my dad in the books I stole from him which were covered with notes in some corners of the pages or his personality underlined in the red delicate pen he always uses, becoming the pillar of a writer's desire. I sometimes wonder if I did this entire trip, all this cinematic escapade, and Kerouac *On the road* fantasy, to try to become familiar with my backgrounds with all those factors that have been surrounding me since the September of 1999, that are pledged guilty on the stand for this built personage. It's not a self-discovery Buddhist expedition, but an understanding of why am I the way I am. I feel like someone else is writing this paragraph for me, like my hands have been stalled by time whilst someone else takes advantage of my distraction.

I'm near Times Square, I can feel it and it's not like the station is very far away, I thought it would've taken longer to distance it from my heels. I've recently walked past Chanel and have realised after visualising Gucci on the other side of the road, and Armani and Prada modelling behind, that I am strolling down 5th Avenue, amongst the socialites of the Upper East Side elite, where women and men become hidden figures from all the bags decorated by fashion signatures that surround them, as if to coat them from the expensive cold that freezes Manhattan every winter. The taxis are barking to become the host of the ladies that hold they're hand up in the middle of the street to be driven to the Upper East Side after their meaningless shopping. They wear red, purple, dark blue, green, black, white, gloves, handbags, heels, boots, sandals, skirts, trousers, jeans, blazers, scarfs, blouses, necklaces, laces, stockings, transparent, opaque, gloves, sunglasses, bracelets, pearls, diamonds. The boutique's crystal entries are slapping one another, and I feel as if 5th avenue was applauding for all the income they were taking by all those heeled steps that cat walked the pavement near to them. You can imagine my position in the middle of all this action, and how fascinating it all appeared; I would've probably been driven insane by this surrounding if it weren't elsewhere than New York. I felt as if it had a uniqueness in its sound and movement to any other commercial bubble in the world. I know I was right, if I weren't, it wouldn't be so melodic to encounter such event, contoured by its diversity of accents, languages and usage of tones. I could feel the pondering drumroll of excitement in my heart; I understood how to be romantic again. I no longer felt unwanted lines distracting me, how they used to curve and squirm, when the only things I was capable of saying was nothing, because I had never fallen in love yet, and the truth is I still haven't because I want a kiss before sex; I want to wake up in New York before falling asleep anywhere else.

I could've written a love song at this point; I could've started writing jazz songs in the corners that jointed with streets such as Bleecker and Houston under the influence of Broadway Av. I felt tunes would follow my beats to the underground metro leading me from the Blue Note's club to Brooklyn and Harlem. I felt like I could paint over Chelsea and find my own gallery, and be seduced by the Meat Packing district cuisine near the Whitney, where once on the rooftop the only way of coming back down again was jumping from building to building as if the whole architecture that maintained the city was summarised in the three opulent blocks in 235 Bowery Street. I wanted to go to Greenwich Village again, that's where we used to have our apartment when we came in December, I wanted to make sure it was still there on the other side of the road from Angelo's Italian restaurant in Little Italy. I could even feel the taste of the Americano my dad used to order in Gasoline Alley Coffee, before going down to Chelsea to meet his gallerist. I could see every past affair slide around me in the shape of a box as I was nearing Times Square, the heart of the futuristic advertisement industry. I could see the light flashes reflect from building to building from a far, and they blinded me. I regretted not having brought my sunglasses, every step I took that brought this alternate three-dimensional space closer to me, as if I was about to enter a videogame I could only get out off if I didn't buy anything. It was the first time I felt lucky for having empty pockets. I had to find my way out of the maze visual images had constructed pixel by pixel.

The thing with this book is that there's no correlation whatsoever, no signs that match one another; it's the water stream in a waterfall, in a river, in the top of a mountain and its detachment in the sea. There is just a person and what delves inside of that person's mind here. I don't want to make sense intentionally, I know unintentionally we are all very capable of doing so, but that is not the case. There is a gap between both concepts, because there is an unknown space between the two creators of such concepts. I am not one of them, I don't believe I ever can or will create anything, because I am not at ease with my own images of myself, I live in a limited illusion of my personage. I know it all sounds very dreamy, as if we've just recently entered somebody's dream by mistake stalked inside a turbulent space—and that is probably what we are: unpaid actors in somebody's expensive dream and they're probably some unpaid actor in ours. I am threatened by the character I've created of myself in this novel, I feel like I no longer recognise her or have any idea of who she is—I only know I'm the one who wrote about her and now she's trying to write me from the cracks, the shape of some letters formulate when typed down, written down, drawn down. I am not mad yet, don't worry, I am confused with the identity that's followed me to New York, when I thought I'd been very careful covering my tracks. Do you believe that things happen for a reason? Yeah, no, me neither. I think they happen because we simply make them happen, because we don't stop until they're a present instant and not just something we want happening some call it the law of attraction.

Anyways, that was my way of representing an interval, you know like the one's at the Opera, I'm giving you time not to think about this, to go downstairs to the kitchen and heat some popcorn in the microwave, drink a glass of water, or if you're someone who like me can't tolerate its taste and needs something that'll flirt with your liver in a near future, open that scotch and drip two drops inside a small glass, and stir it up a little, that's what I do, it softens the taste as if like a baby it'd been rocked it in its cradle and been sang a lullaby, you have to do it right though. Watch out your popcorn doesn't stay too much time in the microwave, they'll get all burnt up like coal and you won't want to eat them anymore, and you'll procrastinate for a while if you should try again with another pack of popcorn or if you should just toast some bread or not toast some bread and make yourself a sandwich. The interval is over in five minutes.

Spontaneous parts of this novel correspond to other parts of itself, and slowly, they'll all compose together and everything will make sense, or they're purposely written in the way they have been to never have to correspond to any other parts and be enough on their own, and one way or another make sense alone and create this novel. At least, that's my understanding of what I've written, although I wouldn't trust my understandings very much if I were you, I am not a very reliable narrator, especially when it's about something that revolves or has any sort of minuscule connection with me. I am not trying to think about what you're wishing I was thinking about like, where am I going to sleep tonight and what is my plan, if even have one after having thrown Nick's phone number in the nearest bin an hour ago. It's probably about five pm by now, heading towards becoming a six, so I guess you do have a point and I should really start concentrating in my actions instead of my city. I don't know if I'm going to meet any new characters that might save me from overflowing in my own made up one, and just like that, I was finally in the middle centre point of the greatest grand Times Square and I felt like a small fraction of LA had snuck itself in my bag and liberated all its fury in this one spot they call Times Square, the plethora of activities and images. I walked in it, bumping into everyone, it's as if Times Square was disconnected from having directions, there was no left, or no right, people just walked and bumped onto one another with all their bags behind them. I regretted getting stuck in this lumbering space, if it could even be considered a space. I felt disgust, I was disgusted by where I was and even more by the fact that my way out of here wasn't going to be easy. I just walked straight with the hope of finding an overture out, like I were in a tunnel in search for a hole of light, to give me hopes there was some way of getting out of there, I wasn't sure if this was the same case. I only saw skin and garments grasping accidently on one another continuously. I felt discombobulated, afflicted by my claustrophobic circumstances, anxious, just terribly anxious. I procrastinated about the possibility of fainting under so much pressure, but the fear of being stepped by all these pigs stabilised my anxiety. I had to get out of here, my advice avoid going inside Times Square, just hamper it—it's an intoxicated lotus flower, just like the one Ulysses ate up, yes that one, the one that looks tempting, entrancing in delicacy but is perilous for it was grown in seditious grounds.

Anyhow, I'm a fast walker and have founded my way out. The difference with Chicago and New York is I know the streets of New York as if they'd been tattooed in the palm of my hand as a map, in a way, I feel safer alone in a city that streams through my veins to my heart. In Chicago, such advantage was an impetuous materialistic want, I could never replace my affection for one city to another. I don't want to control Manhattan, and Manhattan doesn't want to control me, the instant this became true is the moment I fell in love, when I no longer felt any attachment or convenience here but a stream of pureness. These streets piled with mystery, with music, with something greater than greatness, something that isn't dreamed of or considered in expectations, because it is something that summarises in the stroll down the right street joining the right avenue in the right city when all others are right for someone else and you might have a slight chance of coinciding. They're the streets with no destination that only lead you to where your steps will take you to; a constant arrival and unstoppable leave. I tried to make that sound as complicated as possible, I know, but reread it constantly and follow the words with your fingers, trace them down, hell, do what you want to do with them, and imagine this mere sentences as the streets that I am crossing this instant to get to the nearest metro station that'll take me downtown.

Seq. 28 Ext. Greenwich Village

The typical thing we all do when we arrive someplace, is familiarise each little spectre that is part of it to recollect them for further notice. In New York, most people look up to the sky and admire how they can't spot the end of a building for it collides with the clouds in the sky or simple: the sky stops seeming so limitless. At least, that's what most people are doing around me, I've spotted at least a couple to not say a dozen by now who just stand there looking up at the sky, extoling the metallic hands reaching up from the ground. I still haven't done that you know, looking up there. Instead of looking up and appreciating our infinity, I rather delve in the underground and travel to our deepest corners, I want to be downtown already. I need to see if our home is still there, even though no one lives in it anymore—if my soul is still in me even though I've made the residence in me quite uncomfortable. You're probably wondering what I am going to do now. If I'm playing any mind games with you to intrigue you or something of the sort, if I'm trying to take you somewhere only I can go to—but I'm not. I wish I could tell you what's in my mind, but the only thing there is a chaos that's driving me to where I want to be: home. We lived in 145 Mulberry Street, we were there only a month, but for me, it felt like I'd lived there my whole life, I had my own room, with my things, with my views, with my little terrace in the fire escape where I'd hide sometimes at night to smoke a joint or two, or just play with fire trying to illuminate the city that didn't need illuminating. I sometimes closed one eye and put the lighter at a distance from the angle I was looking from, the city appeared to go through the flames of my lighter. It was protected, and you know sometimes I imagined myself as the one protecting it and the one able to destruct it because somehow the city was also translucent through my reflections, visions, through my own opaqueness, as if it was in me. I know how it all sounds, but for me, when I was younger, that was the only thing that mattered: looking at a reflection and being able to sense a flaming city that grew and never came to its ashes, not even the seasons could light it off, not even the months of the year or the rain and snow. I wanted to look through that window again.

I somehow always ended up in train stations, as if unconsciously I was trying to runaway constantly, even in New York I wanted to run away. I didn't even like running but somehow that's how I always ended up—running. I sat down inside the metro after looking at which stop I had to get down at and waited, through all the stops which weren't quite that many but seemed endless every time we entered a tunnel. A woman came in the same wagon as me, she was around her mid-50s but didn't look very well, so I stood up and offered her my seat, to which, she thanked me very touched. I moved away from her then, she reminded me to how my mother must've looked like around now, only she didn't have her eyes, or her nose or any features I could relate to which relieved me, but the sadness in her eyes, the thin blue lining that subdued me even if a thousand people were blocking any possible connection between us. I stood there beside the doors, slowly being trampled and squashed by the sweaty armpits that caged me as well as their skins and breaths, conversations with one another or through their phones and I was there in the middle, and I looked up and I felt how I was slowly diminishing and they were all the skyscrapers I should've looked up to before I went underground, and I could tell they wanted me to look at them because they just stayed there, sweating, being loud and compressing me until they all got out, and I suddenly exploded and went out too because it was my stop. I'd been supervising it since I moved from my seat to the middle of the entrance, and it was finally under the red dot. I walked around the social underground of the city, bumping into singers, musicians and poets all looking at me with a vagrant leer, and I wanted to give them all something, I wanted to leave a piece of me in each of their boxes but I knew they wouldn't appreciate it they just wanted money, and that disgusted me. I picked all their pamphlets and kept them in my bag so someday I could be able to take them out from the limitations of their manufactured aspirations. I stomped on many other artists, dancers with an audience that filmed them but didn't finance them, that thought they were great but only because they were in hiding—because they embodied what to expect when stepping in an underground metro in New York, as if they were a passing spectacle, when they were real. It all felt caliginous and dour down there you know, I felt as if they were rolling a Hitchcock movie, where the lightening was the scene and not the characters in it. I strolled out into what looked like W Houston St, which was just a couple blocks from Mulberry. I recognised the area; I used to walk through here many times, although it looked more familiar at darker hours because it's when we went to the cinema. I needed to find the Angelika Film Centre in order to walk my way home. That's how I knew the streets, not by their names but by the stains of decaying Polaroids. Either way, slowly, I was adapting to the spontaneity of my circumstances, and encountered Angelika on the corner, I knew she'd be standing in taking sips from her coffee mug with her name encrypted in it and selling her tickets through the cabin in the entrance, advertising all the movies you couldn't find anywhere else but there, whether they were avant-garde, French, Bergman's creations or such as *The Artist, Melancholia* or *The Only Living Boy in New York*. I knew she'd be smiling at me, and I wanted to sneak in and watch one of those films she wanted to make sure I watched. It was not the time but I knew I would be back, and continued my walk past it to where it merged with Broadway Av and Lafayette St, and I knew the way from there was just to go through Houston St to Grand and I was already there. I didn't take that route though; I wanted to intentionally get lost before for a while, I wanted to keep things out of my mind. I knew I was going to arrive sooner or later; I just wanted to stall that sooner or later.

I wanted to clear my head; I needed to organise how I was going to contact *The New Yorker* or any publisher such as *Penguin, Simon and Schuster* or *Harper Collins*. I preferred to analyse all these options outside of indoor restrictions before confronting their difficulties and aggravation in a room with four walls, one shut window and one shut door. I guess the desire of wanting to be published was still within me, I could feel that ambition ponder in my head begging me to do the first instinctive thing that came up to my mind, and I knew I would allow it to become an instant than to ignore it. I knew this time I had to ignore it, I wanted to be prudent even though my conscience didn't want me anywhere near prudence She's known to be one of those sneaky ladies or at least that's what her job description describes her as, she's also very expensive. I had my mind under control of having it under control after all this past time, where I'd been reckless to maintain my vitality. I thought of the process of publishing a book, and was excited, I was looking forward to the rejection, to my exhales of desperation, to living under a swimming pool of crumbled pages into balls to play around with, to sleep between them and have my head burst in more of those papers in the shapes of dreams, in my sleep if I were to get any. I wanted to be incapable of sleeping, of moving around the streets like everyone else was right now around me, with their professions intact, with their anxiety supervised by their finances and their quest for maintenance and stabilisation declared a found treasure. I wanted to spend days and weeks in my room or in the living room, or looking out of the reflection in the window, smoking hidden cigarettes so my smoking addiction was my only concern and not the one of those around me, where I could stash all the beverages in my fridge as if it'd gone through a club's alcohol permit and finish it all up slowly or all at once to my sin. I only had that certain in this moment in my life, I wanted to make this book an event the world could explode with. I knew once I arrived home the first thing I'd do is re read all these pages and rip some apart or leave all of it intact and let it be what it is supposed to be, without any essay markings or grades, just a couple of pages that somehow in another life could be read as a novel and I would be considered the writer I think I could ever get to be. That was far away from me now, I just wanted to walk around and for mere seconds disconnect with my spiritual self, let him have a break from so much action, get her or him or whatever it is if it even has a gender to get a sleep or meditate in the temple that resides in it and be left alone, maybe he even wants to go partying or smoke a couple of joints to ease his mind. And that's exactly what I did.

Remember how I told you I was going to take another route to get home, I think that might've not been such a great idea, because I feel like I've outdistanced myself for somehow I am nearing Washington Park in Greenwich, I've just barely noticed I've crossed at least three department buildings of New York University and well I am really staring at the Judson Memorial Church. I am guessing I should turn around again and trace my steps backwards the same way a line traces itself to create a drawing, I needed to draw my presence all over the streets I stepped foot on, to finish my drawing back home. I did just that, wishing deeply that even though I'd never gotten along with time it'd just put itself in my favour for once, for it was already starting to darken and my shadow had left me defenceless. I realise now once in the inner city where everything used to happen and still happens, that it was easier to talk about the city from a distance than once in it. I felt observed as if the city were imminent of each and every word that I'd be writing about it, making sure they're at the standard of its greatness, and it terrifies me that they aren't. I had seduced guys before, random nights out in the Valley or the Pier with my friends but never a city, never a city like New York. I would apologise, but I'm exhausted of doing so if you can't see what I'm seeing through my words, try it from yours or just watch one of Woody Allen's movies, like *Manhattan* or *Annie Hall* and it might be easier for you. Either way, I now regret having thrown Nick's number to the bin, and not have kept Lilou's after Chicago, and sometimes regretting might be just for the best that you've done something right.

There are no longer any opposites, there is no longer a right and a wrong in my state of mind, if I even have one, the only identity there is, is the one that isn't identified, the one that's not an identity. I walk around holding that madness in the paralysed lines on my arms, on my shoulders as they climb up my neck and design my face as they later on roll into the threads of my hair. I'm looking for Barns and Novels again, only that this time I'll actually have chance of finding it. I just want to stand in front of the door, and walk away as I have walked away from everything all my life. I should actually be looking for *The New Yorker*, or *The New York Times* building but I'm very far away now, I'm very, very far away downtown. I want to make a dramatic exit you know, I want to be anonymous for the world, but I'll never be anonymous I've got too much pride, my ego being the only thing I have left constrains me from becoming expired, a momentarily attraction, just another grain of essence in a walking city in which people just stand because even if they're immobilised New York isn't, it takes them to places without them noticing. I want New York to take me home. I know the first thing I have to do is go home, even if home is getting to the end of this book.

I'm going off the rails now, I'm sorry if I haven't talked directly to you for a while, but I can't always be dependant of all those fixed glares on everything I write down, everything I do. I have to make sure I'm not saying some cracked up shit, because I know if I do it'll be the only thing you'll remember about this, or that you'll ever show any interest in. Maybe you want me to give you another interval or just talk about sex a little more, or you just want me to convince you of staying to feel like your presence is important or show you that there's something worth living out there to which my simple plain answer if I was given an interview is yes there is, but only in the people you love without the need of wanting to control them, and the blind assurance that they're not out there to control you.

I've completely isolated myself here, but only because I can't isolate myself of the world, I'll always want to come back I'll always want to be around my friends, around Lilou, even my family, even my encounters in the train. Even in conceived isolation by myself, the only thing I care about, the only thing I can think about right now is all the people who've gone through me and the people who have showed me love in the way they understand it to be. They're the souls that brought the jazz, soul, Funk, Bebop all the way from New Orleans into mine and as the city; are up in protected flames. They're the ones that provoke the fear of a ride on a star without them, or incite the creation of a flowerbed of burning roses in late November if laid among them, you know when there's only fall paint tumbling down from the sky. I like that I can talk about them without needing them, without missing them, without feeling anything towards them but a serenity of having met them in order to be able to be here right now, in this page writing about them as if they'd ever been important even though they haven't. I know I've overused my descriptive imagery, but I am sitting in a bench alone with a weight in my back of the bag I carry with me, and all I have to offer the world in this moment is that I stand up and continue my ambulation home.

"I became aware of just how fleeting the sense of happiness was, and how a flimsy its basis: a warm restaurant after having come from the rain, the smell of food and wine, interesting conversation, daylight falling weakly on the polished cherry wood of the tables. It took so little to move the mood from one level to another, as one might push pieces in a chessboard. Even to be aware of this, in the midst of a happy moment, was to push those pieces, and to become slightly less happy."

—Teju Cole
Open City, 2011

Seq. 29 Mulberry St

I guess it's normal that I compare myself with other writers, or my work with other writers' work and that sometimes my mind blocks, I feel like I'd never be able to express that which I want to express as they do, as they have. I am humiliated, and from that humiliation, I ponder down my blockage aggressively, in merciless inhumane violence, I break through it brick by brick, writer by writer, word by word, and every bloody heartless punch becomes a word, a ferocious word that runs on its own, that backs me up and helps me break through all the other bricks which slowly begin to concentrate on my spine and it all falls to pieces, and there's just this little kid behind all the dust, giggling, laughing just sat there. I'm crossing the smell of brick ovens and Parmesan rain as it parachutes down from a razing punctured aeroplane on Italian cuisine. My stomach growls at me, in anger, I feel how it's trying to push me towards all of the restaurants which have slowly appeared in the streets which corner me on my way to Mulberry St. I walk slower now, I can sense it in my pace and how I am no longer in control of the rhythm of the song I'm closing my eyes to, as I nod my head side to side, up to down in relaxation, even though the song I'm listening to, *Should I stay or should I go* from The Clash. Which to be quite honest with you; makes me feel completely ironic as if somehow the lyrics and my thoughts had been aligned like constellations in a parallel universe from the one I found myself in to mock my way.

I stopped walking, and started rocking an invisible guitar as I tickled the strings and shacked my shoulders back and forth, followed my head rolling from side to side, springing my hair around and around as I whirled my head, creating this space nobody could come close to or they'd have a severe whip. I'd close my eyes, and frequently hunch my back as I twitched my knees up and down, as if I was running but the image of me running was produced under slow motion, so my steps seemed to reach the top of my head and back again even, constantly. I was jittering and dancing backwards as to then sliding forward with my invisible guitar strings in the middle of my torso, and hitting the drums on each side of the road as I slowly, at a pace that made me feel like I'd just had sex for the first time and the glow was doing its part, or got published as I'd dreamed so many times, created the taste of my entrance. I jumped the crossroad, from white to black until I was in Mulberry St, and my presence agitated all the restaurants, that the people walking past stopped and let me through as I ran in small steps as if I'd just had an epileptic stroke I wasn't aware of, for I enjoyed it. It was a strange feeling that I'd never felt before, I felt madness in me, I wasn't controlling my agitations, they were being maneuvered by the retro-punk waves which dazzled my personality to shift into the one of an '80s rock star. I decided as Mick Jones did in 1981 that I was going to go. I continued my stroll whilst miming the lyrics, and replayed the song a couple of times so I didn't stop with my enhancing hyperactive act of a lunatic, as I stuck my tongue out as I looked at the sky that wasn't disturbed by high buildings and hopped on one leg doing so as I stretched my arms, as if I were embracing all of New York. I clapped my hand forward and backwards, and felt like a professional choreographer of a flash mob dance and leaped from one side of the sidewalk to the other and ran freely down the road that hadn't been penetrated by cars yet, and I ran down that road, as I'd skated down Venice Beach's downhill from the pub to the beach and just, simply ran until I was facing 145 Mulberry.

This was the paragraph where my dreams of becoming a rock star, the Jim Morrison of the 21st Century, seemed to have been accomplished even though it was just for the duration of the song, it was the right amount of time because there is no infinite, there is no time longer than the time there is, that's what makes everything worth living for—the limit of time, of love, of reaching the stars, if we could get all those things for as long as we wanted, we'd get sick of them, they'd become used, wasted, they'd disappear and we'd stop seeing them as stars, as love, as anything that could ever evoke beauty in our simple lives, they'd just be more waste, more trashcans, more dark clouds in the sky, more useless divorces, more subdued innocence's, more hate, more hate and hate. That's why I can't stay too long in New York; as Romeo said, I'm not in love, I am out of love, and its simple explanation is if you love, you'll always end up out of love, and I never want to fall out of love with New York, I never want to make it mine, to make it another waste, another crippled plastic bag waiting to be delivered to its execution. I have always been very consistent about my time here, about what that even meant, about not being part of that physical magnitude that measures my every breath, moment, memory, my instants with those I love and reminds me constantly that, soon, I won't have any more left, and I like that adrenaline, that knowledge that even though in me I'll always live outside of it, of the sequences of ticks that play around me; that I won't be limitless in my actual existence. If it weren't for that construction, I'd never have gotten here, I think to myself various times, I've thought it since I left my home in the state of California. I feel like I'm storytelling a fairy-tale, I don't like storytelling, I don't like there having to be an ending and a beginning, and them always starting from the same magnetic points, maybe that's why this book's taking so long to get to its end, maybe it's the exception, maybe the only end it has, has already been written, hinted in pages I don't remember writing in.

Staring at the portal of 145, I'm thinking of ringing the bell, I want someone to answer it if I do, so I ring with the high expectative that a voice will answer it and tell me to fuck off, to go away or something audible similar, to which I'll respond by going up the fire escape and breaking inside, with the aggressive avaricious intention of kicking whoever the voice corresponded to, out. I rang one more time, only this time, I hoped nobody answered, I realised there was a slight possibility that the voice that would answer could come from my mother and that she was hiding out here, with Anthony or Alexander. I stopped ringing just in case it was her. You would've thought after all this wander to get here; I would've felt flustered, enraged and perhaps even choleric to the result of my destination. At first I thought of it too, for the first couple of rings, I could feel my temper rise within me, startling any essence of equanimity that'd ever resided in me, to go to the reception office and create a distraction whilst I bust my ass in the building. I didn't react; I just passed 145 Mulberry, and walked up by Grand St and Broome. Nothing was like I thought it was—'A new generation' that's what I think we are, we are the contemporaries, the days, the one's whose dreams take control of their accomplishments before anyone else does first, there's not much really that we can be put into anymore, not even our own creations can put us into boxes, not even the words I write can define me, illustrate me, evoke ideas about me, even have the arrogance to create me—all I am is who I am, this is just my exercise of trying to make the world identify with the peaks of my liberty. At this moment, I'm guessing you expect my mum to appear, I actually would expect it too but she's not, and that's not the plot twist you must've had in mind. I'm not even sure there even really is a plot twist, or if one is needed.

All I am is an instant of pleasure, that's the only thing I am. This face you've never been introduced to is not my face, I don't belong to its moulded, grown appearance. My name isn't even mine, two hopeless adults in love gave it to me before they fell out of love and the bastards forgot to change my name as a reaction of their difficulties, I didn't even get upgraded in my module or transplanted elsewhere. It all always ends up with your roots, but I don't want any, I don't want to grow new roots to all the places I go to, all the places I'm from. Stars don't have roots; I'm not saying I'm a star that's even too cheesy for me, and the result was a little star had found her place amongst the other stars in the galaxy and they all shone differently *blah blah blah*, where is that even going? I'd apologise now for making fun of all those hopeless romance novels, but I can't. It's okay now, everything is okay, I just have to walk, I have to find the pages you've read till now scrambled in the bottom of my bag buried in pens, in other writers' pages they've been infatuated to in their stay down there, in the bottom of my bag with the dirt, with chewing gum papers, even with sand, with useless coins and dimes that can't buy me nothing, all there is to this book is what is buried at the bottom of that bag, careless without being bottled up. They are rough pages, they are strong, they'll be read because they've been hard to dig out, even though they don't look impeccable and some of them are covered in dirt as brown birthmarks and wrinkles—even they're limitless, even they can decay. I go taking page by page, sometimes I get a couple in a bundle, there might be at least a hundred and something pages, you probably know what a hundred they were if you look down to the number at the end of the page. That number is all there is, once there's no more number under these pages, that'll be the ending.

Pages are heavy once they're all out, and as I'm holding them. I think of what *The New Yorker* could do with them, what *Simon and Schuster* or *Penguin* would do, what would *The New York Times* do? What would the critics do, and the other writers? What would my friends do? What would my generation do? But I don't care about what they'd do, they'd probably do nothing, and I decide to do something. This moment should be filmed, it's probably already been filmed and this song shouldn't be playing now, but it is, and I can't help myself but I have to scream and I do that, I scream, I scream as I hold on each of my hands half a quantity of myself in the aspect of these pages, that are the only description my face will ever physically undertake, or of my name, proof there was a trace of me somewhere once—and I start running ferociously, roaring—

fervent—like a blaze shredding an iceberg, down the first principal road I find, and I barely hear the claxons of all the cars behind me and from the ones confronting me to which I so skilfully in madness of unaccounted heartbeats dodge—fence and I hold on to the pages, at least I try as the wind blows them away, and they all start falling around me and I don't stop to pick them up to take them to *The New Yorker* or to *Simon and Schuster* or to email them to my dad—I let there be snow in New York. I just keep running down that road to which the cars are beeping, dinging, signalling so hesitantly, and to which some people are stopping to watch and they're probably hissing, and whispering whilst to me all they are is mimes and it's all a big commotion of sounds I am not part of because my head is stuck in another tune. I imagined the Kooks to soundtrack me at this point even, or yet to have Creedence Clearwater Revival back me up on this one with *Fortunate Son*, but it was Flora Cash on Jovi's playlist. Thinking about it I recognise Lou Reed's *Vicious*, response to Warhol's idea would've contoured wonderfully, but I knew if Louie had started playing, I would've had a rocking stroke if the following tracks weren't *Rebel Rebel* and *Dani California* or just simply all I would've needed was an Ian Curtis trembling to *Disorder*. Although *Sweet Child O' mine* would've had an ironic twist to my whole situation…so I might stick to that one. There's always a song, we all have that song that for some unexplainable reason is ours, and for however much I wanted to find the song for this moment there wasn't one. None really popped to my mind. I guess I had a sweet loud cacophony of all the songs I've ever heard and that had found a place in my head to stay long enough as to create this orchestra of rock.

(This is my way of telling you ought to listen to these songs, reading this paragraph over and over again with each different one, or your own.)

The people are trying to understand, and maybe they will—it's not that they've never seen pages fly, it's just that these pages are a face, with their own singularities and they aren't flying, they're floating, and we are all walking on water, on vibrations. The pages might rip each other apart once they go too far away. They might end on different streets, and all those streets under names such as Houston, Bowery, Canal, Steinway, Christopher, Madison—are all chapters now. Now, please tell me you feel it to, the racing heart, the scraping in of a fire trying to get out inside, a light, a flame, it doesn't even have to be something bright it could be coal, or a depth of an ocean—but do you feel it, maybe you're tasting it or just listening to it, maybe you've stolen a doctor's stethoscope to listen to your heart, you should, I would if I had one of those. What you can't do to me at this point though, even though you don't feel it, is and I am begging you, you've got me at my knees for this one; please don't imagine a melodramatic eerie image of me flying and having these pages as my wings or that I'm slowly dissolving into those pages as I run, please don't ruin it. Because that is not what happened. The pages slowly let go of me, I didn't let go of them, and once I have nothing left, I continue running down breathless and sprint to the sidewalk where I can take a breath and give my adrenaline an Anaesthetic before I actually get ran over, as I feel my soul out of my chest. I just stand there for a couple of seconds breathing in and out exhilarant—electric sensation.

I wish it was just like in the movies and suddenly a pitch-black screen appeared, and the lights turned on, the exit doors were opened and everyone started to stand up and get the hell out of there. But this isn't a movie, there aren't any sudden black pitches or exit doors opening. There's just me, breathing steadily, just there standing up with my gaze lost on everything that was happening around me, wanting to go home, or a bar nearby I spotted before and order a beer. Maybe two. I'll have to see when I get there.

"…it's hard enough for me to write what I want to write without me trying to write what you say they want me to write which I don't want to write."

—Tennessee Williams
Tennessee Williams's 'The World I live In', 1957

Interview with the Book
About the Author

Let's begin then, thank you for lending us a moment of your time

Well, this interview is really the one giving me more time so lending some of it to you is the least I could do. Thank you for giving me time.

What do you think is the reason you exist or you were written?

To be honest, completely sincere with you, I don't believe I exist as anything. My writer, she had the goddamn balls of never really introducing me as something, I guess some might think I'm a book, or a novel, or even the diary of a teenage girl—which to be honest with you, I am most definitely sure I am not, if that were the case, I would've ripped my own pages a while ago and committed a literal suicide. I really don't understand this interview; you're asking me questions I can't answer. Why do you think you were born?

Would it be easier to answer them if you could somehow, read yourself?

I can't read myself, that'd be like masturbating or ripping an ear off. One of which I would like but would find very difficult to do with you interviewing me. I feel like I'm a mirror, not the mirror you have hanging on your bathroom. I'm just a mirror that's taken a while to polish and now that I finally am, polished, all those reflections some of you look at in bathrooms, or wardrobe doors are just humiliated by their function as limited perceptions of yourselves, while I'm limitless.

Are you saying the only way we can recognise the face in the mirror is if we stop facing it as an image and understanding it as something else?

You're really good at your job, did you know that? I never said that, but I never say anything. I think this is the first time I've been given some privacy since my author is out there taking a beer or a Macallan 98, she likes it on the rocks by the way. I'll answer to your question with this: you got me there. Let me say I am an admirer of your interpretations.

Was it a hard relationship to collaborate with your writer? I mean, I'm guessing you really didn't have a say in choosing her, this young girl to talk about her world through you?

Yes, at first I thought about reporting her of assault, but then again, she never really did go 'through me', at least not literally. I am going off topic, sorry, it's what us books tend to do when we are left alone to deal with the world you egocentrics think you've built. I liked working with her, I liked every word she used, even some of them tickled, and some made me cry, that's why some of the pages are so wet, it's not because she wrote them under the rain but because the rain took over this time and wrote itself.

Aren't you curious to know her real name, or even her face?

I'm not curious at all because I do know her real name, and her face, her face you can only see if you read each page and somehow, align every word with one another like you did in kindergarten to create images, you know? Following the dots with numbers until you look back and see the whole picture. Well, you do the same here.

Do you feel connected with her? As if you were kindred spirits in different forms?

If you're referring to me as a form, I'm going to go straight ahead and tell you I am quite offended. Well, I mean I don't agree with her in most things and she probably doesn't agree with most things I am, or the ways I've been presented before and I like she's given me the freedom to somehow be what I want to be. But we somehow made an arrangement, even though she is very complicated at making arrangements I'll tell you that. 'Kindred spirits', as in soulmates right?

Yes, soulmates...

Well, what does that really even mean? I don't think we can or could ever be soulmates simply because we aren't separate from one another, our soul, our spirit isn't similar, or akin, or even parallel from one another—we are really just the same that's been split into half but still feeling whole with two different reincarnations, I'm made of paper and ink, and she's made of bones and blood, skin and muscles, and all those organs that build her up universe by universe as if trying to carefully resolve a puzzle, but we are the same, we are just ideas that have been given different illustrations to be perceived by the rest.

Now that you've touched the matter, what are your thoughts on solitude?

Well to get to me you have to know what that is, if not how are we gonna feast the way we should. I mean we can't all live everything together always, if not we'd have nothing left. Look at my writer, she needed a split of solitude to look me in the face.

I see, is it hard being a book?

I don't know. I don't even know if I am one, and if I am, this is my first time, but I bet it'll be hard. If not, it isn't worth it. Is it harder to be a writer? I guess I'll never know, we are in two different positions, she writes me, and even tries to sell me so I can write all over you people. It's the type of relation that'd be described as 'complicated' if I were to have a Facebook status.

Would you like to figure out 'whatever it is' you are?

I already did, the day I had the last dot written on me, it hurt and itched like a bitch because, well, people have heart attacks and they simply stop, living, breathing, whatever it is you people do when it's your last metaphorical full stop. But that last dot, that full stop was made of everything that dark bubbled circle wasn't my death, it was simply an orgasm that had to stop for if it had lasted much longer—I really don't know what would've happened. I figured then, this girl and I had more in common than you might've thought, this girl and I had created a world that ended in an orgasm instead of death. Don't you think that's enough to figure out 'whatever it is' that I am? I am pleasure.

Do you believe to be connected with the understanding of pleasure in the society you've been conceived to be read in?

I wish I was conceived in the '80s so I could've met, glorious jewels such as *A moveable Feast* or *The Great Gatsby*…but I guess each century has its golden goddesses, and whilst they're alive, whether their pages have aged, I'd still ask them to dance with me at your famous so-called proms. But to answer your question, yes, I am connected with this society's understanding of pleasure, even though edging towards virtual pleasure, I can break through that. I was born at the pace of this society's movement in my adolescence, where I have stayed.

What does pleasure symbolise for you, sir?

Please, don't call me sir—I could be a Madame for all you know and that'd be disrespectful. Pleasure from my singular perspective symbolises well, me, and all that comes with me and all that comes with all those that are somehow similar to me, some with the same purpose, some with similar lines in them, and some with their targeted audiences or akin attitudes and ideals. The good thing about all that similarity is that it's just that, a similarity, but never really the same thing. Somehow, I believe to be the only individual of my kind, as in my kind there is only one, as in their kind for however similar we may all appear, there is only one. Do you feel the sibilance; do you feel me hissing at you whilst you read me?

Yes, I do. I believe it to be the first time I have only written the questions of my own interview and have been answered by the answers that write themselves. Now to finish, is 'No price, No time', is that your full name?

We thought about being clichés and trying out that minimalist touch, by naming me as what I am supposed to be understood as, 'A NOVEL'. The simplicity of it is beautiful, such an ironic name with its purpose would've been great; it's as if you would've called your daughter, 'a person' or 'a girl'.

Why did you arrange to change it? I believe you must've talked about how you wanted to be referred to with your author?

Well, you see, I didn't have to, you must've understood by now my author has quite the trauma with the idea of names, so she really left it up to me. I flirted once with '99 francs' this French monsieur I met in my visit to Paris, at a little bar called Les Philosophies in Le Marais and just fell infatuated by the way it spoke. The other one was in a road trip I did where I went through Kansas and happened to stumble over '10:04', in the middle of the street and one thing led to another and we ended up at a motel were things got messy in a good way. Besides that, my name is a metaphor; it's an obstacle which doesn't allow us to become the product we are turning into, in me this doesn't happen, you have no price, therefore, you can't be sold and you have no time, therefore, you can't become expired. In a way, my name inclines to manifest infinity.

I'm guessing it was a good shag? (As some might call it)

Oh, not that vulgar! It was a 'good' conversation where not one of us felt the necessity to outshine the other because we had an understanding that each of our egos and each of our ideas could be conversed in detail, and maybe even recycled but not, in any circumstances, compared. But to answer your real question, yes it was.

How would you describe your author? As you're pretty much the only one who really knows who she is.

Maybe, if you read me carefully, and would let yourself be seduced by my margins and commas and specially my words, you would get to know who she really is, but if you did, I think that would break everything, what would there be left of her, what would there be left of me if I just, went ahead and described my author to you? What would all the other 'mes' written by her say? I'd love to betray her, but I can't because it'd be betraying myself. I can describe her to you simply as this: another version of myself that happens to walk around, swim in the ocean, have a couple, to not say many drinks and even fall in love, all those things I can't say about myself unless someone reads them.

So, I see it's going to be impossible to get anything out of you, so I can humiliate your author in the front cover of the magazine I work for?

Yes, I am sorry. It's just because of this terrible personality disorder I have, where I am the author too. But I've got a title you can humiliate us both in, 'No price, No time SOLD OUT!'

Aren't you concerned of the possibility that your author could to be considered mad, crazy, a lunatic for this?

I can only tell you this, is she really the mad one because last time I checked, she isn't the one interviewing a book. Although there is originality in your work, and all there is to madness is that, originality so you may have one or two things in common with her. I guess I'm just going to have to quote this young girl I did in 1865, after I asked her if I'd gone mad and she answered in hype as she took a sip of tea after checking her watch, "I am afraid so, but let me tell you something, the best people usually are,"—in my case, it was books, but you know what I mean. We really are all mad, if you're not mad, you're the one who should be worried, or concerned as you say it, of being considered ordinary, average or even simple.

On that account, I think it'll be all for today, thank you for having me interview you 'No price, No time'.

Stage direction: **Bows** and **exits** the printing conversation.